The Knitting Club

Andie Young

The Knitting Club. Copyright © 2025 by Andie Young. All rights reserved.

Visit Sunflower Lane Press at sunflowerlanepress.com

Visit Andie Young at andieyoungwrites.com

Cover designed by GetCovers.com. All rights reserved.

Edited by Allison Wells.

All Scripture quotations, unless otherwise indicated, are taken from the Holy Bible, King James Version.

No part of this publication may be reproduced, distributed, or transmitted in any form or by any means, including photocopying, recording, or other electronic or mechanical methods, without the prior written permission of the publisher, except in the case of brief quotations embodied in critical reviews and certain other noncommercial uses permitted by copyright law. For permission requests, contact the publisher using the information above.

The Knitting Club is a work of fiction. Names, characters, and incidents are all products of the author's imagination or are used for fictional purposes. Any resemblance to actual events or persons, living or dead, is entirely coincidental. Any mentioned brand names, places, and trademarks remain the property of their respective owners, bear no association with the author or the publisher, and are used for fictional purposes only.

No AI training: Without in any way limiting the author's exclusive rights under copyright, any use of this publication to "train" generative artificial intelligence (AI) technologies to generate text is expressly prohibited. The author reserves all rights to license uses of this work for generative AI training and development of machine learning language models.

ISBN: 979-8-9855615-4-8 (Paperback) ISBN: 979-8-9855615-7-9 (ebook)

Contents

1. Marin . . . 1
2. Frida . . . 10
3. Heather . . . 16
4. Frida . . . 22
5. Marin . . . 27
6. Heather . . . 34
7. Marin . . . 44
8. Frida . . . 50
9. Marin . . . 56
10. Heather . . . 61
11. Frida . . . 67
12. Marin . . . 72
13. Heather . . . 77
14. Frida . . . 84
15. Marin . . . 91
16. Heather . . . 97

17.	Marin	104
18.	Heather	111
19.	Frida	117
20.	Marin	122
21.	Heather	130
22.	Frida	137
23.	Marin	142
24.	Heather	149
25.	Frida	158
26.	Marin	163
27.	Heather	174
28.	Marin	181
29.	Frida	187
30.	Marin	193
31.	Heather	203
32.	Frida	210
33.	Marin	216
34.	Heather	223
35.	Frida	232
36.	Marin	238
37.	Heather	246
38.	Frida	257

39.	Marin	262
40.	Marin	275
41.	Marin	289
Gage's Scarf		297
Acknowledgements		298
About the Author		299
Also by Andie Young		301

"I'm so sorry about your mother, Stella. She was a wonderful woman," Mr. Alfred said. His eyes shifted to Marin, and he raised a wiry white brow.

"Thank you so much," Stella patted the man's arm and rested her hand on his wife's back as they walked forward in line.

Turning to Marin, Stella lowered her overly groomed brows. A second later, Stella's face brightened when she spotted Pastor Mike enter the room.

"Oh, Pastor Mike. Do you have a minute?" Stella walked over to the man.

Marin rolled her eyes. The speed with which Stella switched back and forth between two faces impressed her.

Hanging in the back of the room until the crowd thinned, Marin made her way toward the casket as if she were trudging through thick mud. Each step was more laborious than the last.

Fear had clung to Marin in the days since she'd found her grandma unresponsive. She'd come home from work to her sprawled like a rag doll across the kitchen floor. Her hollow brown eyes emphasized by her pale face—a look now etched in Marin's head. She'd wondered if anyone could bring her grandma back to life for the viewing, but she looked like herself.

Marin swallowed hard as her grandma's face came into view. Light pink blush graced her cheeks, light brown eyeshadow brushed across her eyelids, and her favorite shade of lipstick, peony pink, brightened her lips.

"Have a good day, sweetheart," her grandma said that morning.

"I will, Grandma. I am working until early afternoon." Marin had grabbed her backpack and slipped it over her shoulder.

"Oh good. You'll be home in time for your next knitting lesson." Grandma Judith had smiled and tilted her head toward a basket overflowing with yarn perched on the corner of the fireplace hearth. Marin reluctantly agreed to learn to knit, but she loved that it'd brought her and her grandma closer together.

Chapter 1

Marin

Dark clouds hung in the air, resembling Marin Martin's light drizzle fell from the sky, and she pulled her jacket ti she made her way across the parking lot, the drizzle turned into a downpour, matting her hair to her face. Lowering her head, Mar ened her steps as she approached the front doors of the funeral l

All eyes turned to Marin when she walked into the foyer. around, she spotted a black sign on an easel outside of a room w *Scott* written in white chalk.

Like a hawk swooping down on its prey, Marin's aunt Stell her before she reached the doorway.

"Are you kidding me, Kaylee? Why would you dress like th own grandmother's funeral?" Stella's disapproving gaze slid do

"My name is Marin, and there's nothing wrong with what I'n She refused to be someone she wasn't for the sake of her preter

"Excuse me, *Marin*. You should be ashamed of yourself. Y least wear a pair of jeans and a sweater," Stella said as she follo into the viewing room.

"Hello, Mr. and Mrs. Alfred." Stella beamed, stopping to with the elderly couple standing at the back of the viewing l you for coming."

Now that was gone.

Marin brushed a shaky finger across her grandma's cheek. Except for her cool skin, she looked like she was asleep. An inky tear fell onto the wooden edge of the casket, and she quickly wiped it away. A black tear stain on the white silk lining would give Stella more ammunition against Marin. "I love you Grandma Judith." She covered her mouth to hold back sobs and fled the room.

In the foyer, she garnered a few more stares until she found the sign for the restrooms. Two older women standing at the row of sinks widened their eyes when Marin flung the restroom door open and darted into a stall. A few moments of mumbling between the women went by before they left, and Marin was finally alone. Sliding back the lock, she crept out of the stall and up to the sinks.

Studying herself in the mirror for a long moment, Marin slipped off her black leather jacket and winced. The tattoo of angel wings in the middle of her back still stung. Her parents' initials were emblazoned between the wings. She'd have to go back to the tattoo shop and have her grandma's initials added.

Leaning close to the mirror, she stared at her reflection. Her gaze found each piercing in her face and the piercing in her navel. The new larger gauges were still causing pain in her earlobes. Turning her head from side to side, she looked like Cruella De Vil except her hair was blue and pink. Marin's eyes pooled with tears. Not once had her grandma made a comment about her appearance.

Looping her fingers through the two front belt loops, Marin pulled up her black cargo pants and sighed when the pants slid back down to her hips. She pulled the hem of her black shirt as far down as she could, but it sprang back into place, showing the skin of her midriff. She groaned. At least she was wearing black today, unlike Stella, who was in a pale yellow dress like she was hosting a spring tea party.

Marin pulled out the eyeliner pencil from her jacket pocket and added a fresh layer of black after she wiped away the smudges under her eyes. She took a deep breath and exhaled. Maybe she should skip the burial to keep out of Stella's crosshairs. She needed to look for a place to stay anyway, since Stella said she would put Grandma's house on the market soon. Stella reminded Marin more than once that she was almost twenty years old now and needed to act more like an adult.

Marin headed to the parking lot and slid into the driver's seat of her car. She sat quietly for a while, taking deep breaths to calm down so she could go back inside for the funeral service. Something caught her eye, and she noticed people leaving the building. Soon the pallbearers came out carrying the casket. They transferred it to the back of the hearse and headed to their respective vehicles.

She'd waited too long.

Drawing in a deep breath, Marin cranked her car and waited her turn to join the processional. She owed it to her grandmother to attend the burial, since she missed the funeral service. During the short drive to the cemetery, she continued to take calming breaths.

Marin got out of her car and tugged on the hem of her shirt. She groaned and zipped her jacket. An older couple walked by, and she offered a slight smile. The woman's gaze swept over Marin, and she rolled her eyes. She knew she couldn't make a spectacle at her grandmother's burial and returned to her car.

She was far enough away from the gravesite that it was like watching a muted movie. She didn't have to be present to know the wonderful things that were being said about her grandmother.

Grandma was a pillar in the community and had organized charity events and volunteered her time. But most of all, she was a former first lady of Mississippi. Marin's grandfather, William Scott, had been the governor for eight years in the nineteen eighties and nineties. Stella reveled in her position as a former first daughter.

Through a sheen of tears, Marin watched as they lowered her grandmother into the ground. Gasping, she covered her mouth to keep her grief inside.

When the crowd dispersed, she backed out and headed to work.

The parking lot was full at Charley's Steakhouse, so Marin had to drive around to the back of the building to find a parking space. It was a good sign, and she was almost positive that she could clock in early. She grabbed her apron and made her way inside.

"Hey, girl. How are you?" Madison said when Marin walked into the beverage area. "I'm sorry I missed seeing you at the funeral. I'm sure you and your aunt had your hands full."

If Marin ventured to guess, she'd say there were several hundred in attendance at her grandma's funeral. It would have been easy to miss seeing Madison. There was no way she would tell her friend she'd hidden out in her car during the funeral and burial. Madison wouldn't understand.

"There were a lot of people there, but I was able to say goodbye." It was the truth.

Back in high school, Madison was a classmate. And like Marin's grandmother, she didn't judge Marin by her appearance. Madison was an all-American girl. She had been a cheerleader, homecoming queen, and dated the star football player. But she befriended Marin when she was a new freshman from out of state—a double whammy for a high school student. Madison's acceptance had always puzzled her when they were in school, since they were so different.

"You got table fourteen?" Madison raised her brows as she walked past Marin with a tray full of beverages.

"Yeah." Marin walked over to the table and pulled her order pad from her apron. When she looked up, she was met with four pairs of eyes. Used to the stares, she didn't miss a beat as she gave her spiel on the day's specials and made suggestions of beverages and appetizers.

After table fourteen finished their meals and departed, the busser cleared the table and handed Marin the ticket folder. She held back a smile. The customer had written a note on the ticket and left a generous tip. Despite the typical initial reactions she received from the diners, her tips proved she was a good waitress.

After her shift, Marin headed home. She held her breath when she slid the key in the lock on the front door. She exhaled slowly as the knob unlocked when she turned the key. Stella had not changed the locks yet. She tossed her keys on the coffee table next to a note. Picking it up, her heart pounded hard in her chest.

Kaylee,

I have a real estate agent coming out tomorrow. You need to find somewhere to stay by the end of the week. I want the house ready for showings.

Stella

Marin began trembling. Where would she go? She had little money. Certainly not enough to rent her own apartment. Why did Stella hate her? Over the years, she had paid enough attention to Stella's conversations with her grandma that she knew her mother was the cause. Gemma was five years older than Stella. When Marin's mother turned sixteen, she went wild. Gemma met Marin's father, Kevin, and the two began a whirlwind romance. Only it wasn't a fairytale romance. Kevin was heavily into drugs, and soon Marin's mother joined him. Two weeks before running off with Kevin, Gemma found out she was pregnant with Marin.

Her grandma Judith didn't talk much about her parents. Marin knew it was to protect her. But Stella made snide comments about Gemma. Marin's grandma always quieted Stella when she was around, but sometimes Stella found Marin alone and unleashed her hatred. All Stella could talk about was how horrible Gemma was and how she broke their mother's heart.

The chime of an incoming text drew Marin to the present. An employee had gotten sick, and the supervisor asked Marin if she could cover the rest of their shift. She shook her head, but she needed the hours. No telling where she would be living this time next week. She slipped on her jacket and made her way back out to her car.

Click.

The sound coming from under the hood quickened Marin's pulse. She turned the key again.

Click.

Her forehead fell against the steering wheel. "Please." Tears stung her eyes. She tried again and the engine turned over. "Thank you."

After four more hours at work, Marin got into her car and held her breath as she turned the key in the ignition.

Click.

"No way." Any other time, she'd call her grandma and she'd come get Marin. She tried again.

Click.

A light tap on the window startled Marin. It was Barry, the bartender. Wiping her eyes, she hit the button to lower the window, but the glass didn't move. Sighing, she opened the door.

"Sounds like the alternator."

"Oh." What the heck was an alternator, and how much did it cost?

"I can pull one from a salvage yard and put it in for you."

She knew Barry was into cars, which meant he had connections. He restored cars and could do everything from rebuilding an engine to popping out a dent. But how much would he charge her?

"I can't pay much."

"Don't worry about it. I know you're going through a lot. I'll jump your car and you can follow me to my house. I don't live far. Lizzy can take you home and come get you when the car is fixed. Should be tomorrow."

"Okay. I don't know how to thank you." Marin exhaled slowly. Barry was a lifesaver.

"No need." He grinned. "Just pay it forward."

After Barry's wife dropped Marin off, she stood in the doorway to her grandma's bedroom. She looked around and noticed that her grandmother's jewelry box was missing from the top of the dresser.

Stella.

Did she think Marin would steal items of value? As her grandma's next of kin, Stella had every right to her belongings.

Marin stared at the bed and imagined her grandmother peacefully sleeping. Walking to the edge, she sat down, kicked off her shoes, and slipped off her jacket. She crawled under the covers and laid her head on the pillow. Taking in a deep breath, the faint floral scent of her grandma filled her nose, and she started sobbing.

Barry dropped the car off the following afternoon. Marin carried some of her clothes to the car and laid them across the backseat. She went inside and glanced around for the last time. The past six years played through her mind like a movie. What would her next chapter look like?

On her way out the door, she noticed the basket on the fireplace hearth and stared at it for a moment. The colorful balls of yarn beckoned her. She picked it up and walked out the door.

Locking the front door, she put the key where Stella told her to, then rearranged some things in the trunk of her car. Tucking the basket safely in the corner of the trunk, she headed to work.

Part-time would not be enough to pay rent or buy groceries, much less gas and insurance for her car. She planned to ask for more hours. If she couldn't get more hours, she would need to find an additional part-time job or a full-time job.

Exhausted physically and emotionally after her shift, Marin drove up and down the highway, looking for a place to stay. She found the remains of a building damaged by Hurricane Katrina and parked in the back. In hindsight, she should have made plans to spend the night on someone's couch.

Locking the doors, Marin leaned the driver's seat back. A few moments later, she changed her mind. Climbing onto the backseat, she laid on top of her clothes, covering herself with her winter coat. She didn't want to make herself too vulnerable. Rolling onto her side and using her hands as a pillow, tears filled her eyes. She missed her grandma.

For the first time in her life, Marin was on her own.

Chapter 2

Frida

Pulling back the living room curtains and opening the blinds, Frida Gomez welcomed the warm afternoon sunshine. She walked over to the fireplace mantel and picked up the framed photograph of her husband Max in his Air Force dress blues uniform. She ran her finger over the silver buttons down the front, then the *U.S.* insignia on the lapels. He was such a handsome man with dark brown hair and eyes as black as night.

"*Feliz aniversario, mi amor.*" Frida wiped the dusting cloth over the glass and kissed his face. "Happy anniversary, my love," she whispered.

Frida was at a place where she could celebrate their anniversary with love instead of heartbreak. The first decade after Max died, she didn't acknowledge their anniversary at all. There wasn't anything to celebrate. Frida and Max had been married two years when he received his draft notice for Vietnam. Less than two years later, he was gone. Ripped from her arms; ripped from her heart. She breathed in and slowly exhaled, returning the frame to its place of honor next to their wedding photograph.

The doorbell broke her reverie and she looked at the clock. On time, as usual. She glanced through the peephole and smiled. On the steps stood her niece, holding a large Krispy Kreme box.

"Maria," she said when she opened the door.

"*Tia.*" Maria slipped an arm around Frida's neck. "I brought an afternoon snack." She sat the donut box on the coffee table and followed Frida into the kitchen.

"I see that." Since Maria moved to Mississippi five years earlier, she'd spent the afternoon with Frida on her wedding anniversary every year.

"When do you want to go to the cemetery?"

"In a few." Frida wanted to go alone. Maria had accompanied Frida to the cemetery every year as well. Maybe she could go after Maria left for the day. No, it might be dark. It may hurt her feelings, but Frida needed to tell Maria that she wanted to do this by herself.

"*Sobrina.* I appreciate your compassion, but I would like to go alone this time." Frida was right. Tears gathered in Maria's eyes.

"Oh."

"I'm sorry, Maria. It's just something I have to do this time."

"No, *Tia*, I understand." Maria walked up to Frida and hugged her.

Maria offered to put on a fresh pot of coffee and Frida took a seat in the living room. Glancing out the window, she saw the rose bush out front. Soon, buds would sprout from the branches. A new beginning. That reminded Frida. "How's Phillip?" She smiled at the hint of pink in Maria's cheeks as she walked into the living room with two cups of coffee.

Maria handed Frida a cup. "Black?"

Frida nodded. "Are you avoiding my question?"

"No, *Tia*. Phillip is fine." A shy smile tugged at her lips.

Maria's husband, Mateo, died five years earlier after a brief battle with cancer. She began dating Phillip two months ago when a friend introduced them.

"Sometimes I feel guilty."

"About what?" Frida blew into her cup and took a sip of coffee.

"Moving on. You've stayed single all these years."

Frida and Maria had talked about their kinship. Not just family, but in their grief of losing a husband.

"Maria, you are young."

"I'm thirty-five."

"That's young."

"But you never remarried."

"Your *Tio* Max was the love of my life. I can't imagine myself with anyone else." Frida winced. Maria was with someone else. "But there's nothing wrong with choosing to have a relationship." She reached over and patted Maria's knee.

"I know." Maria bit into a donut and sipped her coffee. "MJ is going to the freshman dance," she said, changing the subject.

"Oh yeah? Did he ask someone?" Frida winked.

"No, he's going with his friends."

"Little Mateo. I can't believe he's old enough to go to a dance. His papa would be so proud."

Maria smiled and finished her donut and coffee. Gathering Frida's cup, she headed to the kitchen. It must be time for her to go. Maria always ended a visit with cleaning. Frida stood and closed the donut box. Maria grabbed her jacket and purse and raised her hand when Frida held out the box.

"You keep it." She smiled and kissed Frida's cheek.

Frida bid her niece goodbye and watched her drive away. Looping her purse strap over her shoulder, she grabbed her light jacket and keys and walked out to her car. She had about an hour before the sun went down.

Frida picked up her jacket from the passenger seat and slipped it on. It was late April, but there was a chill in the early evening air. Taking a guess, she now had around half an hour before dusk settled across the cemetery. The last thing she needed was to head back to the parking lot in the dark and fall and break a hip. Moans and groans coming from a cemetery at night were bound to upset the neighborhood.

Walking down the familiar sidewalk, Frida smiled when Max's headstone came into view. Every year she visited him on his birthday, their wedding anniversary, and the anniversary of his death. More often if she was not doing well emotionally. She reached down and brushed her fingers across the top of the cool granite. Tears gathered in her eyes as she read the words. The same words she'd read for the past fifty years.

Maximiliano Roberto Gomez

Born Feb 16, 1946

Died Sep 3, 1970

Loving husband, son, brother

In the arms of Jesus

She glanced at the blank area next to Max's inscription. One day, her name and details would occupy the space. It was strange seeing where her body would be laid to rest. She sighed. The thought of spending one more day without Max felt like an eternity to her. She never knew grief was palpable until her heart shattered when she was twenty years old. But now that she was seventy-three, she knew they would be together soon. Frida kissed her fingers and touched the top of the stone.

"Goodbye, my love. See you soon." And she would see him soon. It may be for a visit or for all eternity.

Back at home, Frida sat down with the newspaper. *Cinco de Mayo* was coming up, and several celebrations were listed in the Home and Cultural section. Frida's church planned a celebration, and she volunteered to make tamales. When she turned the page, her eyes found a small ad in the lower left corner. She held the paper close to her face and sighed. Slipping on her reading glasses, she read the advertisement.

Are you looking for a way to help our troops?

Join us in knitting socks for troops deployed to the Middle East. Email us at...

Frida shook her head. "Not all of us use email." She raised her brows when she saw a phone number in small print at the bottom. Tearing out the ad, she placed it in the drawer of the side table. She'd look into it later.

Her phone chimed and she picked it up from the side table. Her friend Joyce's name brightened the screen.

Joyce: Are ya busy tonight? Want to play bingo?

Looking at the clock, Frida sighed. It was six o'clock. Bingo started at seven. She still needed to eat dinner and if she was being honest with herself, she wasn't in the bingo mood. She tapped on the call icon. After three rings, Joyce picked up.

"Why did you call me?"

"You know I don't like to text. Too much technology. I'm old school, I guess."

"Bingo?"

"Oh, not tonight."

"Party pooper."

Frida bet that Joyce's free hand was firmly planted on her hip.

"I haven't been home from the cemetery long—"

"Who kicked the bucket?"

Oh, Joyce. Joyce, Joyce. If she wasn't a dear friend...

"Max did—fifty years ago."

"W-what?" There was a moment of silence before Joyce gasped. "Frida. I'm the worst BFF. I'm so sorry. I forgot that today is your anniversary. Do you forgive me?"

"Of course, I do."

"Good. You are excused from bingo tonight. Next Monday?"

"Well, I have to make fifty tamales for next Wednesday."

"I can help."

Joyce was different. Some would say she was eccentric. Her personality was reflected in everything from her bright pink house to her yellow VW Beetle. Her wardrobe set her apart the most. At bingo last week, she wore black pants with giant white polka dots, a white shirt with tiny black polka dots and her favorite red-framed glasses. Despite her quirkiness, Frida loved her friend.

"I would love that."

Frida hung up with Joyce and gazed at her wedding photograph on the mantel. She stood and walked over to the bookshelf next to the fireplace. Pulling out a worn, yellowing white fabric covered album, she sat back down and began browsing her wedding photographs.

"Oh, how I miss you, Maximiliano. Why did God have to take you home so soon?" She wiped tears from her cheeks and spent the next few minutes reminiscing. The last photograph was of the couple eating cake. Frida smiled at the image in the photograph. So young and in love. She touched Max's face.

"Until death parts us. I didn't know it would be so soon, *mi amor*."

A rush of tears fell down her cheeks and dotted the plastic covering the photos. She wiped them away and brought the album up to her face. She kissed Max's face and closed the album. Where was her happily ever after?

Chapter 3

Heather

Heather Zimmerman stood in the laundry room with a toothbrush in one hand and a jelly-stained t-shirt in the other. Grabbing the stain remover, she soaked the stain and scrubbed it, careful to avoid Monty the Monster Truck. If the spray damaged any part of Monty, Jake would have a meltdown. She closed her eyes and inhaled deeply the scent of stew simmering in the slow cooker. The house smelled heavenly.

"Heather?"

She turned and saw her husband, Adam, standing in the doorway to the laundry room.

"Hey. The stew should be ready around five. I'll make cornbread and rice."

Adam stood in silence. Heather's gaze found the overnight bag in his hand and the garment bag slung over his shoulder.

"Are you going somewhere?"

"Um…" Adam shifted his weight from one foot to the other. "Yeah. Troy asked me to go to Atlanta last minute."

"Oh. Okay." Heather rinsed her hands at the sink and dried them on her jeans. Walking over to where Adam stood, she slipped her arms around his waist and kissed him.

Adam stiffened and pulled back. Heather's chest tightened. "I-I'll be home Sunday night." He cleared his throat and blinked.

Heather nodded. "I love you." She opened the door to the garage, and he walked down the stairs.

"You too," he said over his shoulder as he headed to his car.

You too? Adam had never said those words to her. He'd always responded with, "I love you, too."

She watched Adam back out and head down the drive. She hit the garage door button and closed the house door. Walking into the kitchen, she stirred the stew and replaced the lid. The aroma didn't tease her senses like before.

Adam's coffee cup was beside the sink. She washed and dried it and placed it in the cabinet with the others. Gazing out the kitchen window, she watched the breeze push ripples across the surface of the water in the pool.

Something caught her attention and she saw the swing swaying in the slight breeze. Since she was a child, swinging had been a source of stress relief. She slipped on her jacket and made her way out back. Easing herself down on the cedar swing, she set the swing in motion and closed her eyes, enjoying the breeze on her face.

She had wanted a porch swing, but Adam didn't want holes in the ceiling of the front porch. Heather sighed. Resting her hand on the space beside her, her thoughts went to when she and Adam used to swing together while they watched the kids play in the backyard. What was going on with her husband? In the past six months, he'd been distant. And intimacy was nonexistent. Tears gathered in her eyes and spilled down her cheeks.

The back door opened, and Shelly stepped out onto the patio. Heather wiped her face and smiled as her daughter walked up and sat next to her. Shelly looked at Heather but said nothing about her undoubtedly red and puffy eyes.

"Is Daddy working this weekend?"

"Did he call you?"

"No, I saw him at the traffic light leaving the neighborhood."

"Troy sent him to Atlanta." Heather bit her bottom lip to keep from asking Shelly if she knew anything about her dad's behavior.

"Why didn't you go?"

"He didn't ask." Heather used to go with Adam on work trips when her schedule permitted, but like everything else, he'd stopped asking her to go the past few months.

"Oh," Shelly said.

Did Shelly know something? Adam wouldn't talk to their daughter about their marriage, would he? She was an adult at eighteen, but she didn't see Adam confiding in Shelly, although they were close.

"I'm going to call Travis. Is it okay if he comes over for dinner?" Shelly turned her head toward Heather and grinned.

"As long as you make the cornbread and rice."

"Deal." Shelly thrust herself from the swing and giggled as if she was five years old again.

Heather glanced at her watch. She needed to leave to pick up Jake. Heather drew in a long breath and frowned. Adam was supposed to take Jake to see the latest *Monty the Monster Truck* movie. Jake would ask about his father when she picked him up. She rested her hands on the seat on either side of her. That was something else that had been happening more lately. Adam had been forgetting about things he'd promised the kids.

Ethan had gotten his learner's permit, and Adam promised to take him driving on the weekends. That was eight months ago, and he had taken him out a few times. Heather took Ethan out when she had a chance, but he was behind on his hours. Time was running out for Ethan to get his license when he turned sixteen next month. Ethan would be crushed if he wasn't able to get his license when all his friends had theirs.

And Shelly. Heather was sure Adam made promises to her he'd failed to keep. She pushed herself up from the swing and made her way inside. When Heather opened the backdoor, she saw Shelly leaning against the kitchen counter with her phone glued to her ear. She saw Heather and grimaced.

"Trav, I've got to go. See you in a few." Shelly was quiet for a moment. "I love you, too."

Heather's insides knotted. Love was both amazing and heartbreaking. She hoped Travis didn't break her daughter's heart anytime soon. But she knew it would eventually happen. Rarely did a first love last a lifetime.

"Sorry, Mom." Shelly dashed to the pantry and brought out a box of Jiffy Mix and the canister of rice. "Are you leaving to pick up Jake?"

"Yeah. Be back in half an hour."

Shelly nodded and walked up to her mother and kissed her cheek. Her phone chimed. She grabbed it and grinned as pink filled her cheeks. It must be Travis. Funny that they couldn't go five minutes without contact.

As Heather joined the pickup line at Jay Hanna Dean Elementary School, she saw Jake smile and wave. Her sweet boy had a contagious smile that lit up his face.

"Mommy is Daddy home?" Jake said after he climbed onto the backseat.

"No, baby. He had to go to Atlanta this weekend."

"But he promised."

"I know. Mr. Troy needed him at the last minute."

"He's mean." Jake crossed his arms over his chest and huffed.

"Jacob, that's not nice." Heather pulled out of the school parking lot and had an idea she hoped would soften the blow of a broken promise.

"He always takes Daddy away from us."

"Part of Daddy's job is to travel."

Tears stung Heather's eyes. It was true. Maybe Adam could talk to Troy. "How about Dunkin'?" Jake perked up, but not as perky as usual for an afternoon treat that would spoil dinner.

After dinner, Heather helped Jake get ready for bed and tucked him in for the night. She walked out back toward the swing. The lights from the pool illuminated the yard enough that Heather could see where she was stepping. She sat down and looked up. There wasn't a cloud in the sky and the stars twinkled like diamonds. It seemed they were putting on a special show for her.

Adam came to mind as he had been since he left for his trip earlier. She'd realized his behavior changed six months ago when he received a promotion to chief operating officer. The promotion came with an eighty-thousand-dollar bonus. What did he do with the money? He bought a new BMW sports car. She thought of a dozen things that the money could have been spent on.

Maybe Adam was having a mid-life crisis. When was mid-life these days? If he was having a mid-life crisis, it meant he would live to be ninety-eight. Didn't that also mean he'd have a blonde half Heather's age on his arm? His former secretary was in her fifties. She knew nothing about his new secretary. Was there a chance she'd be seventy? Heather looked toward the sky again. What was Adam doing right now? Probably having dinner with his colleagues. Hopefully, with his colleagues and not…

Setting the swing in motion, she thought about their marriage. She firmly believed that Adam would never cheat on her. Both came from a broken home and vowed that they wouldn't follow in the footsteps of their parents. She was overreacting. Standing, she headed to the house and grabbed her phone from the kitchen counter. One text from Adam letting her know he made it. No "I love you." No "I miss you." Just a courtesy text.

A burning sensation filled her chest when she tapped the family location app. He'd been in Atlanta for five hours and had sent the text half an hour ago. She squeezed her eyes shut and wiped the tears that gathered. She typed a reply.

Heather: Glad to hear. I love you.

Staring at the app, a minute went by without a reply. She went upstairs to shower and get ready for bed. Climbing under the covers, she picked up the phone and smiled when she saw a message from Adam. She opened it and her smile fell.

Adam: You too.

Chapter 4

Frida

Frida stood in front of the tiny closet in the spare bedroom. The church asked for donations for the homeless shelter and a box full of clothes she no longer wore was hiding somewhere. She'd already looked in her closet, so it must be in the spare room closet. Opening the door, she pulled out several boxes and placed them on the bed. She began opening them and shuffling through the contents.

She found the elusive box and set it aside. Now was the perfect time to spring clean, and she continued going through the boxes before putting them back in the closet. She found an array of small old appliances, gently used linens, and gifts that she'd received that she had never used. She frowned. Should she donate the gifts? If no one had said a word about the gifts by now, they never would.

In a way, she enjoyed going through the boxes. It was like hunting for Easter eggs, or opening gifts on Christmas morning. Half of the items she had forgotten she owned. She opened the last box and found a few outfits of hers from the nineteen sixties and seventies. She cackled when she pulled out a pair of bell-bottom jeans. Holding them up to her waist, she wrinkled her brow at the bunched up pant legs on the floor. She must have shrunk.

Laying the jeans aside, she peered in the box and froze. Laying on the bottom was Max's neatly folded Air Force dress blues uniform jacket. Memories flooded her mind–the first time she met Max, their first date, their wedding. Then there was the terrible day he received his draft notice. She slowly exhaled and pulled the jacket from the box. Holding it up, it was as if Max himself stood before her. Oh, to feel his arms around her again.

She walked into the living room with the jacket and stood in front of the fireplace. Looking at the photograph of him on the mantel, she draped the jacket across her arm and touched each button and each *U.S.* insignia. She looked up at him with tearful eyes. How could she have forgotten that she still had his jacket?

Back in the spare bedroom, Frida laid the jacket on the bed. She'd check into having it preserved. As she put the last box into the closet, she turned around and saw her knitting basket in the corner. She set aside her knitting a while back because of arthritis in her hands. At her last appointment, the doctor prescribed a new medication and she'd had little pain lately.

Placing the basket on the bed, she browsed through the knitting supplies. She had knitting needles as old as her baby sister. A soft laugh shook her shoulders. The yarn inventory had dwindled, and all she had left was a boring black skein of acrylic yarn. Her eyes brightened and she made her way to the living room.

Opening the drawer in the side table, she pulled out a sales flyer for Cathy's Craft Haven and noticed a small piece of paper flutter to the floor. She picked it up and tilted her head. It was the advertisement she'd torn out of the paper a few weeks ago about knitting socks for the military stationed in the Middle East. The perfect idea came to her. She'd buy a few skeins of yarn and put the new arthritis medication her doctor prescribed to the test. Helping the troops swelled her heart with pride. And who couldn't use a new pair of socks?

She carried the sales flyer and advertisement into the kitchen and picked up the phone. After speaking with a woman named Beth from Socks for Troops, she made a list of the type of yarn and some other supplies she needed. All she had to do was wait until next week's sale. Ten skeins of yarn would be out of the question without the fifty percent off coupon. Frida smiled. It had been a while since she'd felt needed. One of those men or women could have been her Max in Vietnam. She was sure whoever received the socks she knitted would appreciate the gesture.

Frida's phone chimed and she went into the living room to check her messages. Joyce had invited her to coffee. Why not? As she drove to the coffee shop, her mind ran wild with thoughts of the socks she could knit. There were a few old pattern books at the bottom of the basket. Hopefully, they weren't out of style. They were socks. What did it matter? It wasn't like anyone would see them. She grinned.

Joyce was sitting at a table by the window. Frida smiled and shook her head. Joyce wore hot pink pants and a zebra print top. Her friend raised her brows as she watched Frida bounce through the front doors.

"Frida? What's gotten into you?"

"I'm going to knit socks for troops in the Middle East." Frida beamed.

"They wear socks in the desert? Isn't it a hundred and ten degrees over there?"

Frida frowned. She didn't think about the heat. Why did they need socks? Oh yeah. "They wear combat boots all the time. The boots rub their feet so thick socks help."

"You sound like a walking advertisement." Joyce picked up her latte and took a sip. She pushed a plate of scones toward Frida.

"Just a sec. Let me order my coffee." She made her way to the back of the line. Why did Joyce look at her like she was crazy? Maybe she was crazy. She shook her head. No, she wasn't. Knitting would give her hands a workout and help pass the time, and she'd feel useful again.

Frida ordered and returned to her seat across from Joyce. She loved her friend dearly, but she would change the subject. She would not let Joyce rain on her parade.

"So, socks?"

Frida sighed. "Love the outfit."

Joyce smiled and leaned back, running her hand down her shirt. "Thanks. It spoke to me, so I had to have it."

And with that, Joyce went on a tangent from the price of clothes to Gen Z. Kids these days would one day lead the country, which terrified Joyce. The thought had crossed Frida's mind, but she had better things to think about. Socks, for example.

Knitting books and pamphlets covered the surface of Frida's small dining table. She grimaced when she looked at the sock patterns. Argyle, tube socks, ankle socks, and thick wool socks. Maybe too thick. She'd texted her nephew, MJ, and asked him to come over. It was the only way she could get in contact with him. The boy hated talking on the phone.

When he sat in the chair at her computer desk and hit the power button, he looked up at Frida and furrowed his brows. "*Tia*, how old is this computer?"

"Well, probably older than you." He looked at her and scoffed. Frida raised a brow in response.

"I'm sorry. I'll make it work."

Two hours later, between the slow computer and slower printer, Frida had three new sock patterns. Offering MJ a snack, Frida studied the patterns and was confident she could churn out at least ten pairs of socks with what she planned to buy at Cathy's in a few days. She smiled. She couldn't wait to send off her first shipment of socks. Beth assigned her to a base in Iraq. Later, she'd ask MJ to look up the base and give her some information.

"Aunt Frida?"

She looked up and saw MJ staring at her. "Yes, *sobrino*?"

"Do you need your grass cut?"

Frida glanced out the back door. "Do you need some money?"

MJ grinned and nodded.

A few minutes later, he was in her backyard mowing. She watched as he pushed the mower back and forth, cutting perfect lines into the grass. She shook her head. So much loss. MJ was nine years old when his father passed. Her family had suffered several losses over the years. Of course, her parents passed on years ago. Alejandro, her baby brother, died when he was a child. Their father was backing out of the drive. Alejandro was playing behind the car, but her father didn't see him. He never forgave himself and took his guilt to the grave.

There was another loss no one knew about. Not even Max. Shortly after he'd left for Vietnam, Frida became ill and had gone to the doctor. She was miscarrying the child she didn't know existed. She decided not to tell Max, so he wouldn't worry. And she didn't want to tell their families for fear that they would tell Max. When he died, her grief for their child shifted to grief for Max. As the years passed, she saw no need to share her other loss, and it remained tucked deep inside her heart.

Chapter 5

Marin

Marin spent two weeks couch surfing. She'd spent a few nights here and there, but soon her friends grew tired of her occupying their living rooms. Then there was Alpha. She knew him through a mutual friend. He was shady, but she took him up on his offer for her to stay with him and Petra, his girlfriend. June's rising temperatures and the humidity made sleeping in her car miserable. She couldn't leave the car running to use the air conditioner or she'd run out of gas. And she wasn't about to lower the windows. Not even a crack.

The first night she stayed with Alpha and Petra, the three of them enjoyed watching movies and eating pizza. The following day, Petra left to visit her mother out of town, which left Marin and Alpha alone. She woke in the middle of the night to Alpha climbing on top of her. Alpha was tall and built, but she managed to push him off. Most likely because he was high. She sprang from the couch. Grabbing her jacket, she fled the apartment. The past three nights, she was back to sleeping in her car.

Marin pulled into the parking lot at Charley's Steakhouse for her first eight-hour shift. She'd transitioned to full time and now had benefits. But her income wasn't enough to afford an apartment on her own. She looked in the rearview mirror and reapplied her eyeliner.

Stella had called earlier in the day to tell her that her grandma's house sold. It was the first time she'd heard from Stella since her grandma's funeral, not including the note on the coffee table. Marin still had a few things at the house that wouldn't fit in her car. She had picked out what was most important to take with her. Since the house sold, Marin wondered what Stella did with her belongings.

Six hours into her shift, Marin's feet burned as if she was walking on hot coals. The boots she was wearing had no support, but she couldn't afford to buy another pair of shoes. Table ten walked out the door while she was taking table six's order. The busser brought over the ticket folder once he'd cleared the table.

At the register, she opened the folder to turn in the ticket and her lips parted. Table ten left a thirty-dollar tip. Moisture filled her eyes as she read the note written on the side of the ticket.

Excellent service, Marin. We'll be back and will ask to be seated in your section.

With what money she had set aside and the tip, she could buy a new pair of shoes. She helped close for the night and made her way to the parking lot. When she turned the corner, she saw someone leaning against her car, increasing her heart rate. She slowed her steps as she approached. Relief filled her veins when she realized the person was Madison, but her friend's face twisted into a scowl. Madison crossed her arms over her chest. Marin could see her fingers pressing into her sides.

"What are you doing here?" Marin pulled her keys from her pocket.

"I came to pick up my watch from Barry. He fixed it for me." Madison pushed herself away from Marin's car and pointed to the backseat. "Why didn't you tell me you were living out of your car, Kaylee?" Her wavering voice echoed off the dumpsters.

Marin cringed. Stella had been the only person to call her Kaylee in a while. "I…"

"Why Marin?" Madison's eyes glistened. "I thought we were friends."

"We are." Tears threatened to gather in Marin's own eyes.

"Then it's settled. You're coming home with me. Our couch is a sofa sleeper. My roommate is moving out in a few weeks, and we can talk to the office about you taking over her part of the lease."

"Madison, I—"

"I'll help you set up a budget. I can't have you sleeping on the streets. You are one of my best friends."

Marin raised her eyebrows. She liked Madison and appreciated that she treated her no differently than her sorority sisters, but she didn't know Madison felt the way she did about her. Madison walked up to Marin and pulled her into a hug. It took everything in Marin not to bristle.

Marin slid into the driver's seat of her car and followed Madison to her apartment, which was in an upscale part of town. How was she going to afford half the rent? It was probably a thousand dollars a month. She'd be responsible for five hundred dollars. Then there were the utilities. Marin sighed.

Textbooks and notebooks lay scattered across the coffee table, and the dishes were piled up next to the sink. Marin decided she would clean the apartment in appreciation for Madison and her roommate letting her sleep on their couch. She glanced at the couch. It looked brand new.

A red-head walked out of the bedroom on the left and widened her eyes when she saw Marin. Madison smiled and motioned to Marin. "This is my friend, Marin. She's going to be staying with us. I'll talk to management about her taking over your part of the lease."

"Oh, okay. I'm Alicia." Her eyes shifted from Madison to Marin.

Her expression told Marin that Alicia fell into the category of those who prejudged her by her appearance.

"Can I talk to you?" Alicia looked at Madison and tilted her head toward her bedroom. Madison followed.

Marin stepped inside the bathroom and closed the door. Through the walls, she could hear Alicia and Madison's conversation.

"Are you sure she won't steal our stuff?"

"Why would you ask such a thing?"

"Are you blind? She looks like she smokes crack."

Marin's chin trembled and she wiped the tears from her eyes.

"She does not. I've known her since ninth grade. She would never steal from us or do drugs."

"Are you sure?"

"Yes, I'm sure."

"Well, keep her out of my room."

A door slammed, startling Marin. She washed her hands and walked out of the bathroom. Madison was pacing the living room with her arms wrapped around her middle.

"I can leave."

"You are *not* leaving. If needed, you can sleep with me. I have a queen size bed."

"Okay, thank you." Marin brought a shaky hand to her chest.

Madison hugged her. Two hugs in one night were odd for Marin. The only person she'd let hug her was her grandmother. It sort of felt good that someone else cared about her. Her own family didn't.

A week had passed since Marin crashed on Madison and Alicia's couch. She stopped by the store on her way home from work and bought a few groceries. Spaghetti was her specialty and she planned to cook dinner for her roommates. Alicia had been distant, and Marin wanted to do something so their remaining time together was less strained. When she walked into the apartment, she saw the door open to Alicia's room.

Putting the grocery bags on the counter, she drew in a breath and walked to the doorway. Her eyes widened when she saw the empty room. The only things left were the indentions in the carpet, left by the furniture. Alicia told Madison that she would move out next week. Maybe she moved into her new apartment earlier. Marin talked herself out of assuming the worst.

Dipping a spoon in the simmering spaghetti sauce for a taste test, Marin heard the door unlock and watched Madison as she walked in. Madison lifted her chin and sniffed the air.

"Oh my gosh, Marin. That smells so good. Thank you for cooking. I wasn't looking forward to eating cereal again." She laughed.

"My pleasure." Marin dropped the spaghetti noodles into the pot of boiling water. "Should be ready in fifteen."

"Okay, I'm going to change."

Marin watched as Madison strolled into her room. Should she ask? No, let it go. When Madison came back into the living room, Marin's question burst from her mouth. "Um, Alicia moved out already?"

Madison glanced toward the patio doors. "Yeah, her new apartment was ready." She cleared her throat and her gaze dropped to the floor.

Marin turned back to the stove and stirred the spaghetti sauce. She sensed Madison's presence in the kitchen.

"It's me, isn't it?" Marin glanced at Madison as she walked up beside her.

"Marin—."

"It's ready." Marin pulled down two plates from the cabinet and grabbed two forks from the drawer.

The women filled their plates and sat at the small dining table. A few moments passed before Madison spoke.

"I never knew your natural hair color was brown."

Marin touched the top of her head. "Yeah." Hair dye was on the bottom of her list of necessities.

"How long have you been dying your hair? It was like that when you moved here freshman year." Madison studied Marin's hair. "Well, a rainbow of colors over the years." She smiled and twisted spaghetti on her fork.

"About a year before Grandma found me."

"Found you?" Madison's brows drew together.

Marin flinched. She'd kept the truth about how she'd ended up living with her grandmother to herself. It was common knowledge that her parents had died, but she'd told classmates they died in a car accident. Marin opened her mouth and closed it.

"You don't have to tell me."

"No, it's…I-I was in foster care." Marin stuck a forkful of spaghetti in her mouth.

Madison's eyes widened. "I didn't know that."

"Yeah, I don't talk about it."

"You don't have to talk, but if you want to, I'm here." She reached out and laid her hand over Marin's hand.

Should she tell Madison the truth? The thought of opening old wounds exhausted Marin. "Thank you."

They finished eating in silence. Marin washed the dishes and Madison dried and put them away. She was sure a dozen questions were floating around in Madison's head. Marin didn't want to think about her past now, much less talk about it. There was something about seeing pity in a person's eyes. But what she had been through made her stronger. Maybe too strong.

"Hey, want to watch a movie?"

Anything to take her mind off her past. "Sure. How about *Steel Magnolias*?"

Madison laughed. "Sorry. I didn't think you were into chick flicks."

"Goes to show that you should never judge a book by its cover." Marin grinned. "Hey, since Alicia's gone, I'm going to unload my car. That stuff's been in there for over two months. Give me fifteen minutes."

"Want help?"

"It's not much. I can get it."

"Okay, girl. I'll pop some popcorn."

Marin made two trips, unloading her clothes from the backseat. She popped the trunk and covered her nose at the odor. Mold and mildew covered everything on the right side of the trunk and smelled like her grandma's basement after a water leak. Water gushed out as she pulled the rubber gasket back from the trunk. She traced the gasket with her finger and found a long split. Tears stung her eyes. Half of everything was moldy.

Pulling her wet belongings out of the trunk of her car, Marin spotted the knitting basket and bit her bottom lip. As soon as she touched it, she knew the basket and its contents were ruined. She removed the skeins of mildewed yarn from the top. Reaching down to the bottom of the basket, she pulled out a couple of damp skeins. Everything in the basket was wet. A sob caught in her throat, and she sank down to the pavement. The last link to her grandma was gone.

Chapter 6

Heather

"Mommy, where's Daddy?" Jake walked up to Heather, holding his Monty the Monster Truck.

"He should be home soon, baby." Heather tussled Jake's hair.

"Vroom! Vroom!" He crouched on the floor and pushed the truck into the playroom.

The company jet was scheduled to land in an hour. For the past four weeks, Adam had traveled for work every weekend. When she asked him to talk to his boss, Adam said that his new position required frequent travel and there was nothing he could do about it. But all the travel meant he had a few hours with her and the kids on Sundays before their week started all over again.

Heather made her way upstairs to prepare for Adam's return. She showered and chose a casual outfit. He'd appreciate her wearing something besides t-shirts and yoga pants. Adam had shrugged off her advances for the past month. Jetlag was his reason and it made sense. He had been traveling all along the east coast. Branching out recently, the company sent Adam to L.A. this trip. But she hoped this reunion would be different.

She stood at the bathroom counter curling her long blonde hair. Adam had loved it when she let her hair grow. She ran her fingers through her hair to separate the curls. Stepping back, she studied herself. She turned from side to side and sucked in her stomach. She'd wear her shapewear, but Adam wouldn't think it was sexy.

"Mommy! Daddy's home," Jake yelled up the stairs.

Heather grinned and headed down to the living room. Adam's eyebrows raised when he saw her.

"Going somewhere?"

Heather's smile fell. "No, I thought it would be nice to dress up a little."

Did he just roll his eyes?

"Dinner's almost ready. I made chicken marsala."

Adam's face brightened. It was his favorite.

The family sat down for dinner, something that happened less often since his promotion. Heather watched as Adam interacted with the kids. He seemed genuinely interested in Shelly's recent visit to Mississippi State University and Ethan's driving experiences. Once again, he promised to take Jake to see the *Monty the Monster Truck* movie. After dinner, Heather reminded Adam that the movie wouldn't be in theaters much longer. He promised, as usual, to take Jake the following weekend.

Heather stood in her closet and slipped on a white silk chemise. She turned her head upside down and ran her fingers through her hair. Resting her hand on her stomach, she pushed in and sighed. When Heather was forty-three, she missed her period for three months and assumed she was entering perimenopause. During her annual checkup, she'd brought it up and the doctor ordered a pregnancy test. It was positive, and Adam was not happy.

The bedroom door opened, and Heather's pulse raced. She fluffed out her hair again and walked out of the closet into the bedroom. Adam looked at her and turned his head. This time she was certain he rolled his eyes. Moisture blurred her vision. She closed her eyes and wiped the tears away before Adam saw her.

"Heather, I'm tired." He loosened his tie and unbuttoned the first few buttons on his shirt.

"You're always tired. Isn't it supposed to be the other way around?" She tilted her head and smiled.

Adam jerked the tie out from around his neck and his gaze fell to her middle. She swallowed the knot in her throat. Over the years, he'd made comments about her body when she hadn't lost the baby weight after Jake was born.

"You were back to yourself six months after Shelly and Ethan. What's up, Heather?" he had said. He'd refused to factor in her age, which made it harder to lose weight.

One day, he came home and told her he'd bought a gym membership for her. Adam was in excellent shape for a man his age. He'd be fifty next year but looked forty. Heather exercised at the gym three days a week and walked every day, but it had little effect, and Adam noticed.

Adam unbuttoned his shirt and slipped it off. Walking over to her, he kissed her neck, but there was no passion behind his kiss. Heather would take what he offered. Another month could pass by before he paid any attention to her.

This time was different, though. Adam went downstairs as usual, but Heather went into the bathroom and cried. It was something she wanted, but now she realized all he saw her as was an obligation since she was his wife. Was that something she could live with for the rest of her life?

Adam worked half a day on Fridays, but when he left for work, he told Heather he was working until early evening. He had promised to take Jake to the movies, but now that promise, like the others, was broken.

"Mommy? Is Daddy home yet?" Jake ran from the playroom into the living room and leaped onto the couch.

"He called to say he's going to be late."

Jake sighed. "Again?" he whined.

"Yes, again. I know Jake, I'm sad too."

"I'm not sad. I'm mad. He was supposed to take me to see the movie." He crossed his arms over his chest and huffed. Springing from the couch, he ran into the playroom and slammed the door behind him.

An hour had passed since Adam called to say he was running late. Pulling up the family location app, Heather noticed he was at the Italian restaurant close to the office. She furrowed her brows and walked into the kitchen to put what was left of dinner in the fridge. Picking up her phone, she texted him to see when he'd be home. Five minutes passed without a reply, so she opened the app again. Now he was at a hotel. Her heart dropped to her stomach.

Her wandering mind had caused stress over the years. Working hard to overcome her thoughts, she'd been able to reason through her negative thinking. He must have been entertaining one of the company's owners. They visited the office once a month. He probably had his phone on silent and would be home soon. She was exhausted and climbed the stairs to get ready for bed. As soon as she slid under the covers, her mind went to Adam. She took a few deep breaths and closed her eyes.

The light from the hall woke Heather as Adam opened the bedroom door. She glanced at the clock when he went into his closet. It was past one in the morning. Where had he been? He'd never been out past eleven o'clock when the owners visited.

"You're late getting in," Heather whispered when Adam slid between the sheets.

"Mr. Chavez came for a visit and wanted to get drinks after dinner. I took him to the Marriott on Pine Boulevard."

"Why didn't you let me know?"

"Did you want me to yank out my phone and start texting at the table? He's the CEO, for crying out loud."

"You don't have to be a jerk."

Adam huffed. Jake got it honestly.

"Good night," Heather said, her voice thick.

"Good night." He rolled over with his back to her.

Tears gathered in her eyes and slipped down the sides of her face. What did she expect? He hadn't kissed her good night in months. She rolled over and pressed her lips together to keep from sobbing. What was happening? Was their marriage in danger?

Sunday arrived too soon, and they'd be back to the weekly routine. Adam and Jake had gone to see the movie last night. Heather was happy that Jake saw the movie before it left the theater. She cleaned the kitchen after their Sunday tradition of pancakes for brunch. Shelly was spending the day with Travis, and Adam had returned home a few minutes earlier from dropping Jake off at a friend's birthday party. Ethan and his friends were having a video game marathon at his friend Steve's house.

Glancing out the kitchen window, Heather watched a bird fly to the birdhouse and perch. Ethan made the birdhouse with his Boy Scout troop several years ago. A noise behind her drew her attention, and she turned around. Adam stood a few feet away with the large suitcase they used for vacation and a full garment bag.

Heather's lips twitched. She didn't know whether to smile or frown. "Going to a conference?" Heat rolled down her body. She'd say it was a hot flash, but she knew better.

"No." Color left his face, except for his cheeks that were as red as his t-shirt.

She ran her hand down the side of her face. "What's going on, Adam?"

"I...I'm leaving."

"What do you mean, you're leaving?" Her heart climbed into her throat.

"I'm moving out."

"Dad!"

Both Heather and Adam turned to see Ethan standing just inside the mudroom.

"What are you doing home?" Adam snapped.

Ethan bristled. "I got to Steve's and realized I forgot my Switch, so I came back to get it." Red seeped into his face.

Heather backed up against the sink counter to brace herself and lowered her head.

"We'll talk later." Heather looked at Adam when he forced out his breath. He glanced at Ethan when he walked past him on his way to the door to the garage. The mufflers on Adam's BMW vibrated the garage walls when he revved the engine. As the garage door lowered, the sound of Adam's car faded into the distance like his love for Heather.

Her body went numb.

"Mom?" Ethan walked up to her.

Shaking took over her body and white spots distorted her vision. Ethan's arms wrapped around her.

"Mom. Are you okay?" He pushed her hair out of her face.

"Oh, yeah. You should get your Switch. Steve is waiting for you."

"Mom, Dad just walked out on you. On us. You're acting like nothing's wrong." The color of his face had changed from red to white, highlighting his freckles.

Pretending something didn't happen was a coping mechanism. If she didn't acknowledge it, it didn't happen. But it *happened*. Her husband of almost twenty years just walked out on his family.

"I'm sorry, honey. I guess I'm in shock." Out of the corner of her eye, she saw Ethan raise his brows.

"What is Shelly going to say? And Jake. Jake will be devastated. He idolizes Dad, but I don't know why. He's a ba—"

"Ethan Adam."

"Don't call me that," he hissed. "I don't want his name. He's scum." Ethan drew in a ragged breath and flared his nostrils.

"Ethan, don't say that."

Ethan swallowed hard. He still had his arm around Heather.

"You should go to Steve's. I'll be alright."

"No Mom. I'll let him know something came up. You're sick, or something like that."

"Well." She was sick. Heart sick.

When Ethan began texting Steve, Heather walked out back to sit on the swing. He joined her a few moments later.

"He said he hopes you feel better." He gave her a half smile.

Heather's eyes found the bird from earlier. It appeared to be moving into the birdhouse. "Remember that?" She tilted her head at the birdhouse.

"Yeah. It was fun."

"You don't have to stay with me. You know, sometimes a person wants to be alone."

"I'm not leaving you. If you don't want me next to you, I'll go inside and watch you from the sunroom windows."

"Ethan," she patted his leg, "you are so sweet and caring."

Ethan pressed his feet against the ground and pushed off. The back-and-forth motion of the swing soothed Heather, as it usually did. They were quiet until Ethan spoke.

"Things have been different for a while."

"You noticed?" Her child noticed the changes in his father before she did. No, that was a lie. She noticed but was in denial. Tears stung her eyes.

"Yeah." He paused for a moment. "You're not fat."

"What?" Heather glanced in his direction.

"I heard Dad call you fat the other day," his voice broke. The walls had ears. Ethan's bedroom was next to theirs. Adam's voice was probably elevated, as it was more so lately. She breathed in deep and exhaled slowly. "Well, he alluded to you being fat. I don't think he's man enough to call you fat. I'll leave you alone." He slipped his arm around her shoulder. "Text me if you need me." Kissing her cheek, he stood and walked back inside.

As much as Heather wanted to believe it wasn't true, there was only one reason Adam would leave her. She pulled up the location app and tapped his name. He was at the same hotel he was at on Friday. That was all the confirmation she needed, and she was done giving him the benefit of the doubt. Her husband was cheating on her.

As suspected, Jake was crushed. Shelly didn't know what to think, and Ethan was still furious since his dad had walked out two weeks earlier. He refused to spend any time with Adam and would lock himself in his room if Adam was at the house and tried to bridge the gap. It took great effort for Heather to bite her tongue and not tell Adam that Ethan's feelings were a consequence of his actions. What did he expect would happen?

Heather was straightening the playroom when she ran across the doll blanket she knitted for Shelly when she was a child. It was tattered and worn and stained in a few places. She lowered the lid to the toy box and sat down. The blanket brought memories of happier times. She loved knitting. Blankets, hats, socks, and a few sweaters were among the projects she'd made for family and friends.

Tears gathered in her eyes. What would her mother say when she found out Adam had left her? Heather was sixteen, Ethan's age, when her parents divorced. She'd given her mother a hard time and blamed her for many years. Back then, Heather didn't know her father was an alcoholic. She stretched the blanket to get a better look at the stitches. She once loved knitting. Maybe it would soothe her broken heart. She laid the blanket aside and headed upstairs.

Heather opened the door to the attic and stepped inside. Through tears, she looked around and found the area where she packed away supplies from her former hobbies. Tearing open one box, she found the scrapbook kit Adam had given her for Christmas one year. She had many projects in her head, but none made it to paper. She set the box aside to donate. Next, she found the box of embroidery supplies. She was getting closer. The last box held her knitting supplies.

Five years had passed since she last picked up a knitting needle. One after another, she pulled out unfinished knitting projects. Among the pile was a bright yellow scarf about ten-inches-long and a multicolored sock without a mate. Heather laughed at the irony. Digging into the box, she found the zipper bag full of knitting needles. Browsing through the bag, she pulled out the longest needle. For a second, she imagined stabbing the needle into Adam's cheating heart. Not that she would. He wasn't worth her freedom.

The scarf would be easy to finish. She grabbed it along with the ball of yarn it was attached to. Stuffing the projects in the box, she folded the flaps down and went to tuck one flap under another but stopped. Pulling back the flaps, she picked up the sock. It was a long shot, but maybe she'd get lucky and find the same yarn to knit the matching sock at Cathy's Craft Haven.

Chapter 7

Marin

A little over a week had passed since Marin discovered that her trunk leaked when it rained. She searched online and found that bleach killed mildew and could remove some of the stains it left behind. She saved several outfits but ended up trashing the rest. Not ready to part with her grandma's knitting basket, she'd kept it in the trunk for a week. Then it rained again.

Carrying the basket inside, she dumped the yarn into the bathtub and filled the tub with cold water. The instructions for bleaching clothing were for washing machines. She did not know how much water the bathtub held, so she poured what she thought would work and added an extra splash for good measure.

Madison came home and headed for the bathroom, but as soon as she opened the door, Marin smelled the bleach. Madison gagged and coughed. Marin hurried to the bathroom and gasped. The skeins of yarn looked like they were tie-dyed. Madison helped her squeeze out as much water from the skeins as she could. Marin then placed the basket and yarn in the double bagged garbage bag Madison was holding open. Madison hugged Marin as tears rolled down her cheeks.

Marin pulled into the parking lot at work, parked close to the dumpster, and popped the trunk. Heaving the garbage bag in her arms, she walked to the side of the dumpster and paused. It was as if she were at her grandma's funeral again and was about to watch her burial. Except this time, she was the one putting her grandma in the ground.

She balanced the garbage bag on her hip, then shoved it through the opening of the dumpster. Standing for a moment—immune to the smell of rotting trash—she blew a kiss towards the dumpster and whispered, "Goodbye Grandma." Swallowing a sob, she grabbed her apron from her car and headed inside for her twelve-hour shift.

After an exhausting shift, Marin dragged herself up the stairs to the apartment and made it to her dark bedroom. Flopping down on the bed, she laid back for a few minutes, then sat up and turned on the lamp. Madison had placed her mail on the nightstand. The envelope on top was from the car insurance company—a bill she knew was coming. Tearing open the envelope, she pulled out a letter stating that if she didn't pay her premium within ten days, her insurance would lapse. That was the last thing she needed.

Every envelope was a bill. She was behind on her car insurance and a credit card that she signed up for to help her get on her feet. Lot of good it did her. There was a flyer for a craft store at the bottom. Turning it over, she noticed a fifty percent off coupon. Marin heard the front door and Madison appeared in her doorway a few seconds later.

"I see you got the flyer."

"Yeah, what's it for?"

"Well," Madison joined Marin on her bed. "I know it's not your grandmother's yarn, but maybe it can help you connect with her."

"Thank you, but I can't knit."

Madison's forehead creased.

"She was teaching me when she died."

"Oh, I'm sorry. I didn't know."

Marin shrugged. "It's okay. I can't afford it, anyway. I am behind on my bills. They take precedence."

"I get it. It was just a thought." She smiled.

Marin held the flyer in her hand, eyeing the yarn featured on the front when Madison abruptly stood and walked out of the room. She returned a moment later with her wallet in her hand. She opened it and pulled out a twenty-dollar bill.

"Here." She handed the money to Marin.

"No, I can't." Marin held up her hand.

"Yes, you can. You can pay me back later. Is this even enough?"

"I...I think so. There's a fifty percent off coupon."

"Good. You can probably watch some YouTube videos to learn to knit."

When Madison left her room, Marin took a quick shower and pulled up YouTube on her phone. She watched a few videos and made the decision that it was a lost cause. Maybe it would be different if she tried it with yarn. On her next day off, she would go to Cathy's Craft Haven.

Marin's phone rang. She picked it up and groaned. It was the credit card company again. Three days ago, Madison talked her into calling Stella and, of course, she didn't answer. Marin reluctantly left a voicemail. She was sinking into debt. If something didn't change, she wouldn't be able to pay rent soon. As soon as the credit card company hung up, the phone rang again. She was going to let it go to voicemail but took a quick look to see if it was Stella. It was her supervisor from work. Someone was probably sick, and she wanted Marin to cover.

"Hello?"

"Hey Marin. It's Rebecca."

"Hey."

"I know it's your day off, but can you come in for a meeting? Tyrone and I would like to talk to you about something."

Her heart thumped hard inside her chest. "Yeah, sure. See you in a few."

On the way to the restaurant, scenarios raced through Marin's head. She'd had no complaints from diners recently. Actually, she'd had none since she'd been working at Charley's Steakhouse. All her diners loved her. Was business bad and they were about to lay her off? No, it seemed busier lately. Marin's stomach fluttered when she pulled into the parking lot. Taking shaky steps, she walked in and made her way to the office.

Rebecca stood next to Tyrone, who sat at his desk. Tyrone was the owner of the restaurant, and Marin had seen him a handful of times. She tried her best to keep her distance. He reminded her of the principal at her high school. Madison had made the same comment.

Both looked up. Rebecca smiled, and Tyrone's expression held no emotion.

"Have a seat, Marin," Tyrone said, his voice deep and authoritarian. He smiled, but she still trembled a little.

"Marin, honey." Rebecca walked around the desk and patted Marin's shoulder. "It's nothing bad."

"Oh." Marin exhaled and rubbed her palms on her jeans.

"Well Rebecca. Let's put her out of her misery." Tyrone laughed. Marin managed a smile.

"Marin," he continued, "we've seen great things since you've joined us here at Charley's. Nothing but praise from your diners and co-workers."

Where was this going?

"You do your job and do it well. You fill in when your co-workers are sick or can't come in for whatever reason. You have both opened and closed without a hitch." He looked up at Rebecca and nodded.

"Marin, we are offering you a position." Rebecca's face broke into a wide grin.

"Oh. Okay." Marin's heartbeat doubled.

"We are offering a promotion to shift manager." Rebecca looked as if she would squeal.

Marin's head tipped forward, and her eyes widened. "A-a promotion? To shift manager?" Tears filled her eyes, blurring Tyrone's and Rebecca's faces.

"Well, if you don't want it, just say so," Tyrone said.

She looked up and was met with a smile that matched Rebecca's.

"Of course, I'll take it." She held her hand over her smile.

What just happened? She was now a shift manager, which came with a raise. Dare she believe a significant raise? Was her grandma looking out for her from Heaven?

On the way home, she replayed the meeting in her head. A smile lifted her spirits each time she remembered what Rebecca said. *"We are offering a promotion to shift manager."* Shift manager. Shift *manager. Shift manager!* Stopped at a traffic light, Marin glanced to her right and saw Cathy's Craft Haven. Looking in the side mirror, she inched out of traffic and turned onto Shaw Boulevard. No one could wipe the grin off of her face as she walked in the door. She'd be able to pay Madison back sooner than she thought.

Her smile dropped when she realized she didn't have the sales flyer. It would be two weeks before she saw the pay raise in her bank account. The twenty dollars Madison loaned her wouldn't be enough to get everything she needed without the coupon. She spun around to leave but noticed a flyer on the floor under the shopping carts in the corral. Looking around, she pulled out a few carts and reached down to pick up the flyer. She smiled and headed to the needlecraft section.

Chapter 8
Frida

Frida joined her friends for lunch after mass. She didn't want to be rude and rush off, but the flyer for Cathy's Craft Haven was burning a hole in her purse. Technically, she could wait until tomorrow or the next day to buy yarn, but she didn't want to. The sooner she started, the sooner the troops would get a pair of socks. Frida stacked her dishes and placed her used napkins on top.

"Frida, are you leaving already?" Santina's brows shot up.

"Yeah, I've got a few errands to run."

"On Sunday?" another friend replied.

"One of those things. And I need to grab a few groceries."

"*Que tengas un buen dia,*" Santina said.

"*Tú también.*" Frida smiled and headed for her car.

The sliding doors to Cathy's Craft Haven welcomed Frida like open arms. She pulled on a cart, but two carts tried to tag along for the ride. She groaned and jerked the first one free. Several years had passed since she'd been inside Cathy's. Frida started on the opposite side and worked her way around to the needlecraft section since she knew she'd spend longer there.

There were fancy new sewing machines on display. She'd preferred knitting to sewing, but could sew on a button and hand stitch a hem. That was the extent of her sewing skills. The sign for needlecrafts came into view. Frida wanted to take the entire section in, not grab some yarn and go.

She made a quick trip down the embroidery and tatting aisle. Those crafts were beautiful, but Frida didn't want one of those monstrous magnifying glasses strung around her neck. She entered the first of three aisles dedicated to knitting and crocheting. As if she'd walked into a new car showroom, everything was so shiny and new.

She picked up a multipack of knitting needles and gasped. "Good grief. Things have gotten expensive." She hung the package back on the peg. She didn't need any needles, anyway. Time to look at the yarn. She turned the corner and her eyes widened. So many to choose from. Beth had told her tan or black, so Frida browsed the aisle for the wool section. When she reached the end of the aisle, she sighed and turned the corner for the next aisle.

A young woman wearing black stood at the opposite end of the aisle. Frida noticed her hair. Her unconventional hair and black clothing would lead some people to label her as trouble. What Frida saw were vivid shades of pink and blue that stood out against the black. It didn't bother Frida one bit. She'd always looked past a person's appearance to their heart. Take Joyce, for example. If Frida would have judged Joyce by her clothes and the color of her house, she would have missed out on a beautiful friendship.

Surveying both sides of the aisle as she pushed her cart, she noted the wool section next to where the woman was standing. The woman's face was so close to the shelf, either she had vision problems, or she was hiding from someone. Frida took a step closer and realized the woman had a skein of soft yarn pressed against her cheek.

"Excuse me," Frida said as she leaned down to grab a skein of tan yarn.

When the woman turned and stepped back, Frida's heart sank. Her eyes were red and swollen and mascara streaked down her face.

"I'm sorry." She sniffled and looked at the yarn in her hand. "I better put this back." She feigned a smile. When she looked at where she laid the skein of yarn, she grimaced at the makeup that'd rubbed off onto the fibers. "Guess I'd better buy this one." She attempted another smile.

"Are you okay, miss?"

"Oh." She sniffed and pulled up the neck of her black t-shirt to wipe her eyes. "I'm okay." Her bottom lip trembled.

"What's wrong, honey?"

The woman shook her head. A few shoppers wandered into the aisle and didn't hide their curiosity. Frida reached into her purse and pulled out a pack of facial tissues.

"I probably look like I belong in a horror movie. With my mascara and eyeliner and all." A sad laugh came from her broken heart.

Frida watched the woman as she wiped away the trail of black under each eye. Several piercings dotted her face and she wore the type of earrings that made enormous holes in her lobes. She appeared to be in her late teens or early twenties. What could she be struggling with?

"My name is Frida and I have two good ears."

The woman wrinkled her brow.

"I'm a good listener."

A smile brightened her sad eyes.

"I'm sorry. It's just...My grandmother was teaching me how to knit and she died recently. I had the yarn we were using in my car, but my trunk leaked, and it was ruined. I tried watching how-to videos, but it feels hopeless. I figured if I bought some yarn, it would be easier to teach myself how to knit. I saw this yarn and it was soft. It reminds me of my grandmother's hands. They were always soft."

The woman's spirits lifted after she spoke about her grandmother.

"I know what it's like to lose someone you love dearly. Did you know that knitting can be therapeutic? I can teach you."

The woman's lips parted. She looked as if she was considering Frida's offer. "Uh…You don't have to do that."

"I don't mind. I know we don't know each other, but I'd be happy to teach you. We could meet for coffee somewhere and bring our knitting. Or you could come over to my house." Why did she just invite a stranger to her house? Maria would have a fit. Frida dug around in her purse and pulled out her receipt from lunch. She flipped it over and wrote her information. "My name is Frida Gomez. This is my cell and my home numbers." Frida held out the piece of paper.

"Thanks. My name is Marin. Marin Martin."

"Well, what an interesting name. Your parents were certainly creative."

"Not really. My name is Kaylee. I chose Marin as my nickname because I hate Kaylee. I'm obviously not a Kaylee." She gestured to herself and smiled.

"Where did Marin come from?"

"It's Martin without the *t*."

"Well, aren't you a clever one? You'll be knitting before you know it."

Pink brushed across Marin's cheeks when she smiled. Frida spent a few minutes helping her pick out another skein of yarn more suited for a beginner and a set of knitting needles. She watched as Marin walked out of the needlecraft section. She didn't know when, but she had a feeling she'd hear from Marin.

Frida pushed her cart down the aisle and her eyes shifted to a new-fangled gadget on the opposite aisle—a knitting loom. It wasn't traditional knitting but looked interesting. Maybe she'd try it for something of her own. She headed back to the aisle where she met Marin and grabbed a few more skeins of tan yarn and found the black. Then she spotted a blonde woman at the end of the aisle digging around in the bin of sock yarn. A few balls of yarn jumped out of the bin, and she looked at Frida when she picked them up off the floor.

Frida again noticed red and puffy eyes. Two crying women in the yarn section in one day? The woman tossed the yarn back in the bin and moved her search to the lower bin. Frida noticed the sock laying across the woman's purse in the cart and realized what the woman was doing. But why was she going about it in such a violent way? More balls of sock yarn flew out of the bin. Frida pushed the cart towards the woman.

"I can't find it. I've looked in these bins twice." She continued to rummage through the bottom bin.

"What are you looking for?" Frida's gaze followed the woman's frantic hands.

"See this?" She picked up the sock from atop her purse and held it out to Frida. "I bought the yarn for this sock six years ago. Do you think it is discontinued?"

"I'm afraid so."

Frida's eyes widened when the woman slumped and sobbed. A few customers stared at the crying woman as they passed by. Frida pulled the package of tissues from her purse and handed it to the woman.

"Oh, thanks." She took the pack and pulled out a tissue. "I'm so sorry. I'm a mess. My husband just left me."

"Oh, my."

"I don't know why I told you that. I've used knitting to relieve stress over the years and I thought it would help. I haven't knitted for at least five years. I should have known the yarn was discontinued. What am I going to do with one sock?" Her bottom lip trembled. "Make a sock puppet?" She laughed for a few moments.

Frida raised her brows.

"I'm sorry. I'm not crazy. Just heartbroken." She bit her bottom lip. "I'm Heather." She said, holding out her hand.

"I'm Frida." Frida shook Heather's hand. "I'm very sorry to hear about your marriage."

"Thanks." Heather breathed in deeply.

As Frida watched Heather wipe her eyes, she realized she had a sock knitter standing in front of her. No, it wasn't a good idea. The poor woman was going through the wringer right now. But she said knitting was a stress reliever for her.

No, Frida.

"You know?" Heather started. "I don't think I remember how to knit socks. I think it about killed me when I knitted this one. Maybe that's why one is missing." She offered a sad laugh. "Do you know how to knit socks?" Heather lifted her brows.

"As a matter of fact, I do." Frida spent a few moments talking about Socks for Troops. She gave Heather her information and encouraged her to take some time to think about it before she decided. Heather agreed.

As Frida stood in the checkout line, she thought about Marin and Heather. What started out as buying a few skeins of yarn was turning into something more. What? She didn't know yet. The women may never call. If she never spoke to them again, she hoped she provided them with some encouragement. Heather, in pursuing her passion again to help her cope with the end of her marriage. Marin, in connecting with her grandmother, even though she was in Heaven.

Chapter 9

Marin

Marin sat on her bed and leaned her phone against the lamp on her nightstand. Biting her bottom lip, she looped yarn around her fingers and picked up the knitting needle with the other hand. She shifted her gaze to the screen on her phone in time for the video to start.

"Slide the needle behind this area of the yarn and pull it through here and pull tight. You've made your first cast on stitch," the woman in the video said.

"What?" Marin groaned and dropped the knitting needle on her bed.

"You okay?"

Marin looked up at Madison standing in the doorway. "This tiny screen."

"Why don't you use the TV?"

"I think I will." Marin followed Madison into the living room, turned on the TV, and clicked on the YouTube app.

Madison grinned. "I've got to go to work. See you tonight."

"Bye."

Sitting on the floor in front of the TV, she watched the video five times before she could cast a few stitches onto the knitting needle. A little while later, she had knitted four rows. Inspecting her work, she frowned. Something didn't look right. Browsing websites on her phone, it appeared she dropped a stitch. It was ruined.

"*Ahhh.*" She jerked the yarn, ripping out the stitches. Tears rolled down her cheeks, and she flung the yarn and needles across the room. The needles clanked against the wall and hit the floor. It was useless; she'd never learn how to knit. She had let her grandma down.

Grabbing the knitting needles and yarn off the floor, Marin went into her room and threw them in her closet. What was the point? Her grandma was gone. She flopped down on her bed. Who was there to impress? Certainly not Stella. Marin clenched her fists. Stella never acknowledged her voicemail several weeks ago. If she didn't know before, now she knew where she stood with Stella.

Marin turned her back to the bathroom mirror and gritted her teeth as she looked over her shoulder at the updated tattoo. She'd just returned home after having her grandma's initials added. Her eyes shifted between each set of initials. What would life have been like if her parents had gotten their act together? She sighed and pulled her shirt down.

In her room, she found the manilla envelope with her important papers. Getting comfortable on her bed, she pulled out the contents and took her time reviewing each document. First was her birth certificate. One thing she knew, it was a certified copy of the original that the department of children's services obtained when she went into the foster care system. Did Gemma and Kevin have any sense to hold on to important documents, or did they just not care?

Included were report cards and her high school diploma. At the bottom of the stack were photographs. One was of her and her grandma shortly after her grandma gained custody. The other two photos were of Gemma and Kevin when they were dating and them with Marin as a newborn. They looked happy. Grief for what could have been tugged at Marin's heart.

The dryer buzzed. Marin placed the stack back in the envelope and returned it to the closet. Her grandma came to mind when her gaze fell to the yarn and knitting needles on the closet floor.

"Marin, you can do it if you put your mind to it," her grandmother said during Marin's first knitting lesson. She went back to her bed and picked up her backpack.

Shuffling around inside, she searched for the slip of paper. Groaning, she dumped the contents onto the bed and spread everything around. The edge of the paper peeked out from under a makeup compact, and she grabbed it.

In the past, Marin kept people at arm's length—something she was painfully aware of. Frida had seen Marin in a fragile state and hadn't judged her, but showed compassion. A few weeks had passed since she saw Frida in Cathy's Craft Haven. She hoped Frida was still willing to take on a beginner. Marin smiled. She picked up her phone and typed out a text. Editing and reediting the message, she hit send before she could change her mind.

She slipped the knitting in a plastic grocery bag and put the bag in her backpack. Now she was prepared for when Frida responded to her text. Although learning to knit was intimidating, she vowed she would try her best so she would make her grandma proud.

THE KNITTING CLUB

Humidity hung in the warm August air as Marin made her way through the cemetery. Why had it taken four months to visit Grandma Judith? One excuse after another came to mind. Not one of them valid. It took her a few minutes to find the exact location. She knew the general vicinity from witnessing the burial from the parking lot. A vague memory surfaced of going with her grandma to visit her grandfather's grave shortly after Marin moved to Mississippi.

She stood for a moment before spotting a large double headstone etched with *Scott*. A bouquet of fresh cut fall flowers occupied the vase affixed to the base—the bright yellow and orange colors standing out against the gray of the granite. A quick glance around at the other graves told Marin that Stella had been by recently, as no other graves in the immediate area had fresh flowers.

As she approached, the sweet earthy aroma of sunflowers filled the air around Marin. She had to hand it to Stella. The bouquet of dwarf sunflowers and mums made her heart smile. Inhaling deeply, Marin kneeled in front of her grandparents' graves and rested her hand on the stone to steady herself. Tears gathered in her eyes and spilled down her cheeks.

"I'm sorry it's taken me so long to come. I've had a lot going on. You probably know that, though. I'm not really sure how all that works in Heaven. Anyway, I'm doing well. I'm a manager now and I'm making ends meet. I think you'd be proud of me, Grandma. Actually," Marin's voice cracked, "I know you'd be proud of me." She gasped and clenched her jaws to keep herself from breaking down.

"Oh. I'm going to take knitting lessons." She wiped the tears from her cheeks. A slow smile spread across her face when Grandma Judith's face came to mind. Yes, she would be proud of Marin.

Exhaling, Marin stood. "I love you, Grandma." She looked at her grandfather's side of the headstone. "I'm sorry we never got to meet. I love you too, Grandpa."

On the drive home, Marin's thoughts tangled together. She found it ironic how one person's behavior could change the course of many people's lives. Gemma's relationship with Kevin and the decision to run away with him resulted in William Scott dying before he had the chance to meet his only grandchild.

Chapter 10

Heather

"Mommy, how many scarfs are you gonna make?" Jake picked up his Monty the Monster Truck and soared it through the air, making airplane sounds.

"Well, I'm not sure. How many should I make?" She held up the scarf she was working on. She had at least twenty more inches to knit until it was the standard scarf length. Five scarves so far. Maybe she should stop after the sixth. The family already had too many scarves. She'd look into donating the scarves to one of the homeless shelters.

Adam came to mind. While out shopping two days ago, Heather ran into Troy at Starbucks. At first, he seemed nervous and avoided her, but a little while later, he walked over and said hello. He knew. His behavior made it obvious. She'd set aside her anger for a moment and asked about Adam's frequent weekend work trips. Maybe that was what started it all. He'd met someone at an office he visited. Probably a blonde half Heather's age with a toned body. Troy stared at her dumbfounded.

"Heather," he said. "We rarely work on the weekend."

Adam and his home wrecker were going on weekend getaways, and he used work trips as his cover. She bit her lip at the memory. Where did the money for all the trips come from? A flame flickered in her stomach. With his mid-life crisis—she decided that was what was going on—he'd probably used some of his bonus. She did not know how much the car cost. If it was close to eighty thousand, maybe he financed part of the car. Worse, maybe he financed the whole thing. That money should have gone to their family, not to carry on an affair.

Glancing at the basket by her feet, she laid the half-knitted scarf on the couch next to her and rifled through the balls and skeins of yarn; and found the single sock on the bottom of the basket. Like she told the woman in the craft store, she'd end up making a sock puppet. Brushing her hand across the sock, she thought about what the woman had told her. Making socks for the troops wouldn't only take her mind off her troubled marriage, it would help her feel like she was making a difference in the world. She'd been a stay-at-home-mom for eighteen years.

"What do you think, Jake?" She held up the sock. "Do you think this would make a good sock puppet?" He placed his truck on the floor and took the sock from Heather.

"It's sort of small. It could be a baby sock puppet."

"That's a good idea." Heather watched his little finger trace the color pattern.

"Red, blue, purple… What's this color, Mommy?" He pointed to a color between purple and blue.

"Violet, maybe?"

"Violet. Like GG's flowers?"

"Yes. Like GG's flowers." Heather's mother had a collection of African violets.

"I am thinking about making socks for the soldiers overseas."

His face brightened. "Like army men?"

"Yes, and women. Don't forget that women are in the Army too."

"Uh huh." Jake ran to the playroom and returned a moment later with his hands cupped together. He opened his hands and a platoon of plastic green army figures splashed onto the couch. He picked one up and marched it across the couch cushions to where Heather was sitting. "I think that'd be cool, Mommy."

As Heather loaded groceries into the trunk of her Suburban, she heard the unmistakable sound of a sports car driving down the row where she was parked. The driver pulled into a spot three spaces down from her on the opposite side. The car looked like many other BMW sports cars except for the tag. It was Adam's car. He'd gotten a vanity plate with his nickname: *Adman*. A nickname that came from his younger sister's mispronunciation of his name when she was a child.

The flame in her stomach roared to life and burned its way to her throat. Cold chills rolled down her spine, extinguishing the fire, and a coil of panic seized her chest. She didn't want to see Adam now. Tensing, she hurried to load the rest of the groceries. Never one to leave a shopping cart in the parking lot, she pushed it to the corral across the row and glanced toward where Adam parked as she walked back to her car. Her mouth fell open when she saw a woman step out of the driver's side.

And not a skinny twenty something with a perky bosom, but a woman in her late thirties or early forties. Could Adam have let her borrow his car? Her question was answered when he stepped out of the passenger side. He slipped his arm around the woman's waist, and they walked toward the doors. Heather's eyes lingered on the woman. She was thinner than Heather, but not by much.

Heather climbed into her Suburban and cranked the engine. Backing out, the tires screeched when she punched the gas. Tears flooded down her cheeks as she drove to school. She could no longer shop at her favorite

Kroger. If she ran into Adam or his adulteress, she'd end up on the six o'clock news.

Waiting in the pickup line at Jake's school, Heather had to distract herself or her thoughts would drive her crazy. She opened Facebook and scrolled down her timeline. That was a mistake. Everyone was in love, celebrating wedding anniversaries, or wishing their spouses a happy birthday. Birth of babies. Every picture oozed happiness. Heather flinched when the car door opened.

"Hi, Mommy."

"Hi, baby. Did you have a good day?"

"Uh, huh."

Heather wiped her eyes. "Good."

"Are you okay?"

"Oh. Yeah, just not feeling well."

"Look what I drawed." He thrust a coloring page toward her.

She wasn't in the mood to correct his grammar. "Good job, buddy."

Jake chattered from the backseat on the drive home. Heather threw out an occasional "Yeah?" "Is that so?" "Good job, Jake." All the while, her heart was slowly tearing apart.

Jake helped Heather unload the groceries, carrying the lighter bags. She sighed and rested her hands on her hips as she scanned the kitchen. Grocery bags covered all the free counter space. Jake and Shelly occasionally snacked. Ethan was the one that ate her out of house and home.

After putting the groceries away, Heather eased down on the couch. She glanced around the den and saw evidence of their life over the past twenty years displayed everywhere. The kids' baby pictures lined the surface of the sofa table. Their wedding photos hung on the walls. If the kids weren't still living at home, she'd have a bonfire in the backyard and add all the photos of her and Adam.

The scarf she'd been working on was finished and she'd laid it on the side table. She looked around the room and grimaced. The house was becoming cluttered. It'd drive Adam nuts. She grinned. He no longer lived with them, so she could leave things out if she wanted to. She looked at the scarf again. Maybe she should take Frida up on her offer of knitting socks. She reached into the basket, pulled out the piece of paper with Frida's information, and laid it on the end table. She'd call later.

The dreaded day arrived. Adam was picking Jake up to spend the weekend with him. Jake had spent a few hours on Saturday or Sunday, but not overnight. Heather was sure his floozy would be there. The thought of her baking cookies or watching movies with her son made Heather want to vomit. She'd considered demanding that the woman stay away from Jake, but this weekend wasn't about Heather. Jake deserved to spend the weekend with his dad and if the woman was there, so be it.

Heather was sitting on the edge of the pool with her legs dangling in the water. She raised her legs and watched the water drip from her heels into the pool. The backdoor opened and Ethan made his way to where she sat. He eased down next to her and slipped his legs into the water. He still refused to have anything to do with his father. She should encourage him to at least speak with Adam, but Heather was not at that place yet. Admittingly, she used Ethan's disdain to punish Adam.

"It's your fault he hates you, Adam," she said when Adam asked why Ethan wouldn't speak to him.

The sound of Adam's BMW slowing in front of the house twisted the knot in Heather's stomach. *Please. I don't want to talk to him.*

"Mommy! Daddy's here." Jake burst through the backdoor and jerked open the pool gate.

"Careful, Jacob." Heather held her hand over her chest as Jake sprinted around the edge of the pool. He threw his arms around her neck and kissed her cheek.

"Bye Mommy. See you Sunday."

"Okay, sweetie."

"Bye, buddy." Ethan slipped his arm around his brother's waist.

"Are you gonna see Daddy?"

"Not today," Ethan said.

"Oh. Okay. Bye." Jake sprinted back around the pool and in the backdoor.

Heather saw Adam looking in her direction from the kitchen window. His gaze shifted to Ethan, then he disappeared.

"Why does Dad care about us now?"

Heather looked in Ethan's direction.

"I mean. He didn't seem to care until he moved out." Ethan kicked his feet, causing the water to splash on them. He grimaced. "Sorry."

"It's okay. It feels nice in this heat." They were quiet for a moment. Heather wanted to say Adam was too busy building a relationship with another woman to worry about his children–or wife, for that matter. But she said, "That's a question only Dad can answer."

Ethan scoffed. He had a right to feel the way he did about his father. She shouldn't try to convince Ethan otherwise.

Chapter 11
Frida

Frida placed a carafe of coffee on the coffee table and arranged the cups. She adjusted the doilies on the arms of the furniture and repositioned the pillows on the couch. Heather had called earlier in the week and offered to knit socks. She was a talkative woman and gave Frida enough information that told her Heather needed to get out of the house.

MJ was over yesterday to help her with her cell phone. While he tinkered with it, a half dozen texts came through. Marin's text was among the messages. Frida called and left a voicemail after she received the text, and Marin returned her call within a half hour. Frida chose not to tell Maria that she was hosting two strangers in her home. If she did, Maria would invite herself over for each get-together.

The smell of baking Mexican wedding cookies drifted into the living room from the kitchen. Marin said that she had to work at two and they'd planned for a mid-morning get together. The oven timer buzzed, and Frida made her way to the kitchen. The cookies needed to cool for a few minutes before putting them on the serving tray.

Looking down, Frida wiped a smudge of flour from her apron and pulled it off over her head. The doorbell rang. Would it be Heather or Marin? Maybe both. Heather smiled when Frida opened the door. In her hand, she held a large knitting needle case. Frida glanced around out front for Marin, but she hadn't made it yet.

"Come in." Frida led Heather into the living room. "Here's coffee, creamer, and sugar. I have a few tea bags, if you prefer."

"Coffee's fine, thank you."

The doorbell rang when she walked into the kitchen to put the cookies on a platter.

"I can get that for you, Frida."

"That would be great," Frida called out from the kitchen.

"Hello, you must be Marin. I'm Heather. Come in."

Frida smiled to herself as she placed the cookies on the platter.

"Hi," Marin's soft voice drifted into the kitchen.

Frida returned to the living room carrying the tray of cookies. Marin slipped off her backpack and sat on the couch. Unzipping the zipper, she pulled out a plastic grocery bag. The tip of a knitting needle poked through the plastic bag as if it was saying hello. Frida set the tray down next to the coffee and excused herself.

In the spare bedroom, she found two knitting needle cases and combined the needles into one case. When she walked into the living room, she handed the case to Marin. "For you." Frida smiled.

Marin looked at the case as if it were a rare treasure. When she looked up, Frida noticed her eyes glistening.

"Thank you so much." Marin smiled and pulled her knitting needles out of the plastic bag and slid them in the case.

After a few cookies, Frida handed Heather a copy of the sock pattern she'd downloaded from the Internet.

Heather smiled. "Seems simple enough."

"I wanted a simple pattern. That way, we could be more efficient."

"Sounds good." Heather glanced around the living room and into the kitchen. "I love your house. It's so cozy."

"Why thank you. It's a post-World War Two house. It was built in nineteen forty-nine. It is the perfect size for me."

"Is that your husband?" She tilted her head toward the photograph of Max in his uniform on the mantel.

"Yes. My Max. He died in Vietnam."

Marin glanced at the mantel.

"Oh, I'm so sorry," Heather said. Frida handed her a skein of black wool yarn. "Why don't we tell each other a little about ourselves? Only what we want to share. I'll go first. I have three kids. Shelly is eighteen, Ethan is sixteen, and Jake is five. Yes, he was a surprise." She grinned. "I am a stay-at-home mom. Well, for now."

Heather retrieved four sock needles from her needle case and pulled out a long strand of yarn from the skein. Frida watched her cast on stitches and start knitting. Heather said that she had forgotten how to knit socks, but she appeared to know what she was doing.

"My husband of twenty years and I recently separated." Heather continued.

"I'm so sorry, Heather." Frida said, remembering what Heather told her in Cathy's.

"Me too." Heather nodded when she spoke. "I may have to get a job. It depends on what my husband agrees to pay."

Marin removed the yarn from the plastic bag and laid it in her lap. She held onto the needles like someone threatened to take them from her. She glanced at Frida and gave her a tentative smile.

Frida moved to the couch next to Marin and picked up a small ball of yarn from her knitting basket. "I've had this ball for at least ten years." Marin raised her eyebrows. "I'm going to knit along with you."

"Okay."

Frida pulled out a long strand of yarn and said for Marin to do the same. "We are going to cast on using the long tail method." Marin mimicked Frida's movements and cast on several stitches. She showed Marin the knit and purl stitches and before long, Marin had knitted several rows.

Frida watched both Marin and Heather as they knit. Heather was a seasoned knitter despite her five-year hiatus. Marin's teeth had a hold of her bottom lip as she knitted. A habit Frida shared with Marin.

"I guess I'll go next. Max and I married when I was twenty and he was twenty-two."

"So young. Did you remarry?" Heather asked.

"No, Max was my soulmate. Don't get me wrong, I had many a suitor after Max died. Well, they wanted to be a suitor, but I refused." Frida watched Marin for a few moments and leaned over. "Are you sure you are a beginner?" Marin looked at her and smiled.

"Is that your daughter and grandson?" Heather tilted her head toward a photo of Maria and MJ.

"No, my niece and great nephew. Max and I wanted a house full of children, but it wasn't meant to be. Maria is like a daughter."

"What did you do for a living?" Heather asked.

Heather was talkative and Frida would think that she was monopolizing the conversation, but Marin appeared to be a locked journal and had hidden the key deep inside her heart.

"I taught high school Spanish. I retired in 2005 after thirty years."

"Teaching is such a wonderful profession. I never finished college. I was studying for a degree in business. I planned to go to graduate school, but met my husband." She looked at Marin. "What about you, Marin?"

Marin's eyes widened. "Not much to tell. I am a shift manager at Charley's Steakhouse and my roommate is my friend from high school."

"Oh, I love that place. So good." Heather waited for more, but it was obvious that Marin had shared what she was comfortable sharing. Heather returned her attention to her knitting. The sock had already taken shape. Frida was impressed.

The hour and a half the women scheduled for their time together passed quickly. After Heather and Marin left, Frida spent some time straightening the living room and cleaning the kitchen. Both Heather and Marin offered to help, but she figured Heather had enough cleaning of her own and Marin needed energy for her shift at work.

Frida had lived alone for most of her adult life. Maria and MJ visited a time or two during the week, and her other nieces and nephews visited occasionally. Some of her free time was spent on volunteer opportunities through church. Joyce was who she saw most often, but other than that, Frida was alone and that had been okay. But an emptiness settled over the living room now that Heather and Marin had left. She eased down on the chair by the window.

A family walked down the sidewalk in front of her house. Two young children with their parents. Frida had seen the family in the past. Four years ago, she saw pink balloons tied to the mailbox. Many years had passed since she lost her and Max's child, but the sting was as fresh as it was in nineteen sixty-seven. She picked up her rosary beads from the small velvet box on the side table and began praying for Heather and Marin.

Frida had spent time with the two women twice now. Meeting them in Cathy's Craft Haven had been an experience she would never forget. She was feeling close to Heather and Marin, which was odd, since the three of them were still strangers. While Heather was an open book, Marin had built an impenetrable wall around her heart. Frida believed the Lord was leading her to help Marin overcome whatever caused her to keep people at a distance.

Chapter 12

Marin

A pot slipped off the counter and hit the floor with a loud clang. The noise of banging pots and diners' chattering didn't faze Marin. The scarf she'd been knitting since the day at Frida's three weeks earlier was almost finished. Although it was early November, the weather was warm for wearing a scarf in South Mississippi.

She'd been back to Cathy's Craft Haven and bought two more skeins of yarn and joined the frequent buyer program. The scarves she was knitting would be plain and boring compared to a scarf Heather or Frida knitted, but like Frida said, she had to start somewhere.

"Marin."

She looked up and saw Stephanie, one of the waitstaff, standing in the office doorway.

"Sorry to interrupt your lunch, but a diner would like to speak with you."

Since she'd been a shift manager, Marin hadn't had an issue with the staff. Everyone was doing their job well. She laid her knitting aside and followed Stephanie through the kitchen doors where a man stood. He looked familiar, but Marin couldn't place him. He smiled when he saw her.

"Hello Marin. Imagine my surprise when I asked to be seated in your section and was told that you are now a manager. I'm Pete Stone." He grinned and offered his hand.

Pete Stone? Who was Pete Stone? As Marin sorted through her memories, it came to her. She remembered seeing the name on the credit card slip of the man that left her a thirty-dollar tip.

"I knew you'd work your way up."

Marin's cheeks warmed and she fought a smile. "Thanks."

"I just wanted to say congratulations." He smiled and excused himself.

"What in the world?" Stephanie said.

Marin shrugged. No one besides her grandmother had congratulated her. It was nice being acknowledged for something good for a change. Marin returned to the office and picked up the scarf and knitted a few stitches. Her happiness was soon replaced with doubt. Her grandma had to congratulate her because she was Marin's grandmother and Mr. Stone was a stranger. His congratulations didn't count, right?

After the restaurant closed, Marin made her last checks before locking up. The two bussers, Tyler and John, were putting trash in the dumpsters and she heard them laughing.

"Marin knitting is like a death metal band singing *Amazing Grace*." Their laughter echoed off the dumpsters.

She hurried to her car, but not before Tyler saw her.

"Marin. Um. We were just joking." He looked down and shuffled his feet. John stepped into the light and looked down. What were they looking at? Their humanity on the ground?

She held her tongue. Unlocking the driver's door, she slid into the seat and cranked the engine. Tyler's and John's pale faces were intently watching her. Backing out, she headed home with tears streaming down her cheeks.

Stretched out on her bed, Marin balled up the finished scarf and threw it towards the wall. She groaned when it fell into a heap on the floor next to the bed. After one knitting lesson with Frida, she was ready to give up on her new hobby. She picked up one of the knitting needles and ran her fingers across the cool metal. What would her grandma have said about Tyler and John?

"There will always be someone who gives you a hard time. Just remember, it's not you. They are miserable and put others down to raise themselves up."

Did both Tyler and John have low self-esteem? Sighing, Marin picked the scarf up and straightened it. She'd had two or three lessons with her grandma before she died. An hour and a half with Frida and Marin had made the scarf her grandma wanted to make with her. Marin picked up one of the new skeins of yarn she'd bought and cast on another scarf. If she had a family, everyone would receive a scarf for Christmas.

The deadbolt on the front door snapped back, and Marin watched Madison walk in. She put aside her knitting and went into the living room. Madison grinned and tilted her head—a sign that she was up to something. Marin's first thought was to run back to her room and lock herself inside. Madison walked up to Marin with a sparkle in her eyes.

"I met a great guy today. Marin, he's tall—"

"No."

"But you haven't—"

"No, Madison." Marin shook her head. There was no room in her life for a relationship.

Madison rolled her eyes. "Think about it. He's so nice."

"I don't have to think about it. I am not interested in a relationship, Madison."

"Fine." Madison breezed by Marin with her chin held high and went into her room.

Marin cared about Madison and appreciated all that she had done for her, but she could be immature. Heading back to her bedroom, Marin's phone chimed. She picked it up from the side table. Her lips thinned when she saw John's name on the screen.

John: sorry, marin

Either he was truly sorry, or he didn't want her to write him up. Was negative talk about a manager grounds for disciplinary action? It should be. She shrugged and tossed her phone on the bed. She wasn't in the mood to reply.

Marin noticed she'd dropped a stitch on the new scarf she was knitting. Her first thought was to rip it out and start over, but she had knitted at least six inches and couldn't bear the thought of starting over. Knowing herself, she would have rather thrown her knitting supplies back in the closet and forgotten about it. Her phone rang and she glanced at the screen. Frida's name showed, bringing a smile to Marin's face.

A few minutes later, they'd made plans for another get together to knit. Since Frida and Heather didn't work outside the home, Marin chose the time and day to get together. A trace of excitement coursed through her for the first time in as long as she could remember. The desire to box up her knitting—or throw it away—had faded. The day they picked to meet, Marin was off work, and she wanted to spend as much time with Frida and Heather as she could.

Frida reminded Marin of her grandma, even though they were different in many ways. Frida's Hispanic culture was displayed throughout her home, and she seemed to live a simple life. Marin's grandma was involved in several volunteer groups and a member of the country club. Despite their differences, they both looked straight at a person's heart. Neither Frida, nor Heather for that matter, said or did anything that showed that they stereotyped Marin.

Based on the car she drove; Heather's family was well off. But she didn't show it in her personality. Heather was an open book. Marin would never reveal herself as Heather did, but maybe that was what Heather needed because of her marriage. Marin walked to her closet. When she pulled a shirt from the hanger, it caused the hanger to bounce back and knock the large manilla envelope off the top shelf. When she bent down to pick it up, she noticed the corner of her birth certificate had slid out of the envelope. Taking a deep breath, she pulled it from the envelope and ran her finger over her mother's name.

Marin exhaled softly and slipped the birth certificate back in the envelope and laid it on the top shelf. What kind of mother would Gemma have been if she'd cleaned up her act? Marin would have been lucky to have a mother like Heather. Heather's love for her children was obvious in the way she talked about them. Had Gemma loved Marin, or did she see her as a complication? Was that why she didn't care where Marin was or who she was with? A child should never have to question the love of a parent.

Chapter 13

Heather

Shivering, Heather wrapped her arms around herself and stepped into the hall to check the thermostat. She'd forgotten to adjust the heat before going to bed last evening, and the fallen temperature left a chill in the air. Adam was coming over in a few hours to pick up Jake, bringing more chill to the air.

Heather tried to encourage Ethan to speak to his father, but he refused and would either leave or lock himself in his room when Adam came over to pick up Jake. A small part of Heather pitied Adam. A very minuscule part.

From the first weekend with Adam a month and a half ago, Jake had been looking forward to spending time with his father. Instead of every two weeks, Heather agreed for Jake to spend the weekends with Adam. It seemed fair, since she had him during the week. Once they agreed on details of custody, his weekly weekend visits might change. But for now, she had no problem with Jake spending the weekends with his father.

Heather grabbed her robe off the back of the closet door and slipped it on. Passing by Ethan's room, she saw the door was cracked open and poked her head inside. He was curled up under the covers, asleep. Last night, he'd told her that his friends were having another video game marathon. Video games eroded childhoods in Heather's opinion, but what could she say? Ethan was sixteen. Sure, she could make demands. A few weeks ago, Adam insisted that Ethan talk to him, but he had rebuffed Adam. Ethan needed at least one parent.

In the kitchen, Heather prepared the milk mixture for French toast. A *thud* sounded from the stairs, and she stepped into the living room. Jake was coming down, dragging his small suitcase behind him.

"Jake, honey." Heather rushed up the stairs and took the suitcase from him. "That suitcase is as big as you."

He grinned. "French toast, Mommy?"

"Yes, sweetie." Heather had made Jake's choice of breakfast dishes on Saturday morning before Adam picked him up for his weekend visits.

"Yeah." Jake clapped and bounded into the kitchen.

Heather sat a plate of French toast in front of him. He began eating like he was starving. "Slow down, buddy."

"But Daddy will be here soon. See." He pointed to the clock on the microwave. He was right. Adam would be at the house in five minutes. He had always been punctual.

While Jake brushed his teeth and hair, Heather cleaned up the kitchen and leaned against the counter. Usually, after Jake left, she'd spend some time on the swing. But today she was going to Frida's, and she couldn't wait.

The doorbell rang, and Heather made her way to the front door. Jake hurried down the stairs and flew past Heather to open it.

"Daddy." Jake leaped into Adam's arms.

"Hey, little man." Adam stood Jake on the floor and glanced at Heather. "You ready?"

"Yes." Jake grabbed the handle of his suitcase and headed out the door. He turned around, "Bye, Mommy."

"Bye, sweetheart. See you tomorrow."

Adam forced a smile and turned to follow Jake.

THE KNITTING CLUB

Heather pushed the door closed but left enough space that she could see them walk to Adam's new SUV. Last week, he showed up in the brand-new black Chevrolet Tahoe with his girlfriend. When Jake came home on Sunday, he mentioned Amber several times. Heather deduced Amber was the girlfriend. She closed the door and headed to the sunroom to gather her knitting.

"Mom?" Shelly said.

"Good morning. Do you have to work today?"

"Yeah. I'm going in at two."

"I'm going to Frida's today. I can grab a pizza on the way home, if you'd like."

"Travis and I are going out to eat with Dad."

Heather's stomach twisted. Being stung by a hundred wasps would be less painful. "Oh, okay."

"I'm sorry, Mom."

"Don't be, honey. He's your father."

Shelly walked up to Heather and kissed her cheek. "I'm going to grab some French toast before Ethan gets up." She smiled and went into the kitchen.

At least Heather still had Ethan. No, she shouldn't think such a thing. Ethan needed a relationship with Adam. He was Ethan's father, despite his infidelity. She sighed and set her knitting basket on the coffee table and went upstairs to change clothes. Passing by Ethan's room, she saw the open door and knocked. Ethan was sitting on his bed with his phone in his hands. He looked up and smiled.

"Good morning."

"Good morning, Mom."

"What time are you heading out?"

"Around eleven. Steve's mom is buying us a pizza."

"Sounds good."

"What are you doing today?"

"I'm going to Frida's."

"You like going over there, don't you?"

"Yes, I do."

Ethan's phone chimed. He looked at it and scoffed.

"Everything okay?"

"He's crazy if he thinks I'm going to be in the same room with him, much less his sl...girlfriend."

"What?"

"Dad invited me to dinner."

Heather swallowed the knot in her throat. Adam was having a family dinner with his girlfriend?

"I'm tired of him texting me. I'm going to block him."

"Ethan, no."

"How can you stand up for him? He *cheated* on you, Mom."

"Yes. He cheated on *me*, honey. There is nothing wrong with having a relationship with your father."

He rolled his eyes and shook his head. "I'm going downstairs for breakfast."

Heather stood aside as Ethan walked past her. She wouldn't force him to have a relationship with his father. One day, hopefully, he would understand that by having a relationship with Adam, he wasn't betraying her.

Heather pulled into the parking lot of Cathy's Craft Haven to pick up some more yarn and a pack of stitch markers. Frida said that she would provide the yarn, but Heather wanted to add to what they already had. She'd made four pairs of socks since her last visit to Frida's and couldn't wait to add them to the others she and Frida made. Marin was a new knitter, and Heather didn't think she would knit socks soon. But anything was possible.

After she made her purchase, she climbed in her car and made her way to Frida's. When she approached Frida's house, she saw a yellow VW Beetle parked behind Marin's car in front of the house. Maybe the car belonged to a family member. She grabbed her knitting basket from the seat beside her, slid out of the driver's seat, and made her way to the front door.

As Heather was about to knock, the door opened and across the threshold stood a woman wearing black slacks, a white blouse with black lightning bolts, and a pair of red glasses.

A slow smile spread across her face. "You must be Heather. I'm Joyce, Frida's BFF."

"Hello, Joyce."

"Come in. Come in." Joyce held the door open while Heather walked inside.

Heather was met by Frida's warm smile and Marin's reserved one, something she'd gotten used to. The three of them had been getting together to knit for several months now and Marin still kept to herself.

"You can sit here." Joyce picked up her pink jacket and moved to the couch, by Marin.

"Thanks." Heather smiled when she saw Marin raise her brows.

The women talked about what happened since their last get together. Heather minimized venting her frustrations about Adam. She'd admittingly taken over their time together. That meant she was the one talking the most, since Marin was mostly quiet.

Heather sat quietly while Joyce caught her up on the conversation that'd occurred before she arrived. Joyce and Frida had been friends for twenty years. She was a teacher at the same school where Frida taught. Ten years ago, her husband died from cancer, and she spent most of her time volunteering with Frida and playing bingo every week.

Frida took inventory of socks and Marin's scarves. So far, Heather and Frida had knitted twenty pairs of socks and Marin had knitted four scarves. While the socks would be sent to the troops overseas, the scarves Marin knitted were going to the women's shelter.

Heather pulled out the sock she was knitting and settled in for the afternoon. She glanced up and saw a set of sock needles in Frida's hand.

"Are you ready?" Frida said, holding out the needles to Marin.

"Um. Sure, I guess."

"Be confident, even if you don't know what you are doing." Joyce tilted her head.

Marin's lips parted and she took the needles from Frida's hand. "They're so tiny. And there's four."

"They won't bite you, Marin. They aren't baby snakes." Joyce laughed.

Marin bit her bottom lip. "I think I'll stick to scarves."

"Oh," Frida's face brightened. "I forgot about the gadget I bought. Be right back."

Frida disappeared down the hall and returned a moment later, carrying a small wooden box with metal prongs. She handed it to Marin.

"It's a sock loom. You don't have to use needles."

"Oh." Marin surveyed the box.

"They'll be tube socks."

"Cool, I'll try it." Marin's eyes sparkled as she inspected the loom.

A few moments went by as the women concentrated on their projects. Joyce broke the silence. "Can I be a member of your club?"

"Club?" Frida looked up.

"Yeah. You meet every few weeks. That's a club."

"Oh, I guess it is," Frida said.

"I want to be a member. I can't knit, or any of that stuff, so I guess I can be a member for moral support."

Frida looked at Heather, then at Marin. "What do you say, ladies?"

Marin smiled and nodded.

"Sounds good to me," Heather said.

"Good. I'll make a fresh pot of coffee, then we can gossip." Joyce chuckled.

Heather watched Joyce saunter into the kitchen. Joyce being a part of a knitting club when she didn't knit, was like being a member of a photography club without a camera. Though Joyce wasn't a knitter, Heather had a feeling she would fit right in.

Chapter 14

Frida

"When's the club meeting next?" Joyce laid scarves Marin knitted on the table with other donated items at the women's shelter.

"This Saturday." Frida smiled at a little girl who eyed one scarf. "You want it?" The girl grinned and nodded. "It's yours." Frida handed the scarf to the girl and watched her scamper off to her mother.

"Well, strike me pink. I'm going to visit Perry this weekend."

"It will be me and Marin then. Heather is Christmas shopping with her daughter."

Joyce gave a dismissive wave. "Well, maybe you can finally get that girl to talk. She's as quiet as a mouse tiptoeing around a mousetrap."

"Maybe I can." Marin was a closed book. Frida was certain she would have opened up long before now.

Joyce left a half hour later. Frida handed out all four of Marin's scarves and five hats that Frida knitted between club meetings. She smiled. As many times as she'd gotten together with Heather and Marin, she hadn't thought of calling themselves a club.

On the way home, she stopped by the grocery store to buy ingredients for Marranitos and Mexican hot chocolate. Frida loved sharing her culture with Heather and Marin. Spending the day shopping was what Heather needed, but Frida was a little disappointed that she wouldn't be at the get together. Joyce was right about Marin. She was reserved, but Frida had a feeling it was more than a personality trait. Maybe she'd use their time together to crack Marin's shell.

Filling the kettle with cold water, Frida set it on the stove and turned on the burner. While she waited for the water to boil, she walked into the living room and picked up her wedding photo album. Taking a seat on the couch, she opened the album across her lap and smiled as she turned the pages. So many loved ones were now gone. But then again, there were new faces that were not in the photos like Maria and MJ.

The kettle let out a shrill whistle and Frida made her way to the kitchen. As she prepared a cup of tea, her mind went to Heather and Marin. Love for the two women had taken root in her heart, and she looked forward to their time together. With Christmas fast approaching, she wanted to give Heather and Marin gifts—knitting related, of course.

In the spare bedroom, Frida counted socks. Fifteen pairs of socks were piled on the bed. Separating the socks by the knitter seemed like a good idea. Each pair of socks could be put in zipper bags and delivered to the soldiers.

She picked up a pair of socks that Marin knitted. She'd come a long way from when she first started knitting. Marin still used the loom for socks, but Frida planned to ease her into using knitting needles. A multi-colored scarf that Marin knitted lay under the pile of socks. Frida grabbed it and wrapped it around her neck. She smiled. The yarn Marin had chosen was a variegated blue and green.

Less than an hour later, Frida had separated and packaged the socks in zipper bags. A pair of socks Marin had knitted lay on top in the shipping box. Smiling, she picked up the scarf and slipped it in the bag. Laying the card with all three women's signatures on top, she taped the flaps of the box down and affixed the label for their assigned base in Iraq on the top of the box. She rested her hands on top of the box and closed her eyes.

"Dios proteja a estos hombres y mujeres." Opening her eyes, she smiled. God would protect and bless the men and women who would receive the socks—and scarf.

Frida slipped on her coat, picked up the box, and headed to the post office. This was the first of many boxes of socks, she hoped. Both Marin and Heather were currently working on another pair of socks. Frida figured they could send a box every month or so. Pulling into the parking lot of the post office, she smiled as she grabbed the box from the passenger seat. As she stood in line, her heart went out to the men and women away from their friends and families at Christmastime as they served their country. She prayed that the new socks were not only practical but were a reminder that those back home cared about them.

"Where's that doohickey?" Joyce asked, looking around Frida's living room.

"What doohickey?"

"That thing Marin uses. I thought I'd give it a shot."

Frida raised an eyebrow. "The sock loom? She's borrowing it." Joyce wanted to learn to knit? Frida thought she'd never see the day. She tried to get Joyce to knit over the years, but she'd never shown interest. It had to be the knitting club. Maybe she felt left out, which was odd for Joyce. She usually wouldn't give it a second thought.

"Oh." Joyce took a seat on the couch.

"Marin is planning on buying her own when she is paid next. You can borrow it then."

"No hurry." Joyce shrugged. "I figured I'd borrow yours before I buy my own. You know...in case I hate it."

Frida hid a smile and stood. "I think the coffee's ready. Want a cup?"

"As if you have to ask." Joyce grinned.

The women sat in the living room, quietly sipping their coffee. Frida watched Joyce glance around the living room. What else was her friend looking for?

"When are you putting up your Christmas tree? It's usually up by now."

"I thought I'd get a larger tree this year. MJ is going shopping with me Saturday after Marin leaves. He's helping me put the tree up and decorate."

"Oh, really? The poor tabletop tree will be jealous." Joyce laughed.

The last decade, Frida had spent Christmas day with her sister Camilla, Maria's mother, giving her a reason to minimally decorate her home. This year, she was considering asking Marin if she wanted to come over for Christmas. Although Marin didn't talk about anything outside of work, Frida wondered if she had anyone to spend Christmas with. She'd mentioned her roommate a few times, but she wasn't sure if they were close.

"It's because of the girls, right?" Joyce winked and sipped her coffee.

Joyce was perceptive.

"Marin mostly. Heather has her family." A car horn blew, and Frida glanced out the front windows and saw a small dog skitter across the road. "Are you going to Perry's?"

"Yes. Tiff's family will be there." Joyce picked up her coffee cup from the coffee table and took a sip.

"Are you coming Saturday?"

Joyce frowned. "Didn't I tell you? Fran has invited me to go to a craft fair with her."

"Oh, that sounds fun." Frida loved Joyce, but she needed a one-on-one with Marin to chip at the walls around her heart.

Joyce stayed for a little longer, then headed home. Frida stood at the kitchen counter mixing the ingredients for marranitos. The cookies were known to disappear fast. Frida planned to make two dozen for Saturday and maybe another two dozen for the ladies in her church group. She picked up the mixing bowl and inhaled the aroma of ginger and cinnamon. The doorbell rang. She sighed and laid a kitchen towel over the mixing bowl.

Pulling aside the living room curtain, Frida's brows drew together when she saw Maria walking up the sidewalk carrying a cat in her arms.

"Oh, no." Frida drew in a deep breath and opened the door.

"Hi, Aunt Frida." MJ gave Frida a quick hug as he walked past her into the living room.

Maria wore a grin that knotted Frida's stomach. She stroked the white long-haired cat and cradled it like a baby.

"What do you have there?" Frida was almost afraid to ask.

"Here." Maria shoved the cat toward Frida.

Frida took the cat from Maria before it fell to the floor. Surely Maria wasn't giving her a cat. Frida was too busy to care for a cat.

"This is Oscar and he's yours."

"Mine?" Frida held out the cat as if it were a skunk.

"Yes, *Tia*. You need something to keep you company."

"No, I don't." Did she say that out loud?

Maria frowned.

"I don't have time for a..."

Maria cocked her head to the side and pressed her lips together. "You and Frank were so close."

"Frank was a dog and he died eleven years ago. I've been fine without him."

Maria crossed her arms.

Frida sighed. "Come in and have a seat." Frida closed the door when Maria walked into the living room.

"Are you making marranitos?" MJ called from the kitchen.

Frida put Oscar on the floor and hurried to the kitchen. MJ removed the kitchen towel and was running his finger around the lip of the bowl, collecting bits of dough. "Leave that alone. That's for Saturday."

"Your knitting club?" MJ slumped.

"Yes. And the ladies from my church."

MJ looked as if he was about to cry.

"I'll set aside a few for you."

"Thanks, *Tia*." He grinned and hugged Frida. Pulling out his phone, he glued his eyes to the screen and headed to the living room.

Frida shook her head. Kids and their phones these days. She made her way back into the living room, where Oscar was stretched out on the couch. MJ was draped over her chair and Maria was next to Oscar, stroking his back. Frida bit the inside of her cheek and sat on the other end of the couch. She opened her mouth, but Maria's voice cut her off before she spoke.

"Don't worry, Aunt Frida. We have everything in the car. A bed, litter box, litter, bowls, and food." Maria scratched Oscar's head.

She was about to protest Oscar's presence, but it looked as if he was there to stay. Frida looked at the cat as he lay on his side, purring. Pitiful creature. Rolling over, he went to her and peered at her with his round, yellow eyes. His eyes reminded her of the cat in the Shrek movies—wide and pleading. Frida laid a tentative hand on top of his head. He pushed his head against her hand, purring louder.

"*Tia*, he likes you," MJ said. Frida was surprised that the boy pried himself from his phone.

"I guess." Maybe it wouldn't be so bad.

Frida needed to get back to the cookie dough, and it appeared Maria and MJ had come over to bring Oscar and not to visit. MJ brought in all of Oscar's belongings and set up his bowls along the kitchen wall next to the back door. Five minutes later, Maria and MJ were on their way out the front door.

Frida placed the dough in the fridge. She gasped when Oscar brushed against her legs. It would take a while to get used to having someone–or something–around the house. She frowned. Knowing her luck, Oscar would use her furniture as a scratching post. Frida headed back to the living room, straight to her chair. Oscar tried to steal her seat, but she made it in time.

"Ha." She scowled at the cat; he meowed in return. When she picked up her knitting, the creases in her forehead deepened. What if Oscar played with her yarn? She looked at him sitting next to the chair, swishing his tail behind him. That could never happen. She'd worked too hard bonding with Heather and Marin through knitting. Sure, they could start over, but Frida was afraid of how that would affect Heather and Marin. Especially Marin.

Frida glanced down the hall toward the bedrooms. She'd keep her knitting basket behind closed doors. She had a feeling that Oscar would be around for a while.

Chapter 15

Marin

On the way to Frida's, Marin took a detour and drove by her grandma's house. The landscaping had been changed and there was a play set in the backyard. The house belonged to someone else now. She had no choice but to accept that her grandma was gone. For the past six years, she'd had the love of her grandmother and now she was gone. Marin's chest tightened.

She parked in front of Frida's house and grabbed her knitting from the passenger seat. Heather texted her a few days earlier to let her know she wouldn't be at the get together. Marin was both excited and anxious. Heather was a talker and Marin could keep to herself. She couldn't sink into the background today. But since Frida reminded Marin of her grandma, she didn't mind it being just the two of them.

Frida opened the front door as Marin walked up the steps. Her warm smile melted away any trace of apprehension for at least the next few hours.

"Come in," Frida said. Marin followed Frida into the living room. "How are you today?"

"Not bad. My shift starts at four. The restaurant has been busier than usual. Holiday shoppers, I suppose." A fluffy, white cat strode into the living room from the hall and stretched in front of Marin. The cat sprang onto the couch with graceful ease.

"Meet Oscar. My niece thinks I'm lonely." Frida laughed.

Marin sat on the couch and stroked Oscar's back as he laid next to her. "He's beautiful."

"Yes, he is. I've had him for two days. We'll see how it goes." Frida winked.

Frida made small talk about her church group and her family. Marin mentioned the sale of her grandma's house. Compassion filled Frida's face. Marin glanced at Oscar when he stretched and pushed his front paws against her thigh. She smiled and stroked his side.

"He likes you." Frida smiled and held up a nearly finished sock. "Do you have any plans for Christmas?"

Marin's spine stiffened. She liked Frida but didn't want to spend Christmas with people she didn't know, and Frida had told her and Heather that she came from a large family. Madison's family invited her to spend Christmas with them, but as much as she loved the Taylors, she would feel like an outsider. Tears dampened her lashes. This time last year, she was helping her grandma decorate Christmas cookies.

"Are you alright, honey?"

Marin realized the tears had rolled down her cheeks. "Oh. I was thinking about my grandma."

"I know it's hard." Frida stood and walked to the couch. She picked up Oscar, sat next to Marin, and laid Oscar on her lap. Frida rested her hand on Marin's back. Her touch reminded Marin of her grandma. More tears filled her eyes. "Heather has plans with her family and I know this is hard for you since it's the first Christmas without your grandmother. I want to invite you to spend Christmas with me. If you want to, that is. You may already have plans with your roommate."

How could she tell Frida that she didn't want to celebrate with strangers? Marin drew in a deep breath. "Thank you, Frida, but I don't feel like I'm at a place where I can spend Christmas with people I don't know." She twisted a section of yarn around her finger.

"I'm sorry, honey. I meant here at my house."

Marin glanced at her.

"Just us." Frida smiled.

Marin's shoulders relaxed. "I'd like that." Marin's response surprised herself, but it was the truth. She'd love nothing more than spending Christmas with Frida.

"Good." Frida patted Marin's leg. "Ready for those cookies and hot chocolate?"

"Yes, I am." Marin smiled and sat her knitting aside.

Oscar became the focal point while Marin and Frida sat in the living room enjoying cookies and hot cocoa. He stretched and purred when Marin scratched his neck. There was something calming about watching and petting Oscar.

An overwhelming peace washed over Marin, and she had the urge to open up to Frida.

"I know I don't talk much when we knit. It's just..." Marin's mouth went dry.

Frida smiled but said nothing.

"I can't blame it on Heather." Marin laughed.

Frida grinned and stroked Oscar's back when he walked over and hopped onto her lap.

"I keep to myself because I've been through a lot." Marin glanced at Frida, then looked down at the cushion next to her and traced a flower on the upholstery with her finger. "I told Grandma Judith some, but not everything." Marin looked up. She held Frida's compassionate gaze for a moment, something she rarely did when she allowed herself to be vulnerable.

"My grandma told me that my mom met my dad when she was sixteen. He was twenty."

Frida raised her brows.

"I know, right?" Marin took a sip of the lukewarm cocoa. "He was on heavy drugs and got her hooked. She got pregnant not long after they met and then ran off with him."

"Your poor grandparents."

"Yeah. Grandma didn't talk about it much, but when she did, her eyes would tear up. I know they left Mississippi when my mom was pretty far along with me. She used to talk about where all we lived. Tennessee, Arkansas, and Colorado were some states. We ended up in California.

"My earliest memories are of us living in run down houses which I now know were crack houses."

"Oh, *mi querida*." Frida joined Marin on the couch and slipped her arm around her shoulders. "Precious, you don't have to talk about it."

For a moment, Marin feared she would betray her grandma by opening up to Frida. But her grandma would love that Marin had someone she could confide in. "It's okay. Maybe it will help me." Marin smiled.

"If you feel comfortable." Frida moved over and Oscar leaped onto the couch and planted himself between them.

"We were living in a homeless camp when they both died from a drug overdose. I was ten. One of their friends took care of me for a while. I remember her telling me it was no place for a little girl. She took me into the city and pointed to a police car and told me to go up to the door. That's when I went into foster care. I was almost eleven by that time.

"I was in three different homes. There were issues with the first two. I won't go into that now. The third home was wonderful. They had two children they'd adopted through foster care. They started the adoption process for me, but one day, the social worker showed up and took me from the home. I didn't know why. I remember my foster parents standing on the porch holding each other as we drove away. Once we got to the Department of Children Services, a woman I'd never met sat in a chair in the office. She was my grandmother."

"Oh, honey."

"I was angry at first. She ripped me away from the only stable home I'd had. I was with the Copelands for almost a year and a half. But as time passed and I learned about what Grandma Judith had been through, I understood. She'd hired a private investigator not long after Gemma—that's my mom—not long after she ran away. Since we were homeless, it was hard to track us down. It took Grandma Judith fourteen years to find me.

"I knew basic math and could read and write a little. Not because of my parents. In every homeless camp we found, there was at least one person who took pity on me and taught me enough that I could get by. I never went to school until I was in foster care. My grandma hired a tutor to help me. By the time school started that fall, I was proficient enough for ninth grade. I was only one year behind, so I was older than my classmates." Marin stroked Oscar's back. Exhaustion took over, and she leaned back against the cushions.

"Oh, Marin. God was looking out for you." Frida reached over and took Marin's hand in hers. "Fresh cup of cocoa?"

"I'd love some."

Marin rubbed her eyes and closed them for a moment. When she thought about her life, she couldn't help but wonder where God was. Her grandma had always talked about Him. Out of obligation, Marin went to church with her.

Marin glanced at the cross on the wall where she'd seen it each time she'd been over to knit. Frida talked about God often and Marin noticed beads on the side table before. How could she pray to someone who took her husband from her? Especially at such a young age.

Frida walked into the living room and handed Marin a mug. Marin blew into the chocolaty liquid and sipped. "We didn't get much knitting done."

"That's okay." Frida shooed Oscar from the chair and sat down. "Oh, I mailed the first box of socks the other day. The lady at the post office said it should take a week to ten days to get there. Beth from Socks for Troops said that her contact at our base will distribute the socks through the chapel." Frida smiled and sipped her cocoa.

"That's awesome." The idea that socks she knitted would go to a soldier filled Marin with a sense of pride and dread. What if the socks weren't good enough? They looked like a child knitted them. The socks would probably end up in the trash. But maybe they wouldn't. Maybe they'd end up on someone's feet. She smiled.

The women spent the rest of their time together knitting and talking. Several times, Marin's mind attempted to derail the progress she'd made in working through her fear of letting others into the shadows of her heart. But each time the voice in the back of her head told her she'd made a mistake in opening up to Frida, she silenced the voice. And each time the voice whispered; she silenced it again. One day, the voice wouldn't dare to enter her thoughts.

Chapter 16

Heather

Applying a thin layer of red lipstick, Heather rubbed her lips together and grimaced. A quick blot and her lips were a faint hue of red. She ran her fingers through her hair and forced out her breath. Adam would be by any minute to pick up Jake for the weekend. The doorbell rang, twisting her stomach into a knot.

Voices drifted up the stairs. Heather heard Shelly's, Adam's, and Jake's voices. Who did the other feminine voice belong to? Usually, Adam would pick up Jake and be on his way. He wouldn't bring his girlfriend into the house. He wasn't that bold. She sat on the bed procrastinating going downstairs.

Heather was looking forward to spending the day with Shelly. She rarely got Shelly to herself now that she was dating Travis. Glancing at the head of the bed, no one would know that Adam hadn't slept in their bed for months. One thing he left behind were his pillows.

"Mommy!" Jake's feet pounded up the stairs. He blew through the doorway and leaped into Heather's arms. "Daddy wants to talk to you."

Heather tensed and smoothed down Jake's hair. What could Adam possibly want to talk about? Did he want more time with Jake? He was getting him on the weekends. Heather looked up when Adam appeared in the doorway.

"Jake, tell Mommy bye and head to the car."

"Okay, Daddy." Jake wrapped his arms around Heather's neck and gave her an exaggerated kiss on the cheek. "Bye Mommy. I love you."

"Bye, sweetheart. I love you too." She watched Jake race out of the room. Her gaze shifted to Adam. "Was that woman in my house?"

"She had to use the bathroom, Heather. And it's *our* house."

Heather bit her tongue to keep from imitating Adam. "What do you want to talk about?"

"Well...Christmas."

"Christmas?"

"Yeah. Amber's family is getting together Christmas evening and I thought it would be nice if he could join us."

"Christmas is Sunday, and Jake is due home by six."

"I know, Heather. I can have him back Monday before lunch."

"Let me get this straight. You want our son to meet your harlot's family?" She spat the words at him.

"Heather."

"You have some nerve." A fire sparked in Heather's chest and spread throughout her body. "We are going to Mom's and she's looking forward to seeing the kids."

Adam gritted his teeth. "I see this is going nowhere."

"Nope."

"We'll talk about this later."

"*No*, we won't."

Adam shook his head.

"Mom. Dad," Shelly said.

Heather looked up, and Adam turned around.

"You are loud. Steve and Ethan are playing video games in the next room and I can hear you downstairs so I know they can hear you too." Shelly crossed her arms.

"I'm heading out, anyway." Adam kissed the side of Shelly's head and walked out of the room without another look or word to Heather.

Heather burst into tears when Shelly looked at her.

"Mom. It's okay." She guided Heather to the bench at the foot of the bed and slipped her arm around her shoulders when they sat down. "We need to get out of here and hit the mall. Retail therapy always helps." Shelly leaned her head against Heather's.

"You're right." Heather wiped her tears and walked into the bathroom to touch up her makeup. She and Shelly went downstairs, grabbed their purses, and headed to the car.

Heather backed out of the garage and drove toward the entrance to their subdivision. At the traffic light, she gripped the steering wheel tight, whitening her knuckles. Did Adam really want Jake for Christmas, or was he trying to get under her skin? She exhaled and punched the accelerator when the light turned green, causing the tires to screech.

Shelly gasped. "Mom!"

"Your father is a piece of work," Heather said through clenched teeth.

Shelly focused her gaze ahead.

The upcoming traffic light turned yellow, but Heather didn't slow down. Her chest tightened with each heaving breath.

"Mom." Shelly's voice edged on panic.

The light changed to red as Heather drove through the intersection. Out of the corner of her eye, she saw Shelly grab the handle above the door. Easing off the accelerator, she forced herself to slow her breathing.

"I'm sorry, sweetheart. I...I'm so mad. And hurt." Heather wiped the tears from her eyes.

"Me too. I know it's worse for you as his wife. I can't imagine Travis cheating on me."

Shelly's six-month relationship didn't compare to a twenty-year marriage, but she was showing sympathy.

"He's my dad. I hate what he did, but I love him."

"Oh, honey, I know."

"I have animosity for Amber because of what she's done, but I can tolerate her for Dad's sake."

On the tip of Heather's tongue laid a question she wouldn't ask: how did Jake feel about Amber? She knew how Ethan felt. He loathed both Adam and his mistress. At least, that was how he acted. As angry as she was with Adam, Heather continued to encourage Ethan to at least talk to his father.

Heather pulled into the parking lot of the mall. She and Shelly stopped at several stores and ended up at the food court loaded down with shopping bags. The rest of their time together was spent talking about Shelly's plans for her future. She'd graduate in less than six months. Adam was gone and Shelly would move to north Mississippi to attend Mississippi State University. Ethan would follow her in two years and in the blink of an eye, Jake would leave her, too. Heather's family was falling apart.

Five shopping bags laid scattered throughout Heather's bedroom. She went a little overboard shopping for Christmas presents, but she didn't care. Adam was the one paying the bills. Heather picked up one bag and dumped the clothes onto the bed. She grabbed a small pair of scissors from the nightstand and began removing the tags.

The clothes piled on the bed were Christmas presents to herself. She deserved it for putting up with Adam's nonsense. She held up a pair of pants and sighed. She could be the stereotypical wife and go on a diet. Losing twenty-five or thirty pounds would cause Adam to regret his actions and move back home. But she shouldn't care what Adam thought. If she made a lifestyle change, it would be for her and no one else.

Picking up her phone, Heather looked at the time, and her heart pounded. Jake was due home in half an hour. It wouldn't surprise her if Adam stayed in the car and watched Jake walk into the house. Before, the weekends dragged by, and it seemed like Jake had been gone a week. But this weekend flew by. She missed Jake, but she was still reeling from the encounter with Adam.

The aroma of chicken alfredo floated up the stairs. Shelly loved to cook, and Heather looked forward to taking it easy on the nights that Shelly made dinner. Heather made her way downstairs and passed by Ethan and Travis, watching a movie in the den.

Heather walked to the kitchen and glanced at the dining table as she passed by. Shelly had set out seven plates. There were five of them. Surely Shelly hadn't invited her father and she who shall remain nameless. She walked up to the stove where Shelly was standing.

"Here, try this." Shelly held up a spoon full of sauce to Heather's mouth.

Heather took a sip and widened her eyes. "Mmm. So good."

Shelly grinned and turned off the stove burner.

Heart pounding, Heather should mentally prepare herself for Adam and Amber to sit at the table. She could eat in the sunroom or upstairs.

"Ashley and Micah are coming for dinner."

Thank you, God.

"Oh good. I haven't seen Ashley in a while." Heather exhaled slowly.

A car door shut out front, and Heather glanced at the clock on the microwave. Adam was fifteen minutes early. Or maybe it was Ashley and Micah. She walked into the laundry room and separated the blinds. She exhaled as she watched Ashley and Micah walking on the sidewalk to the house. Her eyes widened when she saw Adam's SUV pass by in front of the house and park behind Micah's car. Hiding out in the laundry room was silly, but she'd do it, anyway.

She opened the cabinets above the washer and dryer. There was one jug of bleach, a bottle of stain remover, a box of dryer sheets, and a jug of detergent. Taking inventory was a good excuse to be in the laundry room. Jake's sweet voice filled the living room.

Ethan appeared in the doorway. Closing the door behind him, he walked up to Heather.

"Hiding out?" A restrained smile showed on his lips.

"No." Heather sighed. "Yes."

Ethan slipped his arm around her shoulders.

"It's okay for you to keep your distance, Mom. Dad treated you like garbage." He kissed her cheek.

This time, she didn't chastise him for talking negatively about his father. She would be a hypocrite if she did.

"Mommy," Jake's voice called out. "Mommy?"

"She's in the laundry room," Shelly said.

Ethan walked over to the window and separated the blinds. "He's gone."

The door flew open, and Jake wrinkled his brow. "What are you guys doing?"

Heather looked at the cabinets. "Seeing if we need more laundry detergent."

"Oh." He walked up to Heather and Ethan, wrapping an arm around both of their waists. "I missed you guys."

"We saw you yesterday morning." Ethan patted Jake's back.

"I know. I missed you anyway."

"We missed you, too." Heather lifted Jake's chin and bent down to kiss his cheek.

"Oh. Daddy said to tell you he gave the bank money. He...he put money in the bank." Jake shrugged. "Something about the bank."

"Okay, thank you." Couldn't Adam have texted her or given Jake a note to give her? He just dragged their five-year-old son into their train wreck of a marriage.

Chapter 17

Marin

Marin laid her shopping bag on a free table in the food court and looked around. Madison was probably in the dressing room of one of those trendy stores Marin wouldn't be caught dead in. She sighed. Why did she let Madison talk her into going to the mall five days before Christmas? Tucking a pink tress of hair behind her ear, she pulled out the art supplies she'd purchased.

Not that she'd been in the right frame of mind, but Marin hadn't drawn since before her grandma died. She pulled out a pack of colored pencils and frowned. Her art supplies were one thing she'd left behind when she moved out of her grandma's house. Stella probably trashed her expansive collection of different mediums she'd used to express her emotions.

Closing her eyes, Marin visualized Oscar's yellow eyes and voluminous white coat. She'd never drawn a cat before, but Oscar was as special as Frida.

"There you are." Madison's voice was tinged with exhaustion.

Marin opened her eyes and parted her lips at the number of bags Madison slung onto the table, barely leaving room for their lunch. "Geeze, Madison. Did you leave anything for the other shoppers?"

Madison giggled. She picked up the drawing tablet Marin pulled out of the bag. "I forgot you can draw. Anything in particular?"

"I thought I'd try drawing Ms. Frida's cat. Maybe give it to her for Christmas."

"I bet you can. You're good." Madison pushed her hair away from her face. "What do you want? You can stay with the bags, and I'll get our lunch."

"Um, burritos?" Marin grabbed her backpack from the chair next to her and unzipped the outer pouch on the front.

"What are you doing?"

"Giving you some money."

"I got it."

Marin groaned.

"It can be part of your Christmas present." Madison laughed and disappeared among the throngs of hungry shoppers in the food court.

Part of her Christmas present? Of course, Madison would give her something for Christmas. They weren't just roommates; they were close friends. A month ago, Marin would've been in a panic. But she had gotten caught up on all her bills and had a little money to spare each payday after putting money into her savings account. Now she had to figure out what to get Madison for Christmas in the next five days. Sighing, she shoved the bags aside when she saw Madison heading her way with a full tray.

Settled in her room for the night, Marin tipped the lampshade for more light. She could turn on the overhead light, but the brightness would stifle her creativity. She picked up the black pencil and lightly sketched Oscar's shape. Taking the white pencil, she colored inside the lines and drew faint wisps with the black pencil to define his fur. Finally, she used a blending tool to blur the edges between black and white.

Holding the sketchbook out in front of her, for the first time in a long while, she didn't want to rip one of her drawings to shreds. Moisture filled her eyes, and she rubbed them with the heel of her hand. Her grandmother always told her she had a God-given gift like her mother, and she should share that gift with the world. Marin had believed she was far from gifted, and her sketches had remained hidden in the sketchbooks she'd stored in her closet. They were probably in a landfill by now.

Browsing the pencils, she found the yellows and pulled them out of the box and inspected the different shades. She chose the perfect color—sunburst yellow—and began filling in Oscar's eyes. A few minutes later, she finished the drawing with a blue background—a perfect contrast to Oscar's yellow eyes.

Marin made her rounds in the dining room, visiting guests and making sure they were satisfied with their meals. As she walked into the kitchen, she saw Rebecca walk through the backdoor. Rebecca raised her brows when she saw Marin.

"Just who I wanted to see."

Marin's heart pounded and her mind immediately went to the worst-case scenario. She couldn't read Rebecca's expression. Marin forced out a smile and followed Rebecca into the office. Standing by the desk, Rebecca gestured for Marin to take a seat. She hesitated, then sat down.

"We hired a new shift manager."

Rebecca might as well have slapped Marin across the face. She bit her bottom lip to keep it from trembling. Stepping down to a server position would be an embarrassment. What did she do to lose her position?

"Tyrone and I have given you a set schedule. You will work Monday through Friday, and you'll still have the night shift."

Marin swallowed hard. A normal work week with the weekends off? She allowed a hint of a smile. "Thank you."

"You earned it." Rebecca tilted her head and arched her brows.

After Rebecca left the office, Marin pinched her arm. No, she wasn't dreaming. What would she do with herself on the weekends? The first thing that came to mind was knitting with Frida and Heather. Because of Marin's work schedule, they met once or twice a month if everything lined up. Now that she would be off on the weekends, maybe they could meet weekly. Marin closed her eyes and smiled.

The phone rang and Marin answered. A few moments later, she hung up and sighed. One of the part-time servers called in sick. Since Marin's promotion, she'd had to fill in for a server a time or two. She hadn't minded, but serving and managing at the same time could be stressful. At least it was Monday, their slowest day.

Refilling drinks at table fourteen, Marin noticed a hostess leading a party of three to table ten. She walked over to take their drink order. A man and woman, whose body language told her they were a couple, sat on one side and another man sat on the other. Marin introduced herself and saw the woman smile and raise her eyebrows at the man across from her.

"What can I get you to drink?"

"I'll have a peach sweet tea. What about you, babe?" the woman said and looked at the man sitting next to her.

"I'll take a Dr. Pepper."

"What about you, *Mark*?" The woman emphasized his name.

Marin fought the urge to roll her eyes and turned her attention to the man across the table.

"Coke's fine."

Although she had been looking straight at the man, Marin noticed him for the first time. His eyes were deep blue, and shoulder-length hair was jet black. She was surprised to see that one of his eyebrows was pierced and he wore black eyeliner. Her gaze found a black leather jacket draped on the back of the chair next to him.

As she took mental note of his drink order, she glanced at the couple. The clean-cut man was wearing jeans and a yellow polo, and his blonde hair was cropped close to his head. The woman's long brown hair was pulled back in a high ponytail, and she wore a bright blue top with black jeans. The trio reminded Marin of how she and Madison must look to others in public—a stark contrast to each other.

The woman looked at the man across from her and grinned. A blush skimmed over his cheeks. Marin arched a brow and excused herself to get their drinks.

What was that about?

On her feet for almost forty-five minutes straight, Marin stretched her back and made her way to the dining room. She saw a woman heading towards her wearing a wide smile. As she got closer, Marin recognized her as the woman sitting at the table with the man wearing black. The woman stopped a few feet in front of Marin, causing her stomach to flip.

"Can I get a refill? Oh, and Mark would like another Coke." She grinned. "He's single, by the way."

"Oh. Um, sure, no problem." Marin hoped the stone-faced expression that she'd spent years perfecting was displayed on her face.

The woman smiled again and continued on her way to the restroom. As if it was her first day as a freshman at a new high school and everyone's attention was on her, Marin trembled, and her heart rate elevated to where she might faint. She'd taken painful steps to get her anxiety under control. Would a brunette with a high ponytail undo all her progress? Why was this happening to her? The last thing she wanted was attention from the opposite sex.

She headed to table ten with a glass of peach sweet tea and a glass of Coke. Swallowing the knot in her throat, she smiled and placed the glass of tea in front of the woman's empty plate and the glass of Coke in front of Mark. Picking up the two empty glasses, she took a step back to head to the back when Mark spoke.

"I'm so sorry about my sister's behavior. She's always trying to fix me up," Mark said.

"Yeah, Teena has made it her mission to find Mark a wife. I'm Kenny, by the way."

"No problem." Marin tilted her head toward each man and made her way back to the kitchen as fast as her legs would take her without sprinting. She was surprised she didn't trip or knock anyone to the floor.

When she stepped out of the kitchen to make her rounds and check on diners, she saw Teena head her way again. "You've got to be kidding me," Marin mumbled under her breath.

"Hi," Teena said when she walked up to Marin. "I meant nothing by it. Mark's a good guy that likes to express himself as goth, and I thought since you are goth." She grinned. "And you're pretty." A wide smile filled her face.

Marin's eyebrows knit together before she could stop herself. Teena must be blind.

"Oh, I'm sorry." Teena's smile fell.

"No, it's okay. I must say that this is the first time this has happened to me." Marin swallowed the knot in her throat.

"Well, you never know. I wrote his number on the receipt." She grinned and walked away. Marin groaned and made her rounds.

On the way home, Marin shoved Mark out of her head and thought about the path her life had taken since her grandma died. She went from sleeping in her car to working as a shift manager at one of the most popular steakhouses in town. Where would she be if Madison hadn't insisted that she move in with her? Her mind went to Stella. Why did she hate Marin? What did Marin do to Stella to cause her to throw her out on the streets except being born? What would her grandmother think about Stella's behavior?

Chapter 18

Heather

"**M**onty!" Jake giggled and shook the box that held a remote-controlled Monty the Monster Truck.

"Here, buddy," Ethan said. "I'll set it up for you."

"Okay." Jake clapped and squealed.

Glancing at the clock, Heather held back tears. Adam would be by in an hour and a half to pick up Jake. She'd struggled with Adam taking Jake for Christmas. After an internal battle that lasted a week, Heather reluctantly agreed.

Shelly handed Heather a cup of coffee and sat on the couch next to her. Ethan walked over to Heather holding a small, square wrapped gift.

"Last one."

"Thank you, Ethan." Heather unwrapped the gift and pulled the top off the small box. Inside was a silver bracelet with little dangling figurines. She removed it from the box and held her hand over her mouth. Two boys held Ethan's and Jake's birthstone, and a girl held Shelly's birthstone.

"It was Ethan's idea," Shelly whispered to Heather.

"It's beautiful." Tears pooled in Heather's eyes and spilled down her cheeks. She looked up at Ethan. His smile reached his eyes.

"Thank you, my babies." Heather wiped her cheeks.

Ethan leaned down and hugged Heather, and Shelly kissed Heather's cheek.

"Wait for me, guys." Jake jumped to his feet and climbed onto Heather's lap.

Ethan fastened the bracelet around Heather's wrist. She held her arm up and watched the sunlight streaming through the windows reflect in each gem. Jake let out a giggle as his new Monty truck shot across the room when he pushed the lever on the remote. Ethan took Jake aside and showed him how to use the remote.

"I think it's good you are letting Jake go to Dad's," Shelly said.

Heather turned towards her daughter and arched her brows.

"You're stronger than you think, Mom."

"I don't feel strong." Heather uttered a laugh.

For a moment, they sat quietly, watching Jake and Ethan playing with the remote-control truck across the room.

"If you'd said no, Jake would be heartbroken. He's confused enough as it is. He asked me the other night when Dad is moving back in."

As if steel fingers slipped around her heart and squeezed, Heather rested her hand on her chest. The sound of the doorbell invaded their time together. Heather forced herself to stay put. It was Christmas and would look bad if she ran up the stairs and locked herself in her bedroom.

"Daddy!" Jake shot to the front door and flung it open. "Merry Christmas!"

"Merry Christmas, Jake." Adam hugged Jake, then Shelly, when she walked up to him. He seemed to shrink three inches as he watched Ethan mount the stairs and disappear.

Heather rose and took a few steps away from the couch, keeping a safe amount of distance between her and Adam. She saw him swallow hard when he looked her way.

"Merry Christmas." He tilted his head to Heather. "Thanks again for letting Jake come."

Heather's heartbeat filled the back of her throat, choking off her voice. All she could do was nod.

"See you tonight, Dad." Shelly hugged her father and kissed his cheek. She closed the door behind Adam and Jake. Heather could hear Jake chattering about his new Monty the Monster Truck remote truck on the way to Adam's SUV.

Heather and Ethan planned to spend the day and evening with Heather's mother. Shelly had set up a schedule to divide her time between Travis, Heather, Adam, and her grandparents. The poor girl was already spreading herself thin for a man.

"Thanks, Nana," Ethan said when his grandmother handed him a cup of hot apple cider.

"My pleasure." She sat in an old, faded pink wingback chair and propped her feet up on a tattered ottoman in front of the chair. "How's life treating you, Ethan?"

The room fell silent. Heather sighed to herself. She'd talked to her mother several times about how life had been treating Ethan.

"I'm close to having all my driving hours. Mom's been taking me out as much as possible." An awkward chuckle passed over his lips, then he took a long sip of cider. Too long to be drinking piping hot liquid. The poor kid's lips had to be burning.

If Shelly was there, she'd think of something to say. But she'd left less than fifteen minutes earlier, heading to Travis' house.

"You're mad at your dad like your mom was mad at me," Heather's mother said.

Ethan looked at Heather.

"Dad was an alcoholic, Mom. It was different." Heat filled Heather's chest.

"You were still mad that I asked your father to leave. You accused me of tearing our family apart."

"You knew things I didn't back then. I was young and didn't understand."

Heather's father had hidden his alcoholism well. At least from her. Her mother knew and had finally reached her limit. Her dad passed from cirrhosis of the liver shortly before Shelly was born. Despite his faults, Heather struggled with the fact that her children had never met their grandfather.

"I know Dad cheated. He's certainly not trying to hide it now. Parading all around town with his...his woman." Ethan scoffed.

"It's Christmas. Can we not do this, please?" Heather rubbed her temples. Part of her wished she was sitting in Frida's living room knitting right about now. She loved her mother, but she saw everything in black or white. Gray areas didn't exist in Edith Jordan's book.

"I'm sorry. I was trying to show Ethan that the anger won't always be there."

"Well, this is different. Adam abandoned his family. He walked away on his own. I don't know if Dad would have if you hadn't asked for a divorce. Anyway, it's irrelevant now. We'll never know." Searing pain shot through Heather's temples, and she rubbed them again.

A knock at the front door broke the tension. The trio watched Heather's sister Michelle and her family walk inside. It could go two ways: the topic would change to Michelle, her husband Jason, and their twin teen sons, or Heather's marriage would continue to be the focus of attention. Although Michelle knew Adam had left, aside from asking Heather how she was doing periodically, she didn't dwell on the subject, and for that, Heather was thankful.

"Sissy." Michelle made a beeline to Heather and wrapped her arms around Heather's neck when she stood.

"Hey, girl." The sisters embraced longer than Heather expected, and it felt good.

Ethan and his cousins started a side conversation related to one video game or another and it warmed Heather's heart to see Ethan's eyes light up and a rarely seen smile fill his face.

"How are you?" Michelle asked when the two women sat on the sofa.

Heather glanced in Ethan's direction. He and his cousins were sitting at the island helping their grandmother decorate cookies. Her mind went to Jake. What was he doing now? Decorating cookies with Adam's girlfriend?

"As good as expected, I guess."

"Still knitting?"

"Yes, it's been a lifesaver. I enjoy spending time with Frida and Marin. Joyce too."

"I'm glad. I wish we lived closer. Five hours might as well be fifty."

"I know, me too."

"Have you two talked about the actual divorce?" Michelle sipped cider as she waited for Heather's reply.

"No. It's the elephant in the room. I'm just now getting to where I can tolerate being in the room with him."

"Maybe he's waiting until after the holidays."

"How noble of him." Heather laughed and rolled her eyes. She sighed and tucked her hair behind her ears. "I need to know if I should be job hunting. I don't know who would hire someone with no degree and no job history for the past eighteen years."

"Adam's behavior is deplorable, but I don't see him doing that to you."

"I'd like to say he wouldn't, but I obviously don't know him. I never thought he'd have an affair."

"I know, sis." Michelle patted Heather's leg.

What had changed with Adam? People change over the years as they grow and mature. But most people don't seek new partners. When did he start looking at other women?

Chapter 19

Frida

The oven timer buzzed, letting Frida know that the second batch of sugar cookies was ready. She glanced at the kitchen clock. Any minute Marin would arrive to spend Christmas day with her. She grabbed the potholders and pulled the cookie sheet from the oven. After a few minutes, she slid the cookies onto the cooling racks and placed the icing and tips on the table. She sighed when she thought about the conversation with Maria a few days ago.

"*Tia*, you've never missed Christmas." Maria crossed her arms.

"This year is different, Maria."

"You could invite Marin to Mama's house."

"Marin is not at a place to be surrounded by people she doesn't know. She's very reserved. Maybe next year."

Maria let out a dramatic sigh that Frida guessed Maria hoped would have changed her mind. Well, it didn't. Frida loved her family, but she felt led by the Lord to spend Christmas with Marin and Marin only.

The doorbell brought her to the present, and Frida made her way to the front door. She fought to keep the surprise off her face when she saw the neckband and cuffs of a bright red sweater peeking out from under Marin's black leather jacket. Thinking back, Frida couldn't remember Marin wearing anything besides dark colors.

Marin walked to the couch and slipped off her backpack and jacket.

"Don't you look festive," Frida said.

A shy smile tipped the corners of Marin's mouth. "You too, with your snowman earrings."

Frida grinned and touched the snowman dangling from an ear. "Let's head to the kitchen and get to work." Marin smiled and followed Frida.

Once finished decorating cookies, they settled in the living room with fresh coffee and a few cookies. Frida watched Marin as she looked around the living room at the variety of Christmas decorations displayed. Marin's gaze settled on the crucifix on the wall. They had talked little about faith. Frida mentioned attending mass in casual conversation and Heather talked about her large church wedding.

"Did you have any traditions with your family? Attending Christmas mass is one thing that we always did in my family."

Marin looked at Frida and widened her eyes. "Am I keeping you from mass?"

"No, honey. I can go later tonight. We have several services on Christmas day."

"Oh, okay." Marin smiled. "We went to Christmas Eve service. My grandmother was Baptist. I didn't go to church until I came to live with her."

Marin placed her coffee on the side table and stood, making her way to the Christmas tree. She touched the crown of thorns ornament that Maria and MJ had given Frida for Christmas a few years ago. It was made of resin but looked as if it was actually twisted vines. She reached down and picked up the present she'd brought with her. A wide smile spread across Marin's face when she handed the present to Frida.

Frida took the present from Marin and tore off the paper to reveal a plain white box. When she pulled off the top, she gasped. Holding up the picture frame, she stared at the image. Glancing from the drawing to Oscar and back at the drawing, she looked up at Marin with her lips parted.

"Marin." It was the only word she managed to say. She appreciated artwork but had never received a customized piece of art before. Marin was talented. It was as if Oscar stepped inside the frame and was peering at her with his penetrating eyes. The image was that lifelike.

"Marin, God has truly blessed you with a talent. I have never received such a precious gift." Marin leaned down and hugged Frida. She noticed a hint of a blush in Marin's cheeks when she pulled back.

"I haven't drawn in a while. I thought I'd see if I could draw Oscar."

"You were successful. You even captured his little smirk." Frida laughed.

Marin smiled. She glanced at the floor and back at Frida. "Thank you."

"You are very welcome. Now it's your turn." Frida walked over to the Christmas tree and picked up the large gift that was hidden behind the tree.

"Wow, that's big." Marin smiled. She took her time unwrapping the gift and spent a good minute inspecting each skein of yarn and thumbing through each pattern book in the box. The smile stayed firmly on her lips while she looked over her new knitting supplies. She put everything in the box and sat it aside. When she slipped her arms around Frida's neck, Marin gave her an extended hug. Frida figured part of the hug was meant for her late grandmother.

"Well, I think we had a good Christmas," Frida said.

"Yes, we did." Marin peered inside the box of knitting supplies again. Oscar hopped up on the couch next to her and laid down.

"Would you like more coffee or hot cocoa?" Frida asked.

"I'll take some Mexican hot chocolate if it's not too much trouble." Marin stroked the cat's back.

"Not at all." Frida returned with two mugs of cocoa and handed one to Marin. Taking a seat on the other end of the couch, Frida pulled the pattern books from the box and went through each one with Marin. Marin's eyes widened when Frida pulled out a pattern book for sweaters. She patted Marin's arm and smiled, encouraging her that one day, she'd knit a sweater. Frida was sure of it.

A car door shut, and Frida could make out Joyce's car through the lace curtains stretched across the living room window. Joyce headed to the mailbox. It was something Joyce did if she came for a visit before noon, when Frida usually checked the mail. She didn't mind since it saved her a trip to the mailbox.

"Good morning, dah-ling. Happy New Year," Joyce said as she walked in the door.

"Good morning, and Happy New Year to you too." Frida closed the door behind Joyce and went to the kitchen to pour two cups of coffee. As Frida brought the cups into the living room, Joyce began quizzing her as if she was on a game show.

"What does P.S.C., A.P.O. and A.E. mean?"

"I don't know. What does P.S.C., A.P.O., and A.E. mean?" The letters seemed vaguely familiar to Frida.

"No, this." Joyce handed Frida an envelope. "You got something in the mail with those letters and some numbers. It looks weird."

Frida glanced at the return address and flipped over the envelope. Sliding her finger under the flap, she pulled out a card. She arched her brows when she saw something drop to the floor. Reaching down, she picked it up. Her eyes widened when she saw it was a photo of a soldier wearing the scarf Marin had knitted. She flipped the envelope over and realized the address was for the military base where she'd sent the box of socks.

"What is it, Frida?"

"It's from a soldier that received a pair of socks. I slipped the scarf into one bag of socks that Marin knitted." She handed the picture to Joyce.

"He's a cutie."

Frida groaned.

"Cool it, toots. I'm just making an observation." Joyce shook her head.

Frida opened the card and read the inside.

I want to thank you ladies for sending the socks. The socks we are issued aren't as nice or comfortable as these socks. I really like the scarf too. We don't get a chance to wear winter clothes since it's hot over here now, but it reminds me of my hometown in Montana. I'd love to know which one of you ladies knitted the scarf. I want to thank her personally.

~Gage Harris, Sergeant, U.S. Army

Frida noted an email address at the bottom of the card. She remembered the note she'd included in the box that she'd signed along with Marin and Heather. She ran her fingers over the raised flowers on the front. Should she give the card to Marin? She tended to be hard on herself. Maybe having someone besides Frida and Heather complementing her knitting would help increase her self-esteem. Slipping the card in the envelope, she laid it on the side table. The girls were due to come over within the hour. She had a little time to decide what to do.

Chapter 20

Marin

A yawn stretched Marin's mouth wide. Charley's Steakhouse hosted a New Year's Eve bash two nights earlier, and Marin had been the shift manager. She was no night owl and was having a hard time recovering. As tired as she was, she refused to miss knitting time with Frida, Heather, and Joyce. She grabbed her knitting bag and headed to her car.

Pulling in behind Heather's SUV, Marin picked up her bag from the passenger seat and made her way to the house. As she stepped onto the porch, the front door opened. Joyce moved out from behind the door and grinned at her. Marin couldn't keep her brows from raising at the large, bright red lips on the front of Joyce's white sweatshirt. The shirt, along with Joyce's fuchsia leggings and lemon-yellow loafers, brought out a giggle from Marin.

"Welcome, welcome," Joyce said as she stood aside.

"Thank you. Love the sweatshirt, by the way," Marin said.

"Thanks, doll. I got it on sale."

"Hi Marin," Heather said. Marin hadn't seen Heather in close to a month and had missed her. Marin placed her bag on the floor by the couch and hugged each woman. Six months earlier, hugging was one of Marin's least favorite things and now, each knitting session started and ended with hugs.

"Frida has something for you," Joyce sang.

Picking up an envelope from the table by her chair, Frida walked over and handed it to Marin. Opening the card, Marin studied the photo of the man wearing the scarf she'd knitted. It took reading his words twice for it to sink in that he was looking to connect with her.

"He sure is handsome," Joyce said.

Joyce wasn't wrong, but the man's appearance was irrelevant. All he wanted was to thank her for the scarf. The scarf that looked like a five-year-old knitted it. Or perhaps a blind person. Didn't he see the dropped stitches she tried to correct?

"Are you going to write to him?" Heather asked.

"Oh, I don't know."

"Come on. He's not proposing marriage. Not yet, anyway." Joyce laughed.

If the daggers Frida shot Joyce were real, Joyce would be in a great deal of pain right now.

"How was the New Year's Eve Party?" Heather asked.

"Long." Marin smiled. "I like my sleep and I'm still trying to play catch up. But it was nice. We had a big turnout."

"That's good," Frida said.

Oscar sat at Marin's feet, staring at her, swishing his tail behind him. He looked as if he would launch himself onto her lap at any moment. She'd become his favorite person. Anytime they got together, he was fighting to keep her lap warm. Recently, Marin read an article that animals sensed a person's emotions. Did Oscar know she was broken?

"How have you been?" Marin asked Heather.

"Okay, I guess. Jake spent Christmas with Adam. It was hard, but I'm glad I let him go. He had a good time."

"That's good." Though Jake's parents were separated, at least they both loved him dearly. Marin would have given everything to have had parents who loved her as much as Heather and Adam loved their children.

"Now that we are in a new year, I expect that the divorce will happen this year. I think the sooner the better. I'm ready to get on with my life, whatever that looks like."

"I get that," Marin said.

Frida brought out a fresh carafe of coffee and took her seat. A comfortable silence fell over the room as the women got ready to resume their knitting projects. Marin's mind drifted to Gage Harris. Would she contact him? If so, what in the world would she say?

Marin read the card for the tenth time, or close to it. Closing the card, she ran her finger over the flowers on the front. Why did Frida add the scarf to the package? Gage wouldn't use a scarf in a hundred-degree weather. She pulled up her email on her phone and typed in his email address. Her email would be short and sweet.

Hello Gage,

I sent the socks and scarf. I hope you enjoy them.

Marin

No, that sounded impersonal. But did she want to get personal? Marin sighed and twisted the stud in her nose. She deleted the email and started over.

Hi Gage,

I wanted to do something to help the troops. I'm a new knitter and wanted...

Marin groaned. Why was this so hard? She didn't know the man, so there was no reason for her to be nervous. He couldn't tell she was nervous from an email, anyway. Biting her bottom lip, she deleted what she'd typed and tried for the third time.

Gage,

I wanted to do something for soldiers overseas and I decided to join Socks for Troops. I'm a new knitter and have been making scarves too. Frida, our fearless leader, added one of my scarves to the bag. Thank you for your service. Stay safe.

Marin

She read the email a few times and stopped. Shuffling around in her nightstand, she found a package of notecards that Madison had given her. She pulled one out, grabbed the pen on her nightstand, and wrote what she had written in the last email she'd drafted. Sealing the envelope and writing his address on the front, she looked at it for a moment, then tore it in half. She let out a growl and picked up her phone.

With the draft email open, she tapped the send button before she could change her mind. Nausea bubbled in her stomach. Why did she reply to him? What if he wanted to be pen pals, or whatever it was called nowadays? He probably wouldn't respond anyway, so no reason to get worked up. She went into her sent emails and read the email again. She needed to let it go.

On the drive to work, Gage occupied her thoughts. If he responded, would she? She did not know what to say. Being in the military, he moved around a lot. It didn't matter. It wasn't like they would be in a relationship.

Pushing Gage out of her mind, she clocked in and began the walk through. A full crew was on the schedule for the night. The past week, several employees were out sick because of the flu. A half hour later, the doors were open and soon, the dining room was close to capacity.

In the office, Marin was going over the supply orders for the following week when there was a knock on the door. She looked up and saw Madison standing in the doorway. She wasn't wearing her usual smile.

"What's up?" Marin laid the paperwork aside.

"We have a complaint."

"What about?" Marin's heartbeat picked up speed. It had been quite a while since a diner complained. This was a part of the job she hated. Confrontation wasn't her strong suit. She followed Madison into the dining room and up to a table where a man and woman were seated. The woman's back was to Marin, but she noticed the man's strained expression. When Marin reached the table and glanced at the woman, a knot closed off her throat.

"Kaylee?" Stella's lips parted and her eyes widened. "What are you doing here?" Stella glanced at Marin's nametag.

"I work here. I'm the shift manager." Marin swallowed the knot in her throat. "What can I do for you?" She tensed to keep from shaking.

The man with Stella looked from Stella to Marin and back to Stella.

"Um, his steak is cold and rare in the center." Stella seemed unsure of herself for once.

Marin looked at the man and smiled. "I apologize, sir. I'll take care of that for you."

Stella avoided eye contact, and that was fine by Marin. Madison removed the man's plate and headed to the kitchen. Marin stood for another moment, then excused herself. As soon as she walked through the swinging doors, she headed straight to the office and shut the door.

Trembling, Marin shuffled through the order forms. Maybe Stella didn't get the voicemail. Of course, she got the voicemail. Stella chose not to return Marin's call, which was further evidence she hated Marin.

A soft knock sounded at the door, and Marin looked up. Madison poked her head in. "Who's that couple, if you don't mind me asking?"

"Stella. My aunt."

"Oh." Madison walked in, taking a seat across the desk from Marin. "Are you okay?"

"Yeah. Just a little surprised, that's all. I haven't seen her since Grandma's funeral."

"That was a while ago."

"Nine months."

"You haven't heard from her?"

"Not a peep."

"Your steak is up, Madison," another server said when he stepped in the doorway.

"Okay."

"I've got it," Marin said without thinking.

"Really?"

Marin second guessed herself. She mustered the fraction of strength she needed. "Yes."

"Alright. I'll make my rounds." Madison left the office.

"God, if you're there, give me strength." It was the first time Marin could remember talking to God. She needed all the strength she could get. God was the ultimate strength, according to Frida and Grandma Judith. Marin grabbed the plate with the man's steak and headed to the booth where he sat with her hateful aunt.

A strength Marin couldn't fathom possessing welled up inside. She smiled when she placed the plate in front of the man.

"Please let me know if this is acceptable," Marin asked.

The man cut into the steak and nodded. "Perfect."

Marin turned to Stella and said, "Did you get my voicemail from last May? I never heard from you, so maybe you didn't. By the way, what did you do with the rest of my things when you sold Grandma's house?"

The man made a noise and Marin glanced at him. The look he gave Stella told Marin he didn't know who she was. About that time, Marin noticed the large diamond solitaire ring on Stella's left ring finger. Stella was engaged to this man, and he had no idea what kind of person he was marrying. Did Stella tell him she had a sister named Gemma who died of a drug overdose and that she disowned Gemma's only child? Did he know Stella had kicked her own flesh and blood out of the only home she'd known for the past six years and left her to live on the streets of South Mississippi?

Marin turned to the man and offered her hand. "I'm Marin Martin, Stella's niece."

Stella coughed and took a sip of her drink.

"Chris." The man shook Marin's hand.

"Please excuse me, I need to take care of some managerial things in the back. It was nice to meet you, Chris." Marin tilted her head to Chris and looked at Stella. She still couldn't look Marin in the eye. "You can call or text about my belongings. I have the same cell number I've had for the past four years."

Stella lifted her chin but didn't look at Marin. As Marin walked away, she imagined the conversation Stella and Chris were about to have. Marin was sure her ears would burn for the rest of the night.

On the drive home, Marin replayed the interaction with Stella. She realized she still possessed the strength she'd asked God to provide. Maybe He really was there. All she had to do was ask. A peace Marin had never known filled her heart.

Marin showered and climbed into bed. Before putting her phone on silent, she checked her social media and email one last time. Facebook and Instagram were boring as usual, and she signed into her email. Her throat tightened when she saw an email from Gage. He wasted no time. It took a good ten seconds for her to tap on the email. She held her breath as she read.

Hello Marin. Thank you so much for the scarf. You did an awesome job for a beginner. At least I think so. I will be able to get some good use out of it once I get back to Montana. I admit I looked for you on social media to put a face with the name.

The temperature in the room soared, and Marin pushed the covers off. She closed the email app without reading the rest of the email. Hitting the side button to turn off the screen, she placed the phone on her nightstand and stared at the ceiling. Under no circumstances would she become friends with Gage on social media. She had less than fifty friends as it was, and most of those were from work. And Joyce and Heather. Frida didn't have social media.

Marin rolled onto her side, then back. It was going to be a long night of second guessing her decision to learn to knit.

Chapter 21
Heather

Heather took a sip from the bottle of water provided by the mediator. Adam sat across the table from her. He was dressed in a pale pink, long-sleeved, button-down shirt and relaxed khaki slacks. He looked good and it made her ill. He flashed a smile when she met his gaze. Why was he smiling? They were getting ready to agree to the terms to end their twenty-year marriage. Fighting the urge to roll her eyes, she quickly looked away before she lost the battle.

The folder holding the list of terms she'd brought was on the table in front of her. As if Adam could see from across the wide conference table, each time she opened it to scan the list of requests, she quickly closed it. Glancing at the wall clock, she lowered her brows. The mediator was almost five minutes late.

An exasperated woman walked in and closed the door behind her. She sat at the head of the table and introduced herself as Teresa. She apologized for the delay, explaining the difficulty of the previous clients. Heather glanced at Adam. She hoped they were on the same page or as close to the same page as possible.

"You two have decided to use mediation to agree on the terms of your divorce." Teresa opened the folder in front of her and pulled out her copies of their separate lists of terms.

Both agreed.

"There are three minor children. As a reminder, in the state of Mississippi, for the purpose of child support, the age of adulthood is twenty-one."

Both nodded.

"Shelly Colleen Zimmerman, aged eighteen, Ethan Adam Zimmerman, aged sixteen, and Jacob Allen Zimmerman, aged five." Teresa looked at Heather and Adam above her glasses.

"Jake was a surprise." Heather let out an awkward laugh. Adam raised his brows and looked down at his list of terms. The silent little jabs he'd given her over the years still stung. She knew Adam loved Jake and couldn't imagine his life without him. It was his belief that Jake's existence was all Heather's doing that got to her, as if he had no part in it. Heather looked down at her list and rolled her eyes.

"Alright. Mr. Zimmerman, you've been the sole income earner for your entire marriage?"

"Yes. Heather was a stay-at-home mother. We decided together."

Thank you. It wouldn't have surprised Heather if Adam claimed she'd refused to work.

"Okay. I have your income statement. Your annual income is five seventy-five?"

Heather gulped.

"Yes, ma'am." Adam looked at Heather.

It was obvious Adam thought she had no right to know how much his raise was since he'd planned to leave her. Their earned income for the previous tax year was less than four-hundred thousand. That was one heck of a raise. Heat filled Heather's stomach and inched up to her throat.

They agreed on child support terms and, after a short back and forth, a settlement for Heather. Adam agreed to pay the mortgage and household expenses for up to three years to give Heather time to get on her feet financially. Three years felt like three months, and it terrified Heather.

Who would hire a woman in her late forties who hadn't worked in twenty years?

"Now for the grounds for divorce. Adam, you have irreconcilable differences, and Heather, you have infidelity."

"What?" Heather spat the word. She looked at Adam. "You've got to be kidding me."

"Heather..."

"No, Adam. You walk out on me and our kids and the next week I see you and your girlfriend at the grocery store?"

"Huh?" Adam wrinkled his brows.

"Yes, Adam. I saw you and Amber pull up at Kroger. Maybe it wasn't a week, but you left me for another woman. There are no irreconcilable differences. It's infidelity or we go to court."

Heather leaned back and crossed her arms over her heaving chest. Nausea filled her throat, and she took a few deep breaths.

Adam let out a long sigh.

"It's not like the divorce papers will be framed next to your MBA diploma on your wall at work, but it's quite obvious why we're getting a divorce." Heather exhaled hard and wiped her damp palms on her leggings.

"Fine." Adam scoffed.

They spent a few minutes signing papers, then left the conference room. Heather went straight to the bathroom, locked herself in a stall, and cried. A few minutes later, she refreshed her makeup and made her way to the elevator, where she found Adam waiting for the doors to open. Did he go to the bathroom and cry too? Not likely.

Adam didn't smile this time when he saw her. Touching up her makeup did nothing for her red eyes. The doors opened and they stepped inside—just the two of them.

"Heather—"

"Adam, don't. Please don't say anything. I need time to process my thoughts."

"Okay."

The ride from the third floor to the first went quickly. They walked out the front doors and went in opposite directions. Thank goodness Adam parked elsewhere. It would have been torture if they ended up walking to the same parking lot.

Heather drove home in silence. She couldn't risk a song triggering an emotional breakdown. The last thing she needed was to have an accident because tears blurred her vision. To help her decompress from the day's events, she went straight to the swing in the backyard. Setting the swing into motion, she let the tears freely flow as the swing's movement comforted her.

When Heather tried to imagine what life would look like, her mind kept going back to Adam. She never imagined her life without him. This was not what she signed up for. What was she going to do?

"There you are," Shelly's voice startled Heather. "I was worried. The garage door was up, and your purse was still in the SUV."

"I'm sorry, honey. I had to get my thoughts out." Heather glanced at her watch. She'd been on the swing at least an hour and a half.

"You mean swing out your thoughts?" Shelly laughed.

"Yeah." Heather stopped the swing so Shelly could join her.

"Ethan and I say you are swinging out your thoughts when we see you out here."

"Fitting." Heather laughed and slipped her arm around her daughter.

"How'd it go?"

"Oh, you know. As good as these things can go, I guess." Heather was careful not to berate Adam to Shelly. He was her father, and it wasn't fair to put her in the middle. "Dad's paying the mortgage and living expenses for three years, so I have three years to get it together and move on. I guess I'll look at finishing my degree. Maybe someone will hire a fifty-year-old woman who hasn't worked in two decades."

"Or start your own business. It's very easy to do. I can get you started on social media. It's the way to go."

"I'd need to lose at least fifty pounds before I show my face on social media."

"No, you don't. There are people of all shapes, sizes, ethnicities, ages, even socioeconomic status who are social media influencers. You and the girls can start a knitting channel on YouTube." Shelly grinned. "Or you, at least."

"Nah, I'm good."

"Just a suggestion. Do you still want a business degree? You aren't the same person you were twenty years ago."

"I don't know what I want, Shell." Heather set the swing in motion again. "I have some time to figure it out."

"You can do it, Mom. You are stronger than you think."

"You think so?" Shelly had said it to her before.

"I do." Shelly smiled and kissed Heather's cheek. "I'm going to go get ready for church."

"Church?"

"It's Wednesday. Trav is playing in the praise band tonight."

"Oh, yeah. Have fun, honey."

"Thanks. The invitation still stands."

"I'm still thinking about it." Heather hadn't been to church regularly since she was a teenager. Her dad's new wife was a Christian and he became one not long after they married. She and Michelle attended church during their visits with their dad. He eventually cleaned up his life. Several years later, he ended up developing cirrhosis and had said becoming a Christian didn't absolve him from the consequences of his past sin.

Michelle and her family still attended church. Periodically, over the years, Adam and Heather had taken the kids to church. Shelly and Ethan attended Vacation Bible School every summer when they were younger. Jake still attended. Heather believed in God but didn't feel church was necessary. Even more so now as a divorced woman. The last thing she wanted to be was the subject of gossip.

Heather went inside after Shelly left and walked from room to room, replaying the memories of the years since they'd bought the house. A change of scenery would be good. She couldn't get her own place at the moment, but it would be her goal to get out of the house as soon as she could. First, she should meet with a college advisor to see what it would take to get her degree and decide if she wanted to go that route.

Adam's moving boxes would be delivered in the next day or so. Not that he expected Heather to pack up his belongings, but she could at least pack his clothes to get them out of the master bedroom. Her bedroom. Most of his dress shirts and pants were already at his apartment, along with some casual outfits.

Heather walked into Adam's closet and found his heavy winter coat in the back corner. South Mississippi weather rarely got cold enough to wear a heavy coat. The last time she remembered him wearing it was on a ski trip to Denver years ago.

The urge to wear the coat overwhelmed Heather and she slipped it on, burying her face in the oversized collar. The faint scent of Adam's cologne brought tears to her eyes. Her legs gave way and she fell to the floor, weeping. Why was this happening? What had she done to cause Adam to fall out of love with her?

"Help me move on, God," she whispered between sobs.

Chapter 22

Frida

The doorbell rang, and Frida made her way to the living room. Maria smiled when Frida opened the door.

"*Tia*." Maria hugged Frida. "Something smells good."

"I just pulled a coffee cake out of the oven for this afternoon. You are more than welcome to join us sometime, Maria."

"I can't knit."

"Joyce doesn't knit. Sometimes she uses the loom, but mostly she waits on us." Frida laughed.

"No, *Tia*. It's your thing with your club. Thank you, though."

"Okay, *sobrina*. I have Oscar in his carrier. He'll hate that he's missing Marin. He loves that girl." Oscar let out a long mewl when Frida picked up his carrier. "Thank you for taking him to his appointment."

"Of course, *Tia*. I'll see you later tonight. Save me a piece of cake." Maria grinned and gave Frida a side hug on her way out the door.

It was going to be strange not having Oscar prancing around the living room as they worked. "Okay, honey."

Over the next hour, Frida tidied up the house and made a fresh pot of coffee. She filled an insulated carafe with boiling water for tea. In the living room, she sat in her chair and began praying for Heather and Marin. She included the women in her daily prayers, but she also prayed for them before their time together. Heather surprised her by texting a request for prayers the day before. Heather's mediation with Adam was a few days ago and Frida imagined it was difficult for her.

The doorbell sounded as soon as Frida ended her prayer, and she welcomed Joyce and Heather inside.

"Hello, doll. How are you today?"

"I'm great, Joyce. You?" Frida said.

"Wonderful." Joyce raised her brows at Frida.

Over the years, Frida learned to read Joyce's mood by her wardrobe. The more outlandish the better the mood. Joyce must be in a fabulous mood by her bright purple pants and white long-sleeve t-shirt with tiny multi-colored balls of yarn printed on the fabric.

"Love the shirt," Frida said when she closed the door behind the women.

"Thanks, love. I found it on sale."

"I love it. You'll have to give me the name of the store." Heather said.

"Sure thing, love." Joyce looked around the floor. "Where's Oscar?"

"Maria picked him up. He had an appointment today for his annual exam and I didn't want to reschedule. She took him for me."

"Aw, I'll miss the little ball of fluff." Joyce headed to the kitchen to pour the coffee.

A soft knock sounded at the door, and Frida welcomed Marin. She explained Oscar's absence and noted a slight look of disappointment on Marin's face. Frida also noticed Marin looked off. She'd pull her aside to check on her at the end of their time together. Marin barely sat down when Joyce lit in.

"Did you email the young man?"

Frida noticed Marin tense. She had a suspicion Gage was what had Marin off.

"Yes, and he emailed me back." Marin's response sparked a barrage of commentary from Joyce and Heather. Neither could believe that Marin didn't read all of Gage's email. "It kind of freaked me out. I don't want any kind of relationship."

"It's not like he proposed," Joyce said and laughed. "Well, maybe he did in the part of the email you didn't read." Joyce looked in Frida's direction and grinned. Frida lowered her brows at her friend, and Joyce grimaced. Zipping an invisible zipper across her lips, Joyce tossed the key over her shoulder.

"I'm sorry," Heather said and patted Marin's leg. "We didn't mean anything by it."

"I know." Marin gave Heather a brief smile.

"No, doll. I'm sorry as well."

"It's okay." Marin shrugged.

A quietness settled over the room as the women began their projects. A few minutes later, Heather updated the group on the divorce.

"Another thirty days and I'll be a single woman again. It's strange. I'm almost fifty."

"Heather, Frida and I can give you tips on navigating life as an older single woman," Joyce said. "You are a good bit younger than I was when my husband passed. Frida, on the other hand, has dealt with singlehood as a woman most of her adult life."

Heather looked at Frida and nodded.

"We're similar, but different. I didn't have children to care for. Not only are you dealing with your own emotions regarding the divorce, so are your children. And little Jake must be confused," Frida said.

"Yeah, he's been asking questions. He doesn't realize it's permanent. Shelly said he asked her when Adam was moving back home."

"Maybe look into family counseling. And for yourself as well," Joyce said.

"Yeah, I think I will."

As their time together wound down, both Heather and Marin finished another pair of socks. Marin followed Frida into the kitchen with her and Heather's cups and stopped Frida before she could head back to the living room.

"Will you read his email to me? You know a little more about my history. I want to know what he says, but I feel I need a buffer."

"Of course I will, honey. Let's get Heather and Joyce off, then we'll sit down."

"Okay." Marin smiled. They saw Heather and Joyce off and settled on the couch. Marin brought up her email and gasped. "He sent another email. It looks like it wasn't long after the first one."

"Alright. I'll start with the first one."

"Okay."

"Do you want me to read it out loud or to myself first?"

"Yourself first."

"Okay." Frida began reading with the first email.

Hello Marin. Thank you so much for the scarf. You did an awesome job for a beginner. At least I think so. I will be able to get some good use out of it once I get back to Montana. I looked for you on social media to put a face with the name. I didn't find you, though. I was hoping we could connect so I can learn more about you. I hope all is well with you.

It was presumptuous of Gage to want to get to know Marin. As far as he knew, she could be ninety, with forty-five great-grandchildren. Frida opened the new email and raised her brows.

Hello again. I'm so sorry for trying to look you up. I promise I am not a weirdo. I honestly just wanted to put a face with your name. God bless.

"Hmm."

"What?" Marin leaned over to see the phone's screen.

Frida read both emails to Marin and handed the phone back to her. She watched Marin's demeanor change. Frida didn't know why, but she had a feeling Gage was a good person. They knew nothing about him. He could be an eighteen-year-old kid away from home for the first time. He looked somewhat young in his picture. Maybe he wasn't good at expressing himself.

"Should I email him back?"

"It's up to you, honey."

"He ended with 'God bless.'"

"That's not necessarily a good sign these days, unfortunately," Frida said.

"True."

"You can always pray about it." Frida raised her brows when Marin looked at her.

"Yes, I can." With that, Marin talked about seeing her aunt at work and how she'd prayed for strength before confronting her.

Frida's heart swelled. She'd been open with her faith during her time with Heather and Marin. She prayed a seed had been planted in both their hearts. Frida vowed she'd do what she could to cultivate those seeds.

Chapter 23

Marin

Marin opened the Facebook app on her phone and stared at her profile picture and name. She'd done a good job at remaining anonymous. Marin wasn't a popular name on Facebook. It helped that her last name wasn't on the card Frida included in the package to Iraq. Had the Socks for Troops coordinator at the base passed around the card? Posted it on some bulletin board for the troops to see?

Oscar's piercing yellow eyes stared back at Marin from her profile picture. His face took up the entire image. A pang of grief filled her heart when she whispered her profile name. "Gemma Martin." As far as Marin knew, her parents never married. Using her mom's first name and her dad's last name—her last name—was two-fold. Marin kept her anonymity while honoring her parents.

Sighing, Marin clicked on Madison's profile picture on her friends list. She focused on Madison's brown eyes. The color was not the typical dark brown, but a reddish brown. The color of sun-brewed iced tea was how Madison's mother described her daughter's eyes one time and it had stuck in Marin's mind.

Marin closed the app and opened the camera on her phone and switched to the front-facing camera. She took at least a dozen selfies and decided all were ugly and deleted them. She held up the phone again and posed. Frowning, she put down the phone and removed her brow, nostril, and septum rings. Posing again, now all she saw were the holes she'd put in her face, not to mention her ears. Gage didn't want to put a face to her name. She corrected herself. He didn't want *her* face.

Tossing the phone on the bed next to her, she closed her eyes. A thought came to mind, and she pushed it away. It came right back, taunting her.

No, Marin.

The more she pushed the thought away, the stronger it became. Picking up her phone, she opened the Facebook app, went to Madison's profile, and screenshot her profile picture.

Don't do it.

In the email app, Marin opened Gage's last email and drafted a reply.

Hi Gage, I don't think you are a weirdo. I don't have social media. I guess that makes me the weirdo, huh? I've attached a photo. Now you have a face for the name. How long have you been in the Army? What is your job? Stay safe.

Marin tapped on the paperclip icon at the top of the email and the file folder popped up. She tapped on the photos folder and attached the screenshot of Madison. Hovering her finger over the send icon, Marin paused.

"Don't tap it."

She tapped the send icon and swallowed the knot that had been growing in her throat. She did it. She sent Gage Harris a photo of Madison. Why? Because Gage would never email her again if he knew what she looked like. Tears welled in Marin's eyes, and she quickly picked up the phone and looked in the outbox in her email to see if she could delete the email before it was sent. The outbox was empty. Tossing the phone on the bed, she headed out of her room.

In the bathroom, she studied herself in the mirror. The gauges in her ear lobes drew her attention first. They weren't as big as some people's. The damage they'd caused could be corrected, she guessed. Tears trailed down her cheeks, bringing her attention to the holes in her face. Would the holes close if she didn't put the jewelry back? Raking her fingers through her hair, the part in her hair separating the blue and pink sides was now at least an inch of brown roots. She'd thought about an all-over deep red, but it would cost a fortune at a salon. And home dye wouldn't cut it.

Marin's grandma had always referred to Marin's appearance as an artistic expression. It had been a way for her to express herself, but Marin realized it kept people at a distance. It was her shield, and she'd liked to keep it that way.

Sunrays slipped through the slats in the blinds, waking Marin. Glancing at her phone, she groaned. It was barely seven in the morning. Reaching for the other pillow, she covered her face and tried her best to fall back asleep. The lack of fresh air brought out another groan. She gave up and grabbed her phone again, checking the notifications. Her pulse raced when she saw an email from Gage. Holding her breath, she opened the email and began reading.

Hi Marin!

It's nice to finally "see you". I have never seen someone with the same color of eyes. How unique. Tell me something about yourself. I am the second oldest of four sons. I just turned twenty-six last month. I've been in the Army for eight years and I'm aiming for twenty years. Twelve more years to go. I am a helicopter mechanic. What do you do?

God Bless,

Gage

THE KNITTING CLUB

Marin stared at the words. She should put a stop to this before it went too far. Should she not write back or say goodbye? Sighing, she typed a response.

Hi Gage!

I will be twenty-one next month and I'm an only child. I am a shift manager at a steakhouse. It can be stressful, especially during our busy seasons like the holidays.

She read what she wrote. It looked so impersonal. "It should be impersonal, Marin." She scoffed and typed her name, then hit the send button.

Saturdays were spent cleaning and other household tasks. Inspired, she decided to clean out the cabinets as well. Madison worked Saturdays, so Marin had the place to herself. She connected her phone to the Bluetooth speaker in the living room. Pulling up her eighties playlist, Marin went to work.

An hour later, she took a break, relaxing on the couch. There were several food items that were still good, but she and Madison would not eat before they expired, and Marin planned to donate the items to the food pantry where Charley's Steakhouse donated their overstock. The music quieted for a second—a sign there was a notification on Marin's phone. Checking her phone, she saw another email from Gage.

Thought you'd like to see this.

The sender of the forwarded email was a chaplain, and there was a brief description and an image attached.

Soldiers modeling the hand-knitted socks they received from Socks for Troops...

Marin clicked on the attached image. Several soldiers pulled up their uniform pant legs to show the socks they'd received. Front and center of the group was Gage modeling his socks with the scarf Marin had knitted wrapped around his neck. A smile spread across her face as pride swelled in her heart. Marin typed a reply:

Thank you for sending this. I'm sharing it with Frida and Heather.

Less than a minute later, Gage replied.

Of course! Have a blessed Saturday.

Marin hit the button to reply, but stopped. There was no need to reply. Putting down the phone, she went back to the kitchen. A few minutes later, she had her phone in her hand.

You, too. But I guess it's Sunday there now. Or almost, anyway.

He replied a few moments later.

It's ten thirty Saturday night in Baghdad, Iraq. What time is it where you are?

Biting her bottom lip, she paused.

It's two thirty in the afternoon in south Mississippi. We are in central time zone.

She tapped the send button and waited. Five minutes passed with no reply. Maybe he went to bed since it was late in his time zone. A hint of disappointment filled her chest as the minutes ticked by with no reply. What was she doing to herself? It was best he didn't reply. She put the phone down and went back to the kitchen to find something to cook for supper.

The front door opened and Madison walked in. Her face brightened. "What's that smell?"

"I thought I'd make meatloaf."

"Oh, my gosh. It smells heavenly." Madison went to her room and changed. Back in the kitchen a few minutes later, she asked, "Have you heard from your guy?"

Marin's heart sank. She'd never considered Madison when she sent her picture to Gage.

"Are you okay? You're flushed like you have a fever." Madison touched Marin's forehead when she walked up to her.

Marin took a step back and cleared her throat. "Oh, yeah. Probably standing over these boiling potatoes. Less than ten minutes and it'll be ready."

"Great. I'm starved." Madison went into the living room.

Trembling took over Marin's body as she watched her friend walk away. What had she done?

Marin found it hard to maintain eye-contact with Madison during supper. She was half waiting for Madison to ask about the phrase "I'm a liar" stamped across Marin's forehead. Marin's food went down wrong, and she coughed. Grabbing her glass of sweet tea, she chugged it until the food cleared.

"Are you okay?"

Eyes-watering, Marin nodded. Wiping her eyes, she said, "Yeah, just went down the wrong pipe, as my grandma would say."

"No. You've been quiet. Is everything okay?"

Marin gulped. "Yeah, just a lot on my mind. Gage has been emailing."

A sly smile spread across Madison's face. "Really? Have you sent him your photo yet?" Madison raised her brows and grinned.

Oh, no.

"Not yet."

"What are you waiting for?"

Marin shrugged.

"You're pretty, Marin."

Marin rolled her eyes.

"You are. I can help you do your roots."

Marin looked at Madison and noticed her focusing on Marin's brown roots. "I'm thinking about a change."

"Going natural?"

"Dark red. But I need to save the money. I'll have to have color correction, and that's expensive."

Madison nodded.

"You've been blessed with beautiful natural hair," Marin said, looking at Madison's long, blond locks.

"I guess. Sometimes I think it's too plain," Madison said and twisted a section of hair around her finger.

"No, it's pretty."

"Well, thank you. Finished?" Madison looked at Marin's mostly empty plate.

Marin nodded and Madison gathered their plates while Marin grabbed their empty glasses.

In her room, Marin got ready for bed and checked her phone one last time before putting it on silent. There was an email notification from Gage. Butterflies awakened in her stomach as she read his words.

I'm getting ready for church. I'm attending the traditional service today. I like to alternate between the traditional and contemporary services, but I mostly attend the traditional service as I'm more of a traditional guy. :)

Marin's shoulders sagged. He most definitely wouldn't like someone like her. Madison was more his type. Maybe she should introduce them. She would if it wasn't for Madison's boyfriend. Marin placed her phone on the nightstand and closed her eyes. She was better off alone.

Chapter 24

Heather

Heather ended the call and fought the urge to swear. Not that she used swear words often to begin with, but since going to church with Shelly and joining the women's group, she'd become more aware of her words. She pulled up her contacts and tapped on Dana's name. Dana was a fellow divorcée in the women's group and had become someone Heather leaned on since Dana went through a divorce two years prior.

Heather: Adam wants to talk. Should I? I mean, what could he possibly want to say to me?

Heather exhaled hard as she watched the bubbles bounce on the screen, showing Dana was typing.

Dana: Maybe he wants to apologize.

"Pfff." Heather rolled her eyes and tossed her phone on the couch next to her. She'd never forgive Adam for what he'd done to her. Heather thought about her mother. Mom said she'd forgiven Dad years ago for his alcoholism that had torn their family apart. The therapist she'd seen told Heather that forgiveness was for her benefit more than Adam's benefit.

Forgiveness was the same as saying it was okay, right? Adam's affair was not okay. Sighing, Heather picked up a devotional for divorced women Dana had given her. It was a club Heather would rather not be a part of. She didn't like to be labeled as a divorced woman. Laying the book aside, she checked the time on her phone. A half-hour until she needed to leave for Frida's. Maybe she could help Frida with something before their knitting session. Heather grabbed her knitting and headed for the garage. She needed her girls.

"What'd that sock do to you, Heather?" Joyce asked.

Heather realized she'd been manhandling the sock she was knitting. She grimaced. "I guess I'm knitting out my frustrations. Shelly and Ethan say I swing out my thoughts when I'm on the swing. I guess I'm—"

"Knitting out your frustrations. Clever," Joyce said.

"Adam wants to talk."

"Oh?" Frida said.

On the drive to Frida's house, Heather decided to keep her thoughts to herself. She knew she talked a lot during their time together, and it would be tenfold today with her receiving Adam's text earlier. So much for that.

"My friend says he might want to apologize. If that's the case, I don't know if I can accept his apology. What he did was unacceptable."

"Of course, it was, love. If he was unhappy, he should have asked for a divorce *before* finding someone new," Joyce said.

Frida looked in Joyce's direction and lowered her brows. Joyce was oblivious to the daggers Frida was shooting at her. Heather learned over the past year that Joyce had no filter. Joyce was right, though. But that was not what Adam did. It was not what most unhappy spouses did. The replacement was found first.

"Forgiveness is for you," Frida said.

"That's what my therapist said."

"Good therapist," Joyce added.

Marin was unusually quiet. She mostly kept to herself, but over their time together, she had come out of her shell. Today, however, she seemed like the old Marin.

"You're quiet," Heather said to Marin.

"Oh, just concentrating." She held up the sock attached to four knitting needles.

"Looks like you're getting the hang of it," Heather said.

"Yeah. Slowly but surely."

The room fell quiet as the women worked. Heather's mind wandered to Adam, and that was unacceptable. "Oh, I talked to a college advisor."

"Good for you, toots," Joyce said. Heather watched Joyce wind yarn around the loom on her lap.

"Well, I don't know. I have at least a year and a half ahead of me if I go year around. I have to finish my bachelor's and then there's two years of grad school."

"You can do it," Frida said.

"I don't know. I'll be over fifty when I finish." Heather glanced around the room. As retired teachers, she knew Frida and Joyce had college degrees. She looked at Marin. "Do you have any college?"

Marin looked over at her. "Me?"

Heather nodded.

"As a matter of fact, I do. I lack one class in order to graduate with my associates in art."

"What are you waiting for?" Heather said.

"College algebra terrifies me." Marin arched her brows. "I took it, but made a D, which doesn't count toward graduation."

"Girl, you need to finish. You don't want to be like me—almost fifty with no degree."

"Oh, I don't know. I guess I could take that test that gives you college credit. I can't remember the name."

"CLEP," Frida said. "I think that's a wonderful idea."

"You want to consider taking an actual class since you didn't do well," Joyce said.

"Oh, you're probably right," Marin replied.

"Then you can walk." Heather beamed.

Marin's brows came together.

"Graduate. Walk the stage in your cap and gown."

"I don't care about that."

"You might one day. Look at me." Heather tilted her head. "You never know what you'll regret until you regret it." She laughed. "Oh, how are things going with Gage?"

"We've emailed a few times."

"Ah," Heather said and watched pink fill Marin's cheeks. She couldn't remember seeing Marin blush in the past.

"Nothing serious though."

"Yet," Joyce said and wiggled her brows at Marin. Marin smiled and shook her head, returning her attention to the sock.

The rest of their time together was spent talking about college and the throw blanket Joyce was knitting on the loom. Oscar brought attention to himself a time or two. By the time Heather left, she'd forgotten about Adam. But all the dread came back when she saw a new text notification from him pop up on the screen in her car.

Pressing the voice command button on the steering wheel, she said, "Read new text message from Adam."

"Okay," the infotainment voice responded, and began reading Adam's text. "Shelly and Ethan are taking Jake to see a movie. Shelly said you are on your way home."

Heather gritted her teeth. What on earth did he want to talk to her about that required the kids not to be around? Did Amber leave him now that he was single and was he going to beg to come back? Not if he was the last man on earth.

THE KNITTING CLUB

Heather pushed the voice command button again and said, "Text Adam."

"Okay, what do you want to say?" the voice responded.

"Ten minutes out."

"Message sent."

Adam's BMW was parked in the driveway when Heather arrived home. She thought he'd traded it in for the new SUV. He got out of the car when he saw her and flashed a smile as she passed by on the way into the garage. What did he have to smile about? She hadn't been in the same space as him since mediation. Bees came to life in her stomach, stinging her multiple times. She winced.

"Are you okay?" Adam asked when he walked up to her.

"Yes," Heather said and unlocked the house door.

Adam stood in the mudroom as if he was waiting for permission to enter the main part of the house. Heather shook her head and hung her keys on the keyring by the door. The urge to be hospitable came over her. It was the weirdest thing. Adam knew where everything was. Maybe she should change things around. It was her house now. At least for the next three years.

"Can I get you something to drink?" Heather finally asked.

"No, I'm fine. Thank you, though."

Heather nodded.

"Can we sit down?" Adam's smile was back. Heather figured it was anxiety.

"Lead the way," she said.

Adam walked ahead of Heather into the living room. She should have picked up Jake's toys before she left for the knitting club. A few of her knitting projects were piled on the end of the couch. Her first thought was to apologize for her untidiness, but she stopped herself. She could be untidy all she liked now.

Heather sat on the other end of the couch, and Adam sat in his old recliner. He leaned forward, resting his elbows on his knees, and clasped his hands together.

"I want to apologize to you, Heather."

I knew it. Heather rolled her eyes.

"I never meant to hurt you."

"How cliché of you." The words came out on their own, impressing Heather.

Adam sighed. "I know you're still angry."

"Still angry? Are you kidding me? You destroyed our family, Adam. You better believe I'm angry and will be for a long time." Heather scoffed and shifted in her seat. The first thing that came to mind was to bolt up the stairs and lock herself in her bedroom. A strength she didn't know she possessed welled up inside. "You made a mockery of our wedding vows. You promised me in front of our family and friends and, most importantly, God, to be faithful. What happened? Did you wake up one day and decide you weren't happy?"

"No. I..."

"And don't you dare say it's because of Jake."

Adam sat up straight and opened his mouth to say something but stopped when Heather spoke.

"I didn't get pregnant by myself. You obviously passed high school biology." Heather realized she was trembling.

"Heather." Adam sighed. "I love our children, and Jake is my special little guy."

Adam's love for Jake had been clear since the day he was born. If Jake wasn't the reason, was it Heather's weight gain? Amber wasn't much smaller than Heather. Or did Adam tire of Heather as a person? Tears stung her eyes.

"I told myself that I wanted to be totally honest with you. If you want me to, that is. I know you might not want to know—"

"How long have you been having an affair with Amber?"

"I met Amber six years ago when she started at the company. She works in IT."

That explained it. Amber worked behind the scenes. Most office functions Heather went to were for executives.

"It went from an acquaintance to a friendship after her husband died. Do you remember when the group of employees were in the car accident at lunch?"

The accident happened when Adam was on his two-week paternity leave after Jake was born. Heather's mother came down to stay with the kids so they could attend the funeral of who she now knew was Amber's husband.

"I remember." A hint of compassion for Amber seeped into Heather's heart. She still considered Amber a home wrecker. "When did you start sleeping with her?"

"You probably won't believe me, but that didn't start until the month before I left."

Heather raised her brows. Did she believe him? He'd been lying about working the weekends for months before he left. There was no way they spent all that time alone without sleeping together.

"When did you fall out of love with me?" Tears trailed down Heather's cheeks.

"Heather, I love you."

Heather closed her eyes, pushing more tears down her cheeks.

"I love you because you are the mother of my children."

"You know what I mean." Heather's eyes were still closed when she made the statement. The couch cushion next to her sagged, and she felt the warmth of Adam's presence. Her eyes opened and she glanced at him.

"I realized I loved her around four months before I left. I was so torn. Like you said, I'd made a commitment to you. But I knew my feelings had changed for—"

"How can you be with someone that is okay with being with a married man?" Heather locked her gaze on Adam sitting next to her. He hung his head. She noticed red splotches forming on his neck. It was something that happened when his emotions got the best of him.

He looked at her and wiped the tears from his cheeks. "It kills me that I hurt you."

Heather stood and walked over to the windows, looking out over the backyard. The swing's movement in the breeze caught her attention.

"God says I am to forgive you."

Heather crossed her arms over her chest and rubbed her upper arms. "It's for my own peace, I'm told." She turned to face Adam. He was now standing in front of the couch, watching her. "I'm sure I will forgive you one day, Adam, but I will never forget the unnecessary pain you have caused me."

"I know," he said, his tone low.

"There's no 'should have' in life. But I wish you would have told me how you felt. You killed a part of me when you defiled our marriage. I honestly don't know how I can forgive you for that." She turned back to face the windows and wiped her cheeks. "I think it's time for you to leave."

"All right," Adam said.

She glanced over her shoulder at him. It appeared as if he considered coming to her but changed his mind and left through the kitchen. A moment later, the engine of his car revved and the sound faded as he drove away. Heather dropped to the floor and sobbed until her body convulsed. A few minutes later, she picked herself up and went to the kitchen to splash water on her face before making her way out back to the swing.

With all the thoughts going through her mind, Heather was sure to be on the swing until the wee hours of the morning.

Chapter 25

Frida

The azaleas were thriving in Frida's backyard. If the late June evenings weren't too warm, she liked to sit under the gazebo and listen to the birds as she drank tea. Sniffing turned Frida's head and she saw Maria walking from around the side of the house. Frida placed her cup on the side table and met Maria.

"Maria, honey, what on earth is the matter?" For a moment, Frida's pulse raced. She'd had more than her share of bad news over the years. The sparkling diamond on Maria's left hand caught her attention, and she knew what brought tears to her niece's eyes.

"Phillip proposed," Maria said and held out her hand.

"I see that. But why are you crying?" Frida led Maria under the gazebo, and they sat on the small wicker sofa.

"Why do I feel like I'd betray Mateo if I married Phillip?"

"Oh, honey." Frida slipped her arm around Maria's shoulder and pulled her close. Maria obviously accepted Phillip's proposal. Did she feel pressured at the time?

"I love him. But I keep thinking I should be sitting on the front porch swing with Mateo, not planning a wedding with another man."

"Life doesn't always go the way we think."

Maria sat up and touched Frida's hand. "You would know, *Tia*."

"God has a plan in everything."

"You feel that way about *Tio* Max?"

"I do." Frida picked up the cup of tea and took a sip. "It took years for me to feel this way. If your *tio* hadn't died, would I still be here? In this house?" Frida looked around the backyard and at the back of the house. If not, would she have met the hundreds of children she'd taught Spanish to over the years? And what about Marin and Heather? Would she have met them in the yarn aisle at Cathy's Craft Haven?

"We don't know why people are in our lives. Even those we fall in love with." Frida pointed toward Heaven. "We will know when we join Him." She smiled at Maria.

"Yes." Maria leaned her head on Frida's shoulder. "Will you help us plan the wedding?"

"Of course."

Heather crossed Frida's mind. She'd recently lost her husband. It wasn't a death like Frida, Maria, and Joyce had experienced, but it was still a loss. She imagined it was, in some ways, harder. The person who pledged their love was somewhere else in the world, living life without you. Frida's heart went out to Heather.

"When did Phillip propose? Not an hour ago, I hope."

Maria laughed. "It was last night. I guess it seemed I said yes and came straight here without Phillip. I'm sorry about that. I told Mama. I'm surprised she didn't tell you. But I'm glad she respected my wishes for me to be the one to tell you."

"Yes, your mother is good like that." Frida patted Maria's leg.

"When's the next knitting club get together? Are you still making the socks?"

"Tomorrow afternoon. We filled our quota a while back. Now we are knitting things for the homeless shelters."

"Oh."

Frida raised a brow at the smile on Maria's face.

"I saw a woman's wedding decor on social media. She had the prettiest knitted ring pillow. Phillip and I haven't talked about the type of wedding, but if we have a ring bearer, I'd like a knitted pillow like the one I saw." Maria looked at Frida. "I know you can knit things like socks, sweaters, and scarves, but would you be able to knit a ring pillow?"

"I'm sure I could come up with something. Depending on the date you choose, maybe you can knit your own pillow."

"Maybe," Maria said. Mateo's death had broken Maria. Her reaction reminded Frida of her own reaction to Max's death. Something had come to life in Maria when she met Phillip—love and hope for the future.

"How exciting." Joyce said when she welcomed Maria to their knitting session. "What do you know about knitting, love?"

"Absolutely nothing." Maria laughed. "Aunt Frida is the knitter of the family." Maria greeted Heather and Marin and took a seat on the folding chair Frida placed in the living room to accommodate her.

"I hear congratulations are in order," Heather said.

Frida sensed a bit of sadness from Heather. She imagined engagement announcements on the heels of her divorce could be hard. For Heather's sake, Frida hoped Adam didn't make his own announcement soon. Years ago, a young teacher divorced her husband because of an affair. The ink was barely dry on the divorce papers when he married the woman that he'd had the affair with. The poor teacher had to take a leave of absence. She was so devastated.

Maria recounted Phillip's proposal and talk turned to wedding planning. To Frida's surprise, Heather brought up her own wedding planning. Marin concentrated on the lap blanket she was close to finishing using the knitting loom. She planned to donate it to one of the nursing homes in the area. An idea came to Frida, and she went to Marin.

"Maria wants to make a ring pillow for her wedding. When you are finished, do you think you can teach her to use the loom?"

"The pillow might be lopsided," Marin laughed, "but I'd be happy to."

"It will be perfect." Frida patted Marin's leg.

"How are you, my dear?" Frida asked Heather.

"Adam apologized, but..." Heather cleared her throat. "I'm trying to forgive him."

"It's a process," Joyce said.

"Yes, it is," Heather said. "A long, drawn-out process."

"It's still too raw." Maria offered a smile when Heather looked her way.

Frida had talked some about Heather and Marin to Maria. Heather's divorce was no secret, and Frida didn't believe she'd shared something she shouldn't have.

"Yeah." Heather held up the cowl she'd just finished. They'd decided at their last meeting to get a booth at a local holiday craft fair and donate the proceeds of their knitting to the women's shelter. Heather knitted at least a dozen cowls.

"You look marvelous, Heather," Joyce said when Heather slipped the cowl over her head.

"Why, thank you Joyce. Maybe I'll keep this one for myself. I like the colors."

Frida heard Marin call Maria over and listened as Marin explained how to use the loom. A year ago, Frida couldn't have imagined this day. Marin still had a wall, but Frida found the one loose brick and had been working her way into Marin's heart.

"Is Gage still emailing you?" Heather's question broke through the quiet that had fallen over the room as the knitters concentrated on their work.

"Two more emails since our last meeting," Marin answered.

"Mmm," Joyce's eyes brightened, bringing pink to Marin's cheeks.

"He's a nice guy. At least it seems that way through his emails."

"That's good, honey. Nothing wrong with having a pen pal. I remember having one as a teen. Of course, we wrote letters in the olden days." Frida laughed. "It's all electronic now."

"What all do you know about him?" Heather asked.

Marin shared what she'd learned about Gage. From what Marin said, he seemed like a nice young man. Frida noticed Marin's demeanor perked up anytime Gage became the topic of conversation. Although Gage seemed harmless, it was still wise to be cautious. One could miss something not seeing a person in the flesh. You couldn't see inflection in words on a screen, not to mention the lack of body language. She needed to talk with Marin. The young lady had street smarts, but sometimes that wasn't enough. Frida would never forgive herself if Marin was taken advantage of.

Chapter 26
Marin

For two weeks, Marin and Gage had been emailing at least once a day. Today, he wanted to call. Marin looked at the time on her phone and swallowed the knot in her throat. Four minutes until their scheduled call time. She went to the oscillating fan on her dresser and made two slow turns in front of it, trying to cool off before she passed out.

Stepping into the hall, she turned down the thermostat so the air conditioning would come on again. She'd have to remember to turn it back up to the standard seventy-three degrees. Sixty-eight degrees would shoot their electric bill through the roof. Making herself comfortable on her bed, she counted down the time on her phone until she saw *number unavailable* on the screen a second before the ring tone sounded. This was it. Struggling to catch her breath, she answered.

"Hello?"

Silence was all she heard. About to take another deep breath and repeat her words, she stopped when she heard his voice.

"Marin? It's Gage."

Marin's stomach flipped as if she were on a rollercoaster at the sound of his voice.

"Yes." She glanced up and grimaced at her reflection in the dresser mirror.

"You don't sound southern." He laughed.

"Well, you don't sound like a Yankee." She giggled. "Maybe we have misconceptions."

"Maybe so. But you said you've lived in the south since you were fourteen. Maybe you haven't assimilated yet." He chuckled. "I'm picking with you."

"I know." Marin grinned. "The connection seems good."

"Yeah, it's hit or miss. My mom says sometimes there's an echo. So, what have you been up to?"

"Nothing much. I'll probably work on the drawing of Madison's mom's dog, Bandit."

"That's great."

They were quiet for a few moments. Initially, Gage had wanted to video chat. The suggestion made Marin physically ill. She'd made a list of lies to tell him why she couldn't, but thankfully, neither of their schedules worked.

"I was wondering."

"Yes?"

"Do you have contact with anyone from your dad's family?"

That was out of left field.

"No. My grandma said he had been disowned and was living on his own when my mom met him."

"Oh. That's sad."

"Yeah."

More silence.

"So, Marin Martin, where do you see yourself in ten years?" Gage laughed.

"Am I in a job interview?" Marin laughed along with Gage. "Honestly? I don't know. My life certainly isn't how I'd imagined it would be.

With Grandma Judith dying unexpectedly and me finding myself on the streets—"

"On the streets?" Disbelief colored Gage's tone.

Marin gulped. What she'd shared with Gage up to this point had been basic. Her parents had died, and her grandmother had taken guardianship. She'd left out the part where her parents were drug addicts and their deaths from a drug overdose put her in foster care. Marin told him after Grandma Judith's death, she'd moved in with Madison when Stella kicked her out. She'd skipped the part where she'd lived in her car until Madison made her move in with her.

The box full of her past was now wide open.

Though she was reluctant to be vulnerable, an unfamiliar peace came over her and she began telling Gage her story. He was quiet and after a moment or two, she wondered if the call disconnected, but she realized he'd given her his full attention.

"Goodness, Marin. My heart breaks for you," Gage said after Marin finished.

"I've come a long way in the past year."

"Have you talked to Stella?"

"Not since the night at the restaurant." Did she want to talk to Stella? Marin was at a point where she was taking care of herself financially. One day she would have a place of her own, but for now, Marin was satisfied with being roommates with Madison and it appeared Madison felt the same. A tightness filled Marin's chest. That might change if Madison found out Marin sent Gage her photo.

"Well, all you can do is pray for her."

"Yeah." As if Stella deserved Marin's prayers. A heaviness fell over Marin. Everyone deserved prayer. Even Stella Scott.

"Marin?"

"Yes?"

"I really like you."

Marin's jaw hung open.

"I've never been in a serious relationship. I mean, I've dated a few times, but several years ago, I decided to never casually date again."

What exactly did that mean? Marin had never dated. She'd never even kissed anyone. Here was Gage telling her he liked her more than a friend, at least that was how she took it, and now he said he didn't casually date?

"Gage, I—" A relationship was the last thing Marin needed. She'd have to lower her walls even more than she just did with Gage. Besides, every time she crossed his mind, it was Madison's face he saw.

"It's okay, Marin. I shouldn't have said anything."

Now they both had regrets. Her for being someone she was not and him for revealing his heart too soon.

"No, it's...it's okay. Um, I should probably let you go. It's getting late there."

"Yeah, probably a good idea. I loved talking to you."

"I loved talking to you, too." Marin smiled as if Gage could see her.

They said their goodbyes and Marin laid back on her bed. What was she going to do? Feelings she'd never experienced were coming at her at once. If only she could talk to Madison.

Over the past few days, Gage had been pressing Marin to video chat. The first slew of her excuses included the time difference, her work schedule, and problems with the camera on her phone, which was a flat out lie. He'd asked if she could borrow Madison's laptop, but Marin made up something about the laptop being at Madison's parents' house. Marin had never lied so much in her life.

On their last call, Gage sounded frustrated and brought up buying her a new phone or a laptop. Her twenty-first birthday was next week, and he planned to send something special that he wanted to see her open. Horrified was the only word she could think of at the thought of video chatting. He'd never want to speak to her again if he knew the truth.

To add to her stress, Heather talked Marin into enrolling in college for the fall to finish her associate degree. It was a good stress, according to Heather. In one month, Marin would begin a college algebra class at the community college, and if all went well, she'd graduate in December with a degree in art. She'd thought her artistic abilities had died along with her grandmother, but drawing the picture of Oscar for Frida awakened her desire to create. She'd picked up some commission pieces through Frida. One being a pencil drawing of Christ for Frida's priest.

Marin pulled up the time clock on the office computer and clocked out. She'd gotten an email from Gage earlier and his frustration over her avoiding a video call was clear. Marin had to talk to someone and planned to stop by to visit Frida before heading home.

As usual, Marin was greeted by Oscar and Frida had a plate of fresh cookies and coffee ready for their talk. Marin took a seat on the couch and Oscar hopped up next to her. He purred as she stroked his back. A knot rose in her throat. She was about to admit to one heck of a lie to her dear friend.

"Are you okay, honey?" Frida asked when she handed the cup of coffee to Marin. "You're pale."

"No, not really. I've dug myself into a hole and I don't know how to get out."

"Okay. What's happened?" Frida eased down on her chair and placed her coffee cup on the side table, giving Marin her full attention.

"Um, well, it's about Gage."

Frida nodded but said nothing. Marin wanted the couch to open up and swallow her. "The short of it is Gage wanted me to send him a picture. I tried. I really did, but I..." she trailed off.

"Oh, honey." Frida joined Marin on the couch. It took a bit for Marin to realize her eyes were full of tears.

Wiping her cheeks, Marin drew in a sharp breath and admitted to what she'd done.

"Oh, my," Frida said.

Marin half expected Frida to spew anger, but then again, she was like Marin's grandmother and Grandma Judith would never have spewed anger at Marin. Stella, on the other hand, wouldn't have hesitated.

"And it breaks my heart that he trusted me. We've talked a lot about God and he's going to think I'm..." Marin's shoulders fell. "I don't know what he's going to think about me now. But I know I have to tell him the truth. I don't know how, though. Do I just go for it?"

Frida was quiet for a moment. "Pray about it. God will show you what to do. Why? If you don't mind me asking."

"Why did I send him Madison's photo?"

Frida nodded.

Tears pooled in Marin's eyes, and she pointed to herself. "Look at me."

"Honey," Frida took Marin's hands in hers. "I see a beautiful young woman with a pure heart." Frida caressed the side of Marin's face. "And I believe Gage sees your heart more than he sees what he believes is your appearance."

Marin broke down sobbing. Frida's arms wrapped around Marin's shoulders, pulling her close. Oscar crawled onto Marin's lap and pushed his head against her trembling chin. Frida held Marin until she quieted. Sitting up, Marin sighed.

"I need to tell Madison, don't I?"

"I think that's a good idea. I know you care for her a great deal."

"Like a sister."

Frida patted Marin's leg. "Pray. God will show you what to do."

"God probably hates me."

"No, Marin. He loves you so much and wants what's best for you."

Was God even real? It was a question Marin had wrestled with for years. Especially with her history and her grandmother's unexpected passing. Why would a loving God leave her alone? But then again, she now had Frida, Heather, and Joyce in her life. And look what Madison and her family had done for her.

"How do I know God is real?"

Frida eased back. Marin had just offended her.

"I mean, I know what the Bible says. But some say the Bible is written by man."

"Did your grandmother talk to you about God?"

"We went to church. And I was baptized." Marin told the story of a revival at her grandmother's church. The guest pastor walked out into the crowd and randomly asked people if they believed. Those who hesitated were dragged to the altar. At least, that was how it felt when Marin hesitated.

"Asking Christ into your heart is a personal decision and should never be forced. It's all about the heart. If a person is not ready, saying something like a sinner's prayer is just words. You have to mean it in your heart."

"I don't know if I meant it back then. I have loved talking with Gage—and you and Heather—about God. I feel something here a lot of times." Marin rested her hand on the middle of her chest.

"I believe that's the Holy Spirit." Frida smiled. "You are more than welcome to come to mass with me sometime if you'd like. I like the Catholic church as it is steeped in tradition. And in my culture, most Christians are Catholic. The most important thing is to believe that God sent his only son Jesus to die for our sins. He rose again on the third day and is sitting at the right hand of the Father. He will come again to take all those who believe to Heaven. Is that what you believe?"

Marin considered Frida's words. She'd struggled with what to believe over the years. Grandma Judith had never pressed. She told Marin after the incident of being taken to the altar that if it was not what she felt in her heart, not to go through with baptism, but Marin chose to anyway. Was it from pressure or because deep down, she truly accepted Jesus into her heart?

"Yes." Marin smiled. She hadn't been so sure over the years, but it was how she felt in her heart now.

"Heather has started going to church with Shelly. I believe she said it's a non-denominational church. I'm sure she'd love to have you join them."

"I'll think about it." Marin helped Frida clean up and headed home. She had to tell Gage what she'd done and to let him go. A relationship built on lies would go nowhere. She'd then confess to Madison and pray she'd forgive her. If not—which was Madison's right—Marin would have to look for a new place to live.

When Marin returned home from visiting Frida the previous night, she'd drafted an email to Gage. Instead of sending it then, she kept it in her drafts for the night and planned to reread it before sending it. She pulled up her email and opened the message from the draft folder. Running her fingers through her hair, Marin began reading the words she knew would hurt Gage.

Hi Gage,

I've prayed about how to start this email to you. There's no easy way to say this, but here goes. The photo I sent is not me. It's actually Madison. She has no idea, and it kills me that I've hurt two people I care about. I sent a picture of her because I did not want you to see who I really am. I figured if you saw the real me, you wouldn't want to be my friend (I have pink and blue hair, tattoos, and piercings.)

Marin's thoughts went to Madison. She hadn't cared what Marin looked like. Neither had Grandma Judith, or Frida, Heather, and Joyce, for that matter. Marin continued reading.

I have ruined our friendship, and for that I am very sorry. I wish you the best and you are in my prayers.

Marin

Marin read the words several times. Last night, she'd written at least twice the number of words, supposing her childhood had something to do with what she'd done, but it didn't matter. There was no excuse. She prayed Gage could forgive her and that he'd find someone worthy of his love. Marin drew in a deep breath and held it while she tapped the send button. Now she had to tell Madison.

Having worked until closing last night, Madison hadn't gotten up yet. Marin went to the kitchen to put on a pot of coffee and start building the courage to tell Madison. She begged God for the right words. Coffee in hand, she went to the balcony and settled on the chair. Closing her eyes, she opened her heart to the Father.

God, I'm so sorry. I've gotten myself into this mess. Please give me the right words to tell Madison and the strength to handle the fallout —

A noise inside startled Marin. "Amen," she said and stood on shaky legs. Sliding open the patio door, she stepped inside and smiled at Madison.

"Sorry about the noise." Madison said. "I accidentally knocked the bottle of creamer off the counter. Thank goodness I'd already closed it."

"Yeah," Marin said and laughed a little too hard.

Raising her brows, Madison sipped her coffee as she made her way to the couch. "Are you okay?" she said when she eased down. A yawn spread across her face and held her hand over her mouth.

"No, not really."

"Talk to me." Madison patted the couch cushion next to her. "Is it Gage?"

Marin swallowed hard. "Yeah." She lowered herself to the couch and turned towards Madison.

"I thought things were going well. What did he do?"

"Well, nothing."

Madison's brows came together as she sipped her coffee.

Marin's heart pounded in her ears, and the temperature in the room soared. She swallowed the knot in her throat and caught a cleansing breath.

Here goes.

"We've been emailing for a while."

"You're not video chatting yet?"

"No, I..." Marin focused on her clasped hands in her lap.

"Oh, Marin." Madison reached over and patted Marin's hands. "If he cares about you, he won't care about your quirkiness."

Quirkiness?

"Send him a picture to prepare him for a video call." Madison grinned.

Lord, please help me.

"I did." The words passed through Marin's lips without thinking. Her insides twisted.

After what seemed like a full minute, realization surfaced on Madison's face. Brows lowered over darkened eyes. "You sent him my picture, didn't you?"

All Marin could do was sit, frozen as if she were cast in stone.

"You did *not*."

"I-I was afraid of how he would react to seeing what I look like."

"If you are that ashamed of your looks, why do you insist on looking like a freak?" Red flooded Madison's face and she shot to her feet, glaring at Marin.

A freak?

If Madison thought Marin was a freak, why did she say she was her best friend and want her to live with her? It was all a lie. Madison pitied her.

Without another word, Madison went to her room and slammed the door behind her, rattling the wall. Tears gathered in Marin's eyes, blurring her vision. She went to her room and sat on her bed, imagining packing her belongings. A notification on her phone sounded. Gage replied to her email. Her next steps eluded her.

Chapter 27

Heather

Heather handed Marin a glass of lemonade and a newly opened box of tissues. Marin managed a smile as she accepted the items. Joining Marin on the swing, the two sat quietly, watching a bird flit in and out of the birdhouse.

"Is work going to be awkward?" Heather asked, still watching the bird.

"Madison goes with her family to Augusta every Fourth of July holiday. She left this morning not long after...after the confrontation."

"Did she say anything?"

"I was in my room. I heard the front door and peeked out. Her bedroom door was open, and she was gone."

"Honey, I'm so sorry."

Marin nodded and set the swing into motion. Heather wondered what pushed Marin to be deceitful to Gage and Madison. The Marin she knew wouldn't have done such a thing. But did she really know Marin? They'd been getting together regularly for well over a year. She thought she knew the Marin below surface level.

"Do you mind me asking why?"

Marin pointed to herself.

Heather figured it had to do with more than Marin's appearance. It was about letting someone in; being vulnerable. It took courage to be vulnerable. The first step in vulnerability—at least in Marin's case—was appearance. A good deal of people judged a person on their appearance. Unfortunately, Marin decided Gage was one of them.

"He wasn't pushing for a picture. I guess I kind of freaked out when he said he'd looked for me on social media. I was afraid he'd somehow find me and run in the opposite direction." Marin sighed.

Heather looked at Marin. Her side profile was perfect. The gauges in her ears weren't as big as some she'd seen, and the small hoop in her brow looked fashionable. What was Marin hiding below the surface? Marin turned and looked at Heather, wrinkling her brows.

"You're pretty, Marin. If you're happy with how you look, that's what matters." Heather watched tears pool in Marin's eyes.

"But I'm not happy." She dabbed her eyes with a fresh tissue and hung her head. "Frida knows some of this."

Marin began sharing about her childhood, bringing tears to Heather's eyes. How could a mother leave her child with strangers to party? Heather's thoughts went to her own children. She'd gladly give up her life for her children. Marin's parents gave up their lives, but for their own selfish desires.

"My first foster parents abused me." Tears rolled down Marin's cheeks, but she didn't move. Heather pulled a tissue from the box on the swing between them and wiped Marin's cheeks. "I didn't tell Frida that part."

"Oh, Marin."

"I was with them for six months. My teacher saw bruises and talked to the principal, who called the police." Marin wiped her eyes and told the rest of her story, ending with how her grandmother gained custody.

"It sounds like Grandma Judith loved you very much."

Marin smiled. "She did."

A loud car pulled into the neighborhood, drawing their attention for a moment.

"What am I going to do if Madison wants me to move out? Our lease is up in two weeks."

The bird squawked, and Heather looked toward the bird house. Her gaze fell to the pool house behind the pool. They rarely used it, with the pool being close to the house. She'd need to talk to the kids and Adam, but she didn't see them having a problem. Well, hopefully Adam wouldn't have a problem. Should she bring it up to Marin now or talk to the kids and Adam first?

"Well, if worse comes to worst, maybe you can stay in the pool house."

Marin looked at Heather, then at the pool house. Her brows knitted together.

"I'd need to talk to the kids and Adam. It's his house too. There's a full bathroom and a kitchenette. It's like a studio apartment. We'd need to clean it out. It's been used for storage for the past few years."

"Oh, I couldn't."

"Let me at least talk to Adam and the kids. It can be a fallback. At least for the next three years." Heather laughed. "That's how long Adam agreed to pay the mortgage in the divorce."

"Oh." Marin laughed. "I insist on paying rent. If it comes to that, that is."

"Of course."

A notification sounded on Marin's phone, and she grimaced when she checked it. "Gage has been emailing me. I can't bring myself to read his emails. Maybe I should block him."

"No, there will come a time you'll want to communicate with him if for no other reason than closure. Here," Heather held out her hand, "hand me your phone. I'll create a special folder for his emails. They'll go directly into the folder, so you don't have to see them in your inbox."

"Oh, okay."

Heather began her task, and said, "But I think you should see what he has to say. Goodness, there are half a dozen emails from him."

"I know." Marin sighed.

Heather handed the phone to Marin and stood. "Let's go see the pool house."

Heather lost her sense of security when Adam walked out. With the Lord's help, she planned to do everything in her power to make sure Marin always felt secure.

Ethan talked about the movie nonstop from the time they left the theater until Heather pulled into a parking space at Charley's Steakhouse. Shifting into park, she turned off the engine and smiled when Ethan realized they'd stopped.

"Oh, we're here." He chuckled.

"Yep."

They got out of the SUV and made their way to the entrance. The day before, Ethan brought up the two of them going to the movies since Jake would be with Adam and Shelly was at school. Heather was surprised since she usually wasn't his first choice when seeing one of the popular action-adventure movies. That honor fell to his close-knit group of friends, but she was touched he wanted her to go.

The petite hostess with shoulder length brown hair caught Ethan's eye as she walked them to a booth on the outer wall. It was something Heather struggled with. But her boy was on the cusp of becoming a man and at seventeen, it was normal for a girl to turn his head. They'd barely got settled when Marin stopped at their booth.

"Hello, you two. How was the movie?" Marin asked and looked at Ethan.

He became more animated than usual, and his hands moved about as he talked. Heather bit her bottom lip and wondered if Marin regretted her question right about now. A server stopped and got their drink orders. A full minute later, Marin left with an in-depth preview of the latest installment of *Mission Impossible*.

"So, do you think it will be good to have Marin as a neighbor?"

"Yeah, I think so. She's cool." Ethan eyed the hostess station at the front of the restaurant.

Heather's phone buzzed. A preview of Adam's text showed on the screen, and she swiped to open. It was a selfie of Adam and Jake, with no words. By the trace of chocolate on Jake's lips, she guessed they were at Dairy Queen. She turned her phone around and showed Ethan. He rolled his eyes and turned to smile at the hostess as she walked by.

"Ethan." Heather sighed.

"What?"

Was now a good time to start a deep conversation with Ethan? Anytime she tried to talk to him about Adam, Ethan shut her down. It was like he didn't want to give Adam any grace. Where Adam was concerned, Ethan's behavior reminded Heather of her mother. They both thought in black or white. Adam cheated. End of story. Maybe now wasn't a good time. Ethan seemed pre-occupied with the hostess.

The server walked up with their drinks, pulled out her order pad, and took their order. "Okay, blackened salmon with baked sweet potato and fresh green beans for you, and the T-bone well done with onion rings and fried Brussels sprouts for you," she said, looking at Ethan.

"Yes," both Ethan and Heather said at the same time.

"All right. I'll put this order in and bring a fresh plate of bread and honey butter." She smiled and headed to the kitchen.

"Mom, I—"

"I get it, Ethan."

"Get what?"

"You aren't only hurting for me; you are hurting for yourself."

He looked out the window and shook his head.

The server placed a plate of fresh bread at the table on her way to greet a couple who had been seated across from them. They looked young and a tad uncomfortable. It was probably their first date.

"People don't realize how much damage affairs do. There's the spouse and kids, but there's also extended family, friends, co-workers, church family... The list goes on," Heather said.

"It was a selfish decision. If he was that unhappy, why didn't he talk to you?" Ethan slathered honey butter on a slice of bread and took a bite.

"I can't argue with you there."

"I would never cheat on my wife," Ethan said after he swallowed his food.

"Honey." Heather sighed. "I can guarantee you, your father never in a million years thought he would cheat."

"Well, then, why did he?"

"I don't have an answer for that." Heather almost choked on the words. She wasn't about to tell Ethan she thought his little brother was a possibility. "Anyway, it's not about why. It's about forgiveness."

Ethan scoffed.

Heather saw Marin and a young woman each carrying a plate approach the table. Marin raised her brows when their eyes met. Ethan's reaction to the word *forgiveness* must have been louder than Heather thought.

"For you," Marin said as she placed the salmon in front of Heather. "How's that steak, Ethan?" she asked after the woman placed the plate in front of Ethan.

He cut into the center and nodded. "Perfect."

"Need anything else?"

Heather looked at Ethan, but he was busy pouring Charley's special steak sauce over the top of his T-Bone. "No, we're good." Marin nodded and walked away.

"I'll never forgive him for destroying our family," Ethan said and stuffed a piece of steak in his mouth.

Heather dug around in her potato, mixing the butter and brown sugar. She put the fork down, drew in a deep breath, and rested her hands on her lap. "Ethan, there may come a time in your life when you make a decision that hurts those closest to you."

He looked up and stopped chewing. "Do you forgive Dad?"

"I'm working on it. It may take me years to come to terms with what your father did. But know this. He would never purposefully hurt us."

Ethan looked at his plate and stabbed a Brussels sprout. Laying his fork down, he took a long drink of soda, then nodded at Heather. He heard her, but was he listening? How long would her son resent his father?

Did Heather want to say more? Like grief, forgiveness was a personal journey. It took some people longer than others. Ethan idolized Adam before the affair. How much of Ethan's anger was on Heather's behalf, and how much from his own broken heart?

Chapter 28

Marin

Marin glanced at the clock on the office wall. One hour until they could lock the doors and clean up. She was ready to go home as soon as she walked in the door for her eight-hour shift. It had been two days since the falling out with Madison and she hadn't slept well. An uncertain future tended to keep people up at night. Madison was due home the next day, which added to Marin's anxiety.

"Hey," a hushed voice came from the office door. Stephanie rolled her eyes. "A couple just came in. Sierra sat them in my area." Marin had told Stephanie she could leave early since she had plans with her boyfriend.

Marin sighed. "I've got it."

"Thanks." Stephanie headed to the time clock and signed out.

Marin made her way to the dining area, regretting her decision to let Stephanie sign out early. It had been a while since Marin performed wait staff duties. At least it was only an hour, and the kitchen closed in thirty minutes. She found the couple in Stephanie's section. The woman smiled when she stopped at their table.

"Hello, I'm Marin. Can I get you started with a drink?"

"We're just stopping in for coffee," the woman said.

"And maybe a slice of this Coca-Cola cake," the man added, pointing to the cake on the menu.

"Oh, sure. That cake is to die for. And I'll make sure we have a fresh pot of coffee for you. We rarely have coffee drinkers this late."

"Thank you," the woman said. "It's kind of a special thing." She reached into her purse on the seat next to her and pulled out a worn photo. Handing it to Marin, the woman pointed to the people in the photo. They were sitting in a restaurant booth, much like where the man and woman were currently sitting. A woman and a little girl sat on one side and a man and a little boy sat on the other side. All four wore wide grins.

Marin looked closer at the photo and noticed a menu on the table with *Charley's Steakhouse* printed across the top. She raised her brows.

"That's me and my family. Here. About thirty years ago. I was five in that picture. I'm so glad this place is still around."

"Charley's has been in business for forty-five years," Marin said.

"We drove in from Charleston, South Carolina, yesterday." The woman smiled.

"She's from south Mississippi originally," the man added.

"I'm doing something like a heritage tour. We went to the zoo earlier today. I've got a few things written down that my grandparents told me about or I found pictures of, like this restaurant."

"That's really neat." Marin looked at the woman.

"Oh, I'm Genny and this is my husband Paul," she said, gesturing to the man. "That photo was taken not long before my parents were killed by a drunk driver."

"Oh, my goodness. I'm so sorry."

"Thanks. We went to live with our grandparents in Tennessee and I haven't been back here since."

"Wow." Marin studied the people in the photo closer. The woman was beautiful with shoulder length, dark red hair, like Genny. The man had short brown hair and striking eyes, although she couldn't tell the color. They looked like a happy family.

"Unfortunately, my brother was killed in Iraq in twenty ten. He was my only family by that time. Our grandparents passed over the years. Both our parents were only children, so I have no close blood relatives, besides our oldest daughter, that is."

"I'm so sorry." Marin could relate to losing her parents and grandparents.

"I would have given anything to have aunts or uncles. Cousins growing up would have been nice."

Marin looked at the family picture one last time and handed it back to Genny. Marin had an aunt but might as well have no family at all. She didn't exist as far as Stella was concerned. "Let me go get that coffee started."

Climbing the stairs to the apartment after her shift, Marin unlocked the door. She pushed it closed behind her and leaned against it for a moment, taking in what was before her since she would move soon. Jingling keys and the doorknob turning against her back caused Marin to leap away from the door.

Madison walked in and paused when she saw Marin. The only light was from the lamp by the front door. Madison's tears were unmistakable. Her face twisted, and she blurted out, "I'm so sorry for calling you a freak. You are not a freak, Marin. I was so shocked about what you did, and it was the first thing that came to mind."

Marin gasped when Madison threw her arms around her and pulled her close. The turmoil Marin experienced the past few days melted and tears freely flowed down her cheeks.

"I thought you weren't coming home until tomorrow," Marin said when they separated and wiped her cheeks.

"I had to get back to apologize." Madison pulled Marin into a quick hug. "Let's get settled for the night. We need to talk."

"Okay." Marin's stomach clinched. Madison needed this talk. She deserved this talk. Marin went to take a quick shower and returned to the living room where Madison was waiting for her.

"Here." Madison patted the couch cushion next to her. "Sit."

Marin had a déjà vu moment of their last discussion on the couch. She sat cross-legged and grabbed the couch pillow, hugging it to her stomach. "I'm sorry, Madison."

"I know." Madison reached over and touched Marin's arm. "I've been doing some thinking over the past few days. Are you happy with your appearance?" Her gaze swept over Marin.

"No, I don't guess. Or I wouldn't have sent Gage your picture."

"Why don't you change things up, then?"

Marin shrugged. She noticed Madison looking at her ears. "I don't know what I can do about that." Marin slipped her pinky through the gauge in her right earlobe.

"I have to be honest with you. I was upset and talked to my parents."

Marin cringed inside.

"Dad wants to see you. He said he might can fix your ears if that is what you want."

The thought of being the topic of conversation at the Taylors' Fourth of July celebration turned Marin's stomach, but she knew Madison had been genuinely hurt and would at least talk to her mother about what Marin had done. Mr. Taylor was a well-known plastic surgeon in south Mississippi. Marin was skeptical about what he could do to fix the nickel sized holes in her earlobes.

"I can't afford that."

"He just wants to see you for an evaluation to see if he can fix it. Only if you want to, Marin. Please be the person you want to be. If you want gauges in your ears, then have gauges in your ears."

Who was the person she wanted to be? She'd been Marin the goth, or grunge, or whatever the latest term was for a person who wore dark clothes, had tattoos and piercings, and colorful hair for years now.

"Marin?"

Marin looked at Madison and mustered a smile.

"I love you regardless of how you look. I hope you know that. But if you'd risk our friendship because of your appearance?" Madison sighed. "How did you think this would end?"

"That's the problem. I didn't think."

"What did Gage say when you told him? You told him, didn't you?"

"I emailed him, and I don't know. He's responded, but I haven't read his emails. Heather set up a folder, so his emails go directly in that folder instead of my inbox."

"He hasn't called?"

"He has limited times to call. I expect he will, though."

"Are you going to talk to him?"

"I don't know."

The room fell quiet for a moment. "Okay, I'll call Dad. He can probably come over here. So, what about your hair?" Madison looked up at Marin's blue and pink hair separated by natural brown roots that were close to two inches long by now.

"Why are you doing this, Madison?"

"Because I see you as the sister I've always wanted. I want to help you be your best self. If that's getting your ears fixed and changing your hair, I'm going to do what I can to see it's done. If it's a root touch-up, I'll help you do that too." Madison smiled when Marin glanced at her.

Marin's gaze centered on the TV as if a captivating show played on the black screen and hugged the pillow tighter against her chest. The thought of putting down her shield terrified her. Keeping people at a distance protected her. From what? She didn't exactly know. She'd started coloring her hair in the home of the foster parents who were going to adopt her. It was the first decision she could make for herself. The piercings came along over the years after. The tattoos in the years since she'd turned eighteen.

She looked at Madison. "I'm kind of scared."

"I know. But you're not alone."

Marin smiled at her friend. For the first time since her grandmother died, Marin felt genuinely loved. She might not have family in the conventional sense, but with Madison and her family along with Frida, Joyce, Heather, and now Maria, Marin had a true family. People who loved and cared for her. Peace surrounded her.

Thank you, Lord, for my family.

Chapter 29

Frida

Frida eyed the "Happy Birthday" banner Phillip and MJ were holding above the entry into the kitchen. She figured it was the perfect spot. Marin would see it as soon as she walked through the front door.

"Perfect," she said. The two volunteer party decorators secured their respective ends of the banner and stepped away.

"Anything else, *Tia*?" MJ asked"

"No, that was all I needed you two for." Frida glanced around the living room, noting the stars dangling from the ceiling. Hopefully, they weren't too low. Joyce was the tallest of the guests. If anyone commented, it'd be Joyce. The two nodded and said their goodbyes.

Frida set up a card table in the living room and covered it with a birthday themed tablecloth. She made her way to the second bedroom to bring out the presents. One from her and a special one from Iraq via a U.S. Christian bookstore.

Placing the two gifts on the table, Frida rested a hand on top of each and prayed for Marin. She'd been through so much already. Marin had shared with Frida some of what happened with Madison. She thanked God for mending their friendship. Now she prayed for the relationship between Marin and Gage wherever it went. There had to be a resolution.

Frida picked up Gage's gift again. Though she didn't know what he sent, by the size, shape, and weight, and the type of store it came from, she had her suspicions. A knock sounded on the door. Frida glanced out the front windows and saw Joyce's car. She put the gift down and walked over to the front door.

"But it's not my birthday." Joyce laughed when Frida rolled her eyes. Joyce looked around at the decorations. "Good job. These shooting stars just clear the top of my head." Joyce walked under each dangling star. "It's Fourth of July-ish in here."

"Well, being a few days after the Fourth, I thought we'd be a little patriotic. Plus, it's her twenty-first birthday. She deserves shooting stars."

"That she does, love. That she does. How is our girl doing after her procedure?"

"Good, as far as I know. She said you can hardly tell now. Dr. Taylor put in... Oh I forgot what you call it. Kind of like a placeholder, so her ears are still pierced."

"Oh, how neat. I'm glad it worked out for her."

"Me too. I can't wait to see her. Heather took her to have her hair done yesterday."

"I'm so excited I could squeal." Joyce clasped her hands together and let out a squeal that bounced off the walls.

Frida gasped.

"Oops, sorry." Joyce giggled.

"That's a first." Frida laughed. There was a knock at the door and Frida headed over. Pulling open the door, her mouth gaped when she saw Marin.

"My goodness, Marin." Joyce rested her hand on her upper chest. "You are breathtaking."

Marin's cheeks reddened, matching her new hair color. "Thank you."

Marin walked in, followed by Heather. Frida hugged Marin and pulled back, studying her new look. The only facial piercing was a small hoop in her left nostril. Marin's hair was a deep red that reminded Frida of her mother's red velvet cake. The burgundy sundress complemented her hair and emphasized her deep green eyes. Frida scanned her memories and couldn't remember seeing Marin in a dress before today.

Marin touched her left earlobe. "Dr. Taylor left spacers in my lobes. I still have a few weeks before I can wear earrings."

"They look great, love. If I hadn't seen you before, I'd never have known you had those big dealies in your ears." Joyce inspected both of Marin's ears. "Maybe I should see Madison's dad for a touch up." She brushed her fingers down the sides of her face and laughed.

"Is Maria coming?" Marin asked.

"She sent her apologies. MJ has a play tonight and he has to be there at four. There's a card on the table from her, Phillip, and MJ."

"Oh." Marin noted the two gifts and card on the table and walked over. She smiled at Heather when she placed a gift on the table.

"Oh yeah, I left your gift in the car. Be right back." Joyce headed out to her car.

Marin looked at the gifts, then at Frida and Heather. By her expression, Marin realized there was an extra gift.

"Who is this one from?" Marin pointed to the rectangular gift and looked at Frida.

"Gage."

Marin's eyes widened.

"It came express delivery yesterday." Frida received an unexpected email from Gage two days earlier. It was forwarded by Beth, the Socks for Troops coordinator. In the email, he explained he went that route since he knew there wasn't time for a letter to arrive from Iraq before Marin's birthday. And that Marin had not responded to any of his emails since she admitted what she had done.

Joyce walked in with a large gift bag. She placed it on the floor next to the table so as not to take up too much space. "Don't let the weight fool you. It might be light as a feather, but it cost me a pretty penny." Joyce lifted her brows.

As they'd ventured into knitting garments, Marin learned that good, quality yarn was quite expensive. Frida smiled when Marin's face lit up. Joyce had asked Marin what she wanted for her birthday, and she'd told Joyce about a certain yarn she'd been pining over but put on the bottom of her list because of the cost. Joyce loved gifting people what they least expected.

One gift remained on the table. Marin received her dream yarn from Joyce, and a monogrammed knitting bag from Heather. Frida had given Marin a gold charm bracelet with two charms—a cross and a ball of yarn—to start her off.

Marin cradled the gift from Gage in her lap. The three other women watched her intently as she traced her fingers over the paisley printed paper.

"Are you going to open it or just admire it?" Joyce asked.

Marin looked up and parted her lips. Gingerly, she pulled at the tape, careful not to tear the paper.

"You weren't that easy on their gifts." Joyce tilted her head to Heather and Joyce. "And you practically ripped mine from the bag."

Marin flashed a smile and laid the paper aside. She pulled the top off the box, revealing a mauve, leather Bible. Frida noticed *Marin Martin* embossed on the lower right corner of the cover. Marin removed the Bible from the box and rested it on her lap.

THE KNITTING CLUB

"That's a beautiful Bible," Heather said.

"It is," Joyce agreed.

Marin opened the cover and slowly turned the first few pages. Frida spotted the handwriting on the presentation page. Gage must have asked the bookstore to fill it out for him. Marin paused on the page a moment, then looked up at Frida, holding the Bible out.

Frida took the holy book from Marin's hands and read what Gage requested to be written.

Presented to: Marin Martin

By: Gage Harris

On the Occasion of: Your 21st birthday to encourage you as you seek God

Date: July 10, 2023

Frida noticed tears on Marin's cheeks. "Oh, honey." She rested the Bible on her lap and slipped her arm around Marin's shoulders.

"How can he still want anything to do with me after what I did to him?"

"It's called forgiveness," Heather said. "I'm working on it myself." She smiled when Marin looked up at her.

"But I pretended to be someone I wasn't."

"No, doll. You were you. He got to know your heart. He may have imagined Madison's face when he thought of you or you were talking, but trust me, he got to know that kind, beautiful heart of yours," Joyce said.

"How can he trust me? I've lied and deceived him."

Heather reached over and rested her hand on Marin's knee. "We know why you did it, but he doesn't."

Marin pushed out a breath and ran her hands over her face. "I'd have to let him in. It's too hard."

"Yes, you'd have to be vulnerable," Heather said. "It's terrifying. I was vulnerable and look at what happened. But my relationship with Adam wasn't in vain. We have three beautiful children. Don't get me wrong, I never imagined being close to fifty and divorced."

"But..." Marin exhaled softly. "Everyone I love dies."

"Oh, honey." Frida pulled Marin close. "I can certainly relate to that."

"I need to pray about it."

"That's right," Joyce said. "Seems that's what Gage wants you to do." She pointed to the Bible on Frida's lap. "Seek God."

"I do like him. And I've never liked anyone before. Not like this, anyway."

"If he's the one, he'll honor your request for patience," Frida said. "If he pushes boundaries—"

"He ain't the one, toots." Joyce gave a curt nod.

"Happy birthday, Marin," Frida said.

"Yes, doll, happy birthday," Joyce said.

"Happy birthday." Heather patted Marin's leg.

"Thanks." Marin took the Bible from Frida and slowly thumbed through the delicate pages.

Frida and Joyce began cleaning while Heather and Marin talked about Marin's upcoming move. Madison and Marin had decided not to renew their lease. Madison recently graduated and accepted a job as a nurse in Mobile, Alabama. Marin was not in a place financially to take over the lease on her own. Frida was as excited about Marin's next chapter as much as Marin was.

Chapter 30

Marin

How often did the average person use algebra? To Marin's surprise, she'd been maintaining a B average. It was the third week of the term, but who was counting? She smiled and closed her notebook. She had an hour before she needed to leave for class.

Curiosity got the best of her, and she opened her email app and went to the folder Heather created for Gage. She counted twenty-six emails, with the last one being two days ago. She still couldn't bring herself to read them. She closed out of her email and opened the voicemail app. Tapping the voicemail message on her birthday, she held her breath as she listened to Gage's voice.

"Happy birthday Marin." A five second pause, then a deep breath. Marin had listened to the message too many times to count and memorized each word, pause, and breath. "I don't know why you aren't responding to my emails, but please know I forgive you. Please email me back. God bless."

By his tone of voice, it was obvious how much Marin's silence hurt Gage. He deserved a response. Marin's gaze went to the Bible on her nightstand. She'd searched the internet about what the Bible said on forgiveness. It was pretty much mandatory. God had forgiven us for our sins, and we must forgive those who sinned against us. Gage forgave Marin because he had to as a Christian.

Marin sighed. If that were true, that meant she had to forgive Stella. She rolled her eyes. The look on Stella's face the night at Charley's had been seared into Marin's memory. It was a look of shock, surprise, and, most of all, guilt. Frida said Stella's behavior was of someone lost. Part of Marin wished she'd stay lost. But that was not what God wanted, was it? She could write Stella a letter. Let her know how her behavior had hurt Marin. But that would be admitting Stella had power over her. Marin groaned. She couldn't win for losing, as Grandma Judith used to say. She should probably take Heather up on her offer to see her therapist.

Tapping on the oldest email in Gage's email folder, Marin bit her bottom lip as she read.

Marin, I'm surprised you'd do something like that, but I don't care what you look like. Honest. I want to call. When are you available?

Tears gathered in Marin's eyes. Gage had tried to call several times over the past month. In the beginning, he'd leave a short voicemail. A few times were calls with no voicemails. The last time he tried to call was three weeks ago. She went through each email. Most were him begging her to reply, with one being a simple *Hello?* She tapped on the last email from two days ago.

Please don't shut me out. I forgive you seventy times seven. I'm calling Tuesday at ten your time. Please talk to me.

Today was Tuesday. Marin looked at the clock. It was nine fifty-nine. She gulped and stared at the clock on the top left of her phone's screen. She squeezed her eyes shut when the numbers changed.

10:00

The ringtone opened her eyes, and the air left her lungs when *Unknown Number* showed on the screen. Marin felt as if her arms were not attached to her body. Her heart wanted to answer, but she couldn't make her arms move. After six rings, the phone went silent. Usually, a notification sounded around ten seconds later if someone left a voicemail. Marin counted the seconds for Gage's voicemail. If he left a voicemail this time.

One, two, three —

The phone rang again, and Marin gasped at *Unknown Number* on the screen. Why wouldn't her arms work? Was she having a stroke? *Please God.* Finally, she got her thumb to swipe to answer and brought the phone to her face.

"Hello," she squeaked out.

"Um... May I speak to Marin?" Gage asked, unsure of himself.

"It's me."

"Oh," he let out an awkward chuckle. "It didn't sound like you at first."

Silence.

She opened her mouth, but nothing happened. Now her tongue refused to work. Her heart was screaming for her to speak, to tell him how sorry she was and that he meant the world to her, but she couldn't get her mouth to cooperate.

"Marin?"

"I'm here."

"Are you?"

Confused at first, Marin realized the meaning behind Gage's words. "Yes," she whispered. For the first time, she was being her authentic self. Faux red hair, piercings, and tattoos included.

"I'm glad to hear that. You've put me in a good bit of turmoil over the past month. My heart is happy now. Confused, but happy."

Marin grimaced. She'd caused this man a great deal of pain. Why did she have to be the way she was? Why couldn't she be normal? What was God's purpose in all of her suffering?

"I'm sorry, Gage. So, so sorry." She gasped and swallowed a sob.

"Oh, Marin. I know you are, and I forgive you."

"You *have* to forgive me."

"What?"

"Christians have to forgive. We are directed by God to forgive because He forgives us," Marin said.

"Yes. I forgive you because God commands it, but even if He didn't, I'd forgive you."

"Why?"

"Because I've gotten to know your heart and I know what you've been through and how it can affect your thinking."

Gage knew her better than she knew herself, it seemed. It was time to admit what she'd kept hidden in her heart. "I'm scared," she whispered.

"I get it. There's a song 'Fear is a Liar' by Zach Williams. Look it up and pay attention to the lyrics."

"Okay." Marin made a mental note to look up the lyrics. "I have realized recently that being vulnerable terrifies me. Heather has offered to help me get set up with her counselor."

"I think that's a good idea."

"Grandma Judith took me to counseling for a little while after she got custody, but I was too angsty to participate."

"I can imagine."

Marin needed to concentrate on healing. As much as she liked Gage—and she liked him a lot—she had to admit she was in no place to be in any kind of relationship. "I need to focus on me now. Healthy Marin wouldn't have sent someone else's picture."

Gage was quiet, then said, "You do what you need to do to be healthy. But I'm not going anywhere."

"I don't expect you—"

"I'm not going anywhere, Marin."

Marin could imagine the determined look on Gage's face. As long as he respected her boundaries, she'd be happy to have him in her life.

"I wish I could be there for your graduation in December. I regret volunteering to extend this deployment now. I'll miss your graduation by less than a month."

"Yeah, it would be nice to see you in person." Butterflies sprang to life in Marin's stomach at the thought of meeting Gage face-to-face. She pushed her fist into her stomach. Maybe one day. Her watch buzzed, letting her know it was time for her to leave for class. "I hate to, but I need to get going. Class starts in an hour."

"Sure thing." Gage paused for a moment, then said, "If you feel comfortable, would you consider sending me a picture?"

Marin's eyes widened.

"If not, can you at least tell me the color of your eyes?" Gage's smile was evident in his voice.

"Green."

"Green," Gage repeated. "I like that."

Marin was a mix of giddiness and dread on the way to class. Gage had forgiven her, which she was thrilled about, but admittingly, she was a little nervous that he wanted to stay in her life. Why? Marin pushed the one-word question away. Why did she find it necessary to question everyone's motives?

The small waiting room held a sofa and two upholstered wingback chairs. A variety of artwork hung on the walls and a short bookshelf full of self-help books was positioned under the front windows. Marin read the sign perched on top of the bookshelf: *Clients: help yourself to our lending library. Please see your therapist to check out a book.* Marin guessed she fell in the category of client. Or would after today. She looked at the empty chairs across from her. *Thank you, Lord, for me being the only one in this waiting room.*

"Kaylee?"

Marin cringed inwardly and smiled at the woman who called her by her birth name.

"Hi, I'm Barb. This way, please." The woman waited for Marin to join her, then led her to the office at the end of the hall. Marin glanced at the nameplates of the other therapists outside the doors she passed.

Barb pointed to the small sofa against the wall. Marin sat stiff as a board and forced her spine to relax. Barb picked up the laptop from the small desk in the corner and eased down on an armchair caddy-cornered from the sofa. Marin figured it was a strategic position. Barb's eyes scanned the laptop screen.

"Marin, I'm so sorry. I overlooked your preferred name on the paperwork."

"It's okay."

"I'm going to go over some of the policies and agreements you signed online, then we'll get started."

Marin nodded and watched the woman as she read from her laptop screen. Funny, she didn't look like a Barb. Marin always imagined a ninety-year-old bent over with white hair when she heard the name Barbara. This Barb was around Heather's age. Did Marin look like a Kaylee? Was that the true reason she went by Marin? Or maybe, just maybe, she was—

"Marin?"

"Oh, I'm sorry. What did you say?"

Barb smiled. "Just share what you are comfortable with."

"Okay." Marin blew out her breath and started with the story she'd known her whole life. Gemma met Kevin. Kevin was no prince charming. Marin was conceived and Kevin talked Gemma into running. As she shared, Marin realized the beginning of her story was from her grandmother's perspective. Marin's memories were sporadic until shortly after her parents died, when she was ten.

A tear trailed down Marin's cheek and fell to her hands resting on her lap. Plucking a tissue from the box on the table next to the sofa, Marin dabbed her cheeks. Barb shifted in her chair and laid the notebook Marin hadn't realized she'd been holding on the edge of her desk.

"You've suffered a lot of loss. That, along with a lack of control, can impact how you process your feelings. You witnessed the death of your parents, though you didn't know it at the time. Your ten-year-old mind knew something was wrong. Probably other deaths as well because of your living situation. Then you go from the only people you knew to the first foster placement, which ended up being abusive.

"Finally, you settle into a normal home only to be yanked away to the home of a woman you didn't know. It didn't matter that she was your grandmother." Barb raised her brows.

"No, it didn't." Marin pushed out an awkward laugh.

"And then?" Barb tilted her head to the side.

"I find myself on the streets."

"So many things are out of your control."

"Yes." Marin dabbed her cheeks.

"Madison. God bless her, but she left you no choice either, did she?" Barb laughed.

"I guess not." Marin hadn't thought of that. She wasn't mad that Madison practically made her move in with her. But she hadn't given Marin a choice in the matter.

"Tell me about Gage."

Surely the hour was over by now. Marin looked at her watch and raised a brow. She still had twenty minutes.

"Well." Marin talked about how she'd met Gage and their communication and growing relationship. "I think I like him more than a friend. No, I know I like him more than a friend. He's always here." Marin touched her head. "And here." She touched her heart. "I don't know why I have this block in him knowing what I look like."

"It's something you *can* control."

But it's Gage.

"Hmm?" Barb arched her brows when Marin looked up at her.

"Maybe?" Marin said.

"You don't seem sure of yourself."

"I don't know if it's a lack of control. It's like there's a wall between us."

"Definitely a few oceans," Barb said. "You said he's in Iraq?"

"Yes."

"It's not like you'll run into him somewhere locally, or a chance he'll come in for steak. He's literally depending on you to show yourself to him."

Marin looked at her wrist and touched the yarn charm on the bracelet Frida had given her for her birthday. "How can I overcome this?" she asked when she looked up at Barb.

"Well, maybe a form of exposure therapy."

"Exposure therapy?"

"In exposure therapy, the individual would slowly expose themselves to what causes them anxiety. For instance, a person who is afraid of flying. Their first step would be to look at photos of planes, then videos, then see a plane in real life. Some people would break it down into two dozen steps or more. They would look at tickets online, go to the airport and walk around. The ultimate goal would be to go on a flight."

Marin nodded. How would that work in her situation?

"Does he know anything about your appearance?"

Marin talked about her recent makeover. "When we talked a few days ago, he asked for a picture. I thought I was going to throw up." Marin grimaced. "He said he understood if I was uncomfortable and asked what color my eyes were. I told him."

"How did that feel?"

"Not bad." Marin laughed. "By the way, I didn't tell him I had a makeover."

"Why not?"

"I didn't want him to think I did it for him."

"Did you?"

"No."

"You didn't hesitate with your answer." Barb smiled.

"My friends helped me see I had been using my appearance to protect myself from being hurt. People kept their distance because I was..., well..., weird."

"It sounds like your friends care a great deal about you."

Marin smiled. She felt very much loved by her friends. Except for Madison, they weren't the typical friends of a twenty-one-year-old. Heather was old enough to be her mother. Her mother would have been closer to Maria's age if she'd lived, and Marin knew Maria was in her mid-thirties. Frida and Joyce were her grandmother's age. Marin wouldn't have it any other way.

They ended the session with a homework assignment. As comfort allowed, Marin was to reveal her appearance to Gage a little at a time, whether in photos, emails, or during their phone conversations. In the meantime, they were going to work through Marin's childhood trauma. Every ounce of Marin's being wanted to never set foot in Barb's office again, but she knew in order to be healthy, she had to work through her past. And that included dealing with her parents' death and the abuse at the hands of her first foster parents.

Matthew nineteen, verse twenty-six, had spoken to Marin during her study time and she'd made it her life verse. She'd written it on sticky notes and placed them everywhere. Glancing at the neon pink sticky note next to the gas gage on the instrument panel of her car, Marin said, "'With men, this is impossible; but with God, all things are possible.'"

With God and her friends' prayers and encouragement, she'd get through this.

Chapter 31

Heather

With the second coat of sea pearl paint dry, Heather held up one panel from a set of curtains her mother made over the window. The hint of blue in the paint complemented the small flowers in the curtains. Marin had done a good job picking out the fabric.

The door of the pool house opened, and Heather was about to ask Marin how she liked the paint color, but closed her mouth when Adam walked inside. She blinked. Through prayers, she'd gotten to the place where she could stand to breathe the same air as him. Why was he standing in the pool house?

"Is Jake okay?" Heather draped the curtain panel across the back of the chair.

"Yes, I.., I needed to talk to you." Adam glanced around, his gaze finding the small couch she'd picked up second hand for Marin.

Heather glanced at the back of the house and saw Jake in the sunroom. She could make out the shape of his Monty the Monster Truck as he drove it through the air. When she turned back to Adam, he had moved to the couch and sat down, resting his elbows on his knees and his hands clasped. Heather's brows drew together.

Raking his fingers through his hair, Adam drew in a deep breath. "There's something I need to tell you." He shifted on the couch and rubbed the back of his neck. Before Heather could speak, he sprung to his feet and began pacing. She'd known this man for over twenty years. When he behaved this way, it was serious.

Heather's arms went weak. Adam had proposed to Amber. Easing out a breath, she took small, deep breaths to calm her racing heartbeat. It made sense. That was what happened in an adulterous relationship. Those that cheated married once the ink dried on the respective divorce papers. The kids were gaining a stepmother.

"Amber's pregnant," Adam said.

Heather's legs buckled and she managed to get to the chair and braced herself before she fell. "What?"

Adam stopped pacing and sat on the couch. "It wasn't planned. Obviously."

Amber was in her forties and Adam was knocking on fifty-one's door. They weren't naïve teenagers. They knew how this worked. She glanced in the sunroom windows at Jake. He would forever be her baby, but he was no longer Adam's baby.

"I don't know what to say."

"I just wanted to let you know since the kids will start talking."

"You told them?"

"Not yet. I wanted to tell you first."

How thoughtful.

As the news settled in, the memory of Adam's reaction to her discovering she was pregnant with Jake came to the surface. There was anger. Genuine anger. Adam's face turned red, and he'd raised his voice. That was putting it nicely. He'd down right yelled at her, blaming her for the pregnancy.

Heather wanted to ask Adam how he felt. Was he angry? Disappointed? Dare she say happy?

Adam stood. "I'll let you get back to whatever you were doing."

"Thanks for agreeing for Marin to rent the pool house."

"Of course. If you say she's a good person, I trust you." Adam offered a slight smile and turned to head to the door.

"Adam?"

He stopped and turned back to Heather.

"Are you happy? About the baby?"

Adam slipped his hands in the pockets of his pants and his eyes shifted to the floor.

"You said we were too old to have another baby when we found out about Jake."

Adam pushed out a long breath. "Amber knew for eight weeks before she told me."

Heather's lips parted.

"She admitted her first thought was to have an abortion without telling me she was pregnant. She never really wanted kids. She finally told me she was thinking about an abortion but wanted my input. I couldn't help but think of Jake." Adam glanced at the house. "I wanted you to get an abortion."

Heather's heart rose to her throat. Hearing those words from Adam back then turned her stomach. And he'd said it more than once.

Adam looked at the house again, then at Heather. "I'm glad you stood your ground. I can't imagine my life without that little guy." His voice cracked.

Heather bit her bottom lip. "Me neither." She exhaled slowly and said, "Well, congratulations."

Adam offered a slight smile. "Thanks. See ya."

"Bye."

As Adam walked away, Heather guessed there'd be a new Mrs. Adam Zimmerman soon. What would the kids think? Jake was six now. He might be happy about a baby. Shelly would probably be excited. Ethan? She did not know how he would feel.

Heather had been talking more to Ethan about Adam, gently encouraging him to communicate with his father. She'd told Ethan he didn't want any regrets. Ethan stayed in the living room when Adam picked Jake up the other day. Adam said hello and Ethan's response was a chin lift as his eyes stayed glued to his phone screen. It was the first time he'd been in the room with Adam since Adam had left over a year earlier. Heather prayed the baby wouldn't be a setback for Ethan. Children were a blessing from God. Even children born in the wake of a bitter divorce.

Looping the tieback around the curtain panel, Heather secured the ends and repeated the process with the three remaining curtain panels. She took a step back to inspect her work. The curtains looked great. Her mom had done a good job of bringing her vision to life.

Amber's pregnant.

She'd repeated Adam's words every minute, it seemed, since he'd told her an hour earlier. Her emotions were twisted together. One second, she was happy for the new life, and the next, she was having flashbacks to the not-so-nice things Adam said to her when she was pregnant with Jake.

The door opened and in walked Marin, wide eyed as she looked around. "I've only been gone eight hours and you've painted, hung curtains, and…bought a couch?" she said when she noticed the small cream-colored couch that matched the curtains and paint color. She pointed to the room divider. "What's that?"

"It's a folding room divider. I figured it would give you some privacy, so your bed isn't visible."

Marin walked around the room divider and gasped. "And new bedding?" She came back to the living area with her mouth gaping. "Heather. You didn't have to do all this."

"I wanted to. It's kept me busy, so I don't think."

Marin lifted her brows and she rubbed her finger repeatedly down her cheek. What on earth was she doing? "You've got..." She pointed to Heather's cheeks. "There's a black smudge down your cheek. I didn't notice it when I first came in."

"Oh." Heather rubbed her hand over her cheek and grimaced when Marin shook her head. "I think I know what it is. Mascara. I've been crying."

"What's going on?"

Heather walked over to the sink, wet a piece of paper towel, and wiped her cheek. "Adam dropped a bomb."

"Uh, oh."

"Amber's pregnant."

"What?" Marin winced. "I didn't mean to be that loud. Pregnant?"

"Yeah." Heather sat on the couch, and Marin joined her. She told Marin what Adam said.

"Wow. How do you feel about it?"

"There's an innocent life on the way. I can't be mad at that." Heather sighed. "But it has taken me back to how Adam treated me when I found out I was pregnant with Jake. He was not happy. Jake wasn't planned. I actually thought I was going through menopause. I mentioned it to my doctor at my yearly physical, and she ordered a test. It was positive."

"I bet that was a shock."

"That's putting it mildly. At one point, I didn't know if Adam was going to be with me in the delivery room. I had my mom on standby."

"Really?"

"He came around. He's not acting like he did back then and he's over six years older. I don't get it. One thing he said about Jake was how his retirement plans would be ruined."

"Maybe he's still in shock about the new baby."

"Maybe."

"Maybe he has changed and is genuinely happy."

Heather looked at Marin and arched her brows. Could Adam be happy about this new child? Adam would be almost seventy years old when the baby graduated from high school.

Would Amber lose her figure? It was hard to bounce back after having a baby in your forties. More hurtful words from Adam came flooding back. And the disgusted looks on his face anytime he'd see her in her underwear. Tears burned Heather's eyes.

"When's the baby due?"

"You know, I didn't ask. He said she was eight weeks when she told him."

"Wow, really?"

Heather nodded. "Maybe he's known for a few weeks. You know, working up the nerve to tell me."

"Yeah, maybe," Marin said.

"Enough of that. How's Gage?" Marin's expression at the mention of Gage's name lifted Heather's spirits.

"He's great." Marin's update on Gage transitioned into her disdain for college algebra and disappointment in Madison's replacement at Charley's Steakhouse. It was clear how much Marin missed Madison. Maybe Heather would suggest a weekend visit. She could use a change of scenery.

Heather and Marin said goodnight and Heather headed to the house. Shelly was with Travis, and Ethan and Jake were watching a *Monty the Monster Truck* movie. A cup of chamomile tea sounded good. In the kitchen, she turned on the electric kettle and prepared her cup with a tea bag and a pinch of sugar. On the kitchen counter, her phone rang. Adam's name brightened the screen. Why was he calling at eight on a Friday night?

"Hello?"

"We're at the hospital. Please pray," Adam said between sobs.

"Adam, what's wrong?" Heather peeked at the boys and walked into the laundry room for privacy.

"It's an ectopic pregnancy. Amber's in emergency surgery." He gasped.

"Uh."

Hang up, Heather.

The nerve of Adam to call *her*. Why didn't he call his mother? The whistle of the kettle brought Heather away from her thoughts.

"Of course."

"Thank you. Thank you so much. I need to go. I'll keep you updated."

"Okay."

Heather went to the kitchen, turned off the kettle, and went back to the laundry room to pray. One thing came to mind when she finished. Why was she the first person Adam thought of?

Chapter 32

Frida

A veil of grief had fallen over the women as they worked on their respective knitting projects. Heather had called last Saturday morning to ask for prayers for Adam and Amber. They lost their child to an ectopic pregnancy. Amber had lost a lot of blood but was stable. Frida feared Heather was dealing with a mixture of grief and guilt.

Frida's grief for her own loss stung harder than usual. It happened anytime she heard of the loss of a child. Frida glanced at Joyce. She bit her bottom lip as she used the loom hook to pull yarn over the pegs of the loom. Joyce had been Frida's dearest friend for well over forty years and she did not know Frida lost a child.

Frida glanced around the living room. Marin guided Maria in using the knitting loom to make potholders as practice for the ring pillow. She'd made a stack of three asymmetrical potholders that were supposed to be square. Frida smiled at the mismatched stack. Her smile fell when she noticed Heather staring off into space, her cheeks damp. Frida picked up the box of tissues on the table next to her chair and made her way to Heather.

"Oh, gosh," Heather said as she grabbed a tissue. "I didn't realize I was crying." She patted her cheeks and eyes. She grabbed a tissue and blew her nose. "I'm such a mess. Praise God, I have a therapy appointment on Monday."

"That's two days away." Joyce raised a brow. "You've been carrying all this for a week?"

She dabbed at her eyes again. "I just called yesterday. I think I would have been okay if Adam hadn't kept calling me."

"Oh, my," Frida said. Why wouldn't Adam have called his family or Amber's family? Poor Heather.

"We all have two good ears," Marin said and gave Frida a knowing smile. Frida said the same thing to Marin the day they met in the yarn aisle at Cathy's Craft Haven.

Heather grimaced. "I don't think y'all want to hear the thoughts going through my head."

Every hand stilled and every eye turned to Heather.

"Honey, you're human. You're allowed to have a whole slew of thoughts—good, bad, and downright ugly," Joyce said.

"Oh, there's been some ugly ones." Heather's eyes widened and she focused on her knitting, though her hands stayed still.

An uneasy silence filled the surrounding space. Heather blotted more tears and glanced at Marin. She drew in a deep breath and said, "I was shocked when Adam told me Amber was pregnant. I didn't know why he told me at first, but it hit me later. The kids would have a new sibling." Heather swallowed hard. "Here are my thoughts in no particular order. Please don't judge me."

"We won't judge you, sweetheart," Frida said. Everyone agreed.

"They aren't teenagers. Technically, they are old enough to be grandparents. I know accidents happen. I have one that's six years old. Adam treated me so badly when we found out about Jake. Let's face it, he treated me horribly until the divorce. I could have added alienation of affection as grounds for divorce, but..." Heather glanced out the window. Gathering her knitting project, she laid it aside and braced to stand, saying, "I think I need another cup of coffee."

"I got it, honey," Frida said.

"Oh, okay." Heather leaned back against the chair.

"I'll put on a fresh pot." Frida went to the kitchen to prepare the coffee. Heather continued sharing her thoughts and feelings. Frida winced when Heather mentioned Adam wanted her to have an abortion when she found out she was pregnant with Jake. She rested her hand on her heart when Heather said Adam thanked her for not giving into him.

Frida raised her brows when she heard Marin's voice. She stood still as she listened to Marin's take on Heather's feelings. The broken young woman she'd found in the yarn aisle had come a long way. Each woman sitting in Frida's living room had her own take on grief and loss. Frida, Joyce, and Maria lost their husbands through death. Heather had lost her husband through divorce. Marin lost her parents as a child, then the foster family that wanted to adopt her. And her grandmother.

Frida filled Heather's cup before the coffeemaker finished brewing and brought it to her. The room was quiet again. Heather smiled when Frida handed her the cup.

"I know he called me because he knew I'd pray for them." Heather blew into the cup and took a small sip. "He gave me permission to tell Shelly. He hadn't told the kids about the baby yet. She was surprised, but the gravity of the situation took over. We got a prayer chain going that night." Heather looked Marin's way. "And I started making calls Saturday morning." She smiled at Frida.

"The one thought that kept tormenting and taunting me was..." Heather cleared her throat and looked at each woman. "At first, she was going to have an abortion." She gulped. "Now she didn't have to." Heather hung her head and sobbed.

"Heather," Joyce said. She was sitting closest and got to Heather first. Slipping her arms around her shoulders, Joyce pulled Heather close and kissed the side of her head as she sobbed.

"Why was that my first thought? They'd decided to keep the baby. I'm such a horrible person," Heather pushed out between sobs.

"No, love, you are human." Joyce tightened her arms around Heather. "Adam has caused you so much pain, love. It's no wonder that was your first thought."

"But it's not the way a Christian should think," Heather said.

"Even as a Christian, you are a human first." Joyce looked at Frida and lifted her brows as if Frida would contradict what she'd said.

"You know what Barb told me? She's our therapist," Marin said to the women. Heather looked her way. "Thoughts and feelings are like roadblocks on the journey to healing. You have to acknowledge them in order to process them and move forward."

"And no one likes a roadblock. Especially when you have to lean over to search through your glove box for your registration." Joyce laughed. "Kind of like searching through those tightly sealed boxes in your heart."

Heather mustered a smile. "I love all of you."

"We love you too, honey," Frida said.

"We are here for you, Heather," Maria said.

"Anytime. And you know where I live." Marin winked, bringing out another smile from Heather.

Their time together ended. Heather assured everyone she was okay. She and Marin had ridden together, and Marin told Frida she'd keep an eye on Heather. Life was hard. Frida didn't know where she would be without God and the people He'd put in her life.

"Hello, my love," Frida said as she brushed debris from the top of Max's headstone with a whisk broom. "It's been a while. I've been so tied up with the girls. I don't mean for that to be an excuse. Time gets away from me with all that has been going on."

The slight breeze provided no relief for the mid-September heat. Frida fanned herself with an old sales flyer from Cathy's she'd brought from her car for a minute before cleaning up around the gravesite. She placed the new silk flower arrangement in the vase attached at the base of the headstone. The woman who'd made the arrangement did an excellent job making the flowers lifelike.

Frida opened the portable stool and eased down. In her younger years, she'd sit on the ground and cross her legs. Those days were long gone. She'd have to call 911 for help to get to her feet if she sat on the ground now. She laughed. Fanning herself, she read the details of Max's life etched into the stone—the same words and dates she'd read for the past fifty-one years.

Her thoughts drifted to Maria and Phillip. Wedding plans were in full swing. They'd planned a December wedding—three months to go. Mateo crossed her mind. Frida believed some people had more than one great love, and Phillip was Maria's second great love. Frida didn't feel there was anyone else out there for her. No man could have lived up to Max. Frida was sure she would have compared every word and every action to Max. It wouldn't have been fair to any man in her life.

Frida's phone dinged, and she pulled it out of her pocket. Marin sent a screenshot of what looked like a sales flyer.

Marin: Just got this sales email from Cathy's. Yarn is 50% off!!!

Was Gage Marin's soulmate? From things Marin shared, he reminded Frida of Max. A caring, thoughtful, God-fearing man. And Marin lit up like a Christmas tree every time she talked about him. Yet, she'd been keeping him at arm's length. She still hadn't shared a photo of herself. All Gage knew was Marin had green eyes. Frida shook her head. Marin was using healthy boundaries. Frida prayed Marin's boundaries wouldn't become walls.

The heat hung in the air around Frida, and a bead of sweat trickled down her back. Reaching under her, she used the seat of the stool to push herself to her feet. Kissing her fingers, she touched the top of the cool granite headstone. "Until next time, my love. I promise it won't be so long."

On the drive home, Frida's thoughts centered on Marin. She'd gotten close to Marin and Heather over the last year and a half. While Heather had her mother, Marin had no one. Frida could never replace Marin's mother or grandmother, but she held a special place in Frida's heart. A place that'd been empty for far too long.

Chapter 33

Marin

Marin signed the beverage vendor's invoice and turned her attention to the computer screen. She had been rearranging the schedule to cover the shift of a server who had come down with the flu.

"Marin," Stephanie said, poking her head in the office's door. "Here's the mail. That padded envelope is for you."

Marin noticed a large padded manilla envelope on top of the stack of mail in Stephanie's hand.

"Thanks." Marin raised her brows at how the envelope was addressed.

Kaylee Martin, C/O Charley's Steakhouse

Her eyes drifted to the top left corner of the envelope. What she saw twisted her stomach.

Stella Scott

What could be in the envelope? Marin gave the envelope a gentle squeeze, then squeezed up and down the length. It felt like a knitting needle holder full of knitting needles. But surely not. Using a letter opener from the desk drawer, Marin gently sliced open the envelope and pulled out the contents, along with memories of her grandmother. In her hand was Grandma Judith's knitting needle holder with an array of knitting needles. Tears burned Marin's eyes as she ran her finger over the *JS* embroidered on the outside.

"Judith Scott," Marin whispered. She closed the office door and opened the needle holder. The knitting needles were of varying sizes and lengths. Several appeared to be older than Marin. Tears coursed down her cheeks. Peeking in the envelope again, Marin noticed a small, folded sheet of notebook paper. She pulled it out, unfolded it, and gulped. It was a handwritten note from Stella.

Kaylee,

Marin rolled her eyes. She'd let her birth name on the envelope slide since Stella sent it to her place of employment, but now Stella was being passive-aggressive.

I found this when I was going through some of Mom's things. I thought you might like to have it.

Marin reached up to twist the stud in her nose but found the hoop. She ran her finger along the cool metal edge and shook her head. Stella? Thoughtful?

I have a question.

Marin arched her brows.

I am in therapy now, working through some things. I was wondering if you'd be willing to come to a session with me.

Marin's mouth hung open and she scoffed.

My therapist thinks it's a good idea.

Marin stared at the words and reread the last three sentences twice. Then a third time. Stella was the last person Marin wanted to be behind closed doors with. But if she was working on her issues…. Marin shook her head. Folding the note without reading the rest, she slid it along with the knitting needle holder back in the padded envelope. She couldn't do this now.

She glanced at the wall clock. Thirty minutes until she could go home and leave this day behind her. When she walked into the restaurant seven and a half hours earlier, she didn't know she'd have to deal with Stella. At least it was towards the end of her shift.

Marin walked into the pool house and hung her keys up on the holder by the door. She'd just kicked off her shoes when she heard a knock at the door. Separating the slats of the blinds, she saw Ethan holding a large manilla envelope. Two in one day? This one better not be from Stella as well.

"Hey," she said when she opened the door.

"Hi. Mom said to bring this to you when you get home. She's at her Bible study."

"Thanks, Ethan." She smiled and took the envelope from him and closed the door. One of those yellow forwarding address labels was over the original address. Marin could make out the first two numbers of the street address of the apartment she'd shared with Madison. The envelope wasn't padded, but it was thick. She looked at the sender's name: *Charles Clarke, Estate Attorney*.

Estate attorney? Easing down on the couch, she slid her finger under the flap and opened the envelope. On top of the stack of papers she pulled out was a letter from Charles Clarke. *Last will and testament* and *minor trust* appeared throughout. By the time Marin reached the end, her hands were shaking. There was lots of legal jargon, but from what Marin could make out, Stella kept what was rightfully hers from her.

Marin's phone chimed, and she saw a preview of the text before the notification disappeared.

Heather: Did you get the envelope from the attorney?

She swiped the screen and replied.

Marin: Yes. Do you have a few minutes?

Heather: Of course

Marin: Be right over.

"I'm no attorney," Heather said when Marin showed her the letter from Mr. Clarke. Heather noticed the papers stapled together behind the letter. "But this is a copy of your grandmother's will." She thumbed through them. "Marin," Heather looked at Marin, "it says you and Stella are to share her estate."

"What?" Marin took the will from Heather. It might as well be a foreign language to Marin, but she saw her name alongside Stella's throughout.

"I think you should call Mr. Clarke tomorrow." Heather handed the letter to Marin.

"Yeah." Marin slipped everything back in the envelope.

At the pool house, Marin searched online for Mr. Clarke's practice hours and set an alarm on her phone. It was going to be a long night.

As Marin stared at the ceiling, a realization came to her. Did Stella want her to join a therapy session because she knew Marin would receive the letter and copy of Grandma Judith's will? Was it Stella's way of making nice? And why didn't Stella mention the will in her note?

"The note." Marin turned on the lamp and flung the covers back. She found the envelope from Stella and pulled out the knitting needle holder and note. Settled on her bed, she leaned close to the lamp to read the rest of Stella's note.

I have made some poor choices where you are concerned.

"You think? I had to sleep on some creep's couch and get groped by him in the middle of the night, Stella." Marin yelled at the note. She balled it up and threw it across the room. Grabbing the knitting needle holder, Marin instinctively held it to her nose and inhaled. A faint scent of her grandmother's house filled her senses, pushing tears down her cheeks. She turned off the lamp and held the knitting needle holder next to her face as she fell asleep.

"Hold please, while I put you through," Mr. Clarke's receptionist said.

"Okay," Marin gulped.

Mr. Clarke picked up on the first ring. "Marin, nice to finally hear from you. I was beginning to wonder." He chuckled.

"I recently moved, so the package was forwarded." Marin realized Mr. Clarke had not called her Kaylee.

"Ah, good, good. So, the abbreviated version of events. I have been your grandmother's attorney for a long time. In her previous last will and testament, the estate was to be distributed evenly between her two daughters: Stella and your mother, Gemma. When Judith discovered your mother passed and she'd brought you home, she'd changed it to Stella and you, with Stella holding your share in trust until you attained the age of twenty-one."

Marin's brows lifted. "Not eighteen?"

"Mississippi law states the age of twenty-one."

"Oh, okay."

"And with your birthday this past July tenth, I assumed I'd hear from you. I couldn't get ahold of Stella when August rolled around with no contact from you. I kept leaving messages with Stella."

Heat billowed in Marin's stomach.

"My receptionist finally tracked you down somehow. That's how we got that address."

Mr. Clarke gave an estimated timeline for the inheritance and talked about the process. Marin's head spun as he talked. All this time, she'd assumed Grandma Judith's estate would go to Stella, as her next of kin. Marin didn't know that her grandmother included her.

"Wait," Marin said.

"Yes?"

"So, Stella had control of my trust, which meant she could have given me money?"

"Yes. For necessities like food, clothing, shelter, education."

Shelter.

"Marin?"

When Mr. Clarke said Marin's name, she felt the tears that gathered in her eyes fall down her cheeks. "I was homeless for two months."

"My word," Mr. Clarke said.

"She kicked me out of Grandma Judith's house so she could sell it."

"Marin, I am so sorry."

Marin wiped her cheeks.

"Mr. and Mrs. Scott had some problems with Stella after Gemma disappeared."

Marin tilted her head and wiped away fresh tears.

"I'm not a therapist, but a lot of my clients talk about their personal lives. It's tied up in the type of law I practice. The Scotts were no different."

Marin let what he said sink in. It was something that had never crossed Marin's mind. How did her mother's running away affect Stella?

"Okay, well. Your grandmother had a considerable estate, Marin. Certainly, more than my average client that comes in for estate planning."

"She did?"

"Between the life insurance, bank accounts, the proceeds from the sale of the house, investments…"

Marin's thoughts refused to come together and comprehend what Mr. Clarke was saying. Each time Marin tried to make sense of the figures he was tossing out, her mind went blank. A soft chuckle brought Marin to the present.

"I don't want you to be shocked at the amount on the check."

"Oh, okay." She'd rather have Grandma Judith in her life than a bunch of zeroes on a check.

Chapter 34

Heather

Heather scrolled through the texts between her and Adam, reading a few relevant ones to her therapist, Barb.

"Did you and Adam lose a child?"

Heather looked up mid-scroll. "No."

"I wondered if that could be a link, but since you haven't, I think Adam is relying on you for emotional support because you allow it."

Heather's brows came together, and she tensed. Since Adam called the night he'd taken Amber to the emergency room, she'd made herself available to him. She'd answered texts and calls throughout the day and evening and provided comfort when he'd stopped by the house to pick up or drop off Jake. Her gaze dropped to the text chain, and she sighed.

"Why?" Barb asked.

Heather looked up again.

"I'm not looking for an answer. It's just something for you to think about. In the meantime, I think you should establish some firm boundaries. Suggest that he seek a professional. It's understandable that he's struggling. But you've made so much progress in healing. I don't want to see you lose that."

Barb wasn't lying. Heather had made progress and encouraged Ethan to interact with his dad. Then Adam told her about the pregnancy. She'd barely had an hour to process the news when he'd called from the hospital.

Barb changed the subject, and they talked about how Heather had been dealing with Shelly's move to attend college. She engaged in conversation with Barb, but Heather's mind kept going back to what Barb said at the beginning of the session. The realization hit her square in the face: Heather was enabling Adam.

Heather's mind wandered as she drove home. Should she make herself less available to Adam little by little or cut him off immediately? She pulled into the garage and walked through the mudroom. A noise in the laundry room drew her attention and she peeked in. Marin's smiling face lifted Heather's mood.

"Would you like a cup of tea?" Heather asked.

"I'd love some. Let me finish folding this load and I'll meet you in the..."

"Sunroom?"

"Okay." Marin held up a bath towel and folded it in half.

Heather glanced at her phone as she waited for the water to boil. Three hours until she had to pick Jake up from school. Ethan had play practice or he'd pick up his little brother. The kettle whistled and she poured boiling water over the chamomile tea bags. A text notification sounded, and she grabbed her phone.

Adam: Amber called out again today.

Heather sighed. It had been a month since Adam and Amber had lost their baby. Amber had gone back to work Monday, but called out Wednesday and Thursday, and apparently today.

"Bad news?" Marin said as she walked out of the laundry room on her way to the sunroom, balancing a laundry basket on her hip.

"It seems Amber went back to work too early. Adam said she's called out again today." Heather carried the cups of tea behind Marin and handed Marin a cup when they settled on the couch.

"Oh." Marin sipped her tea. She arched her brows nearly to her hairline. Was it because the tea was hot or Amber? "This may be none of my business, but..." Marin placed the cup on the side table and glanced Heather's way. "Adam sure does text you a lot."

"Did Barb call you?" Heather laughed at Marin's wrinkled forehead. "We were talking about that in my session."

"Oh, okay." Marin laughed.

"I need to set some boundaries."

"That's a good idea."

"I just don't know how to go about it. Do I cut him off, so to speak, or do it slowly?"

"Tell him you can't talk about Amber and the baby. Just your kids."

"Yeah. I don't know why this is so hard."

"Kind of like sending Gage a picture. I should just do it, but... Barb said it's something I can control. Good old childhood trauma." Marin rolled her eyes.

"I can see that." Heather's phone chimed and she went to the kitchen to get it. It could be Shelly or—. She shook her head when she saw who'd texted her.

Adam: Just checking to see if you got my text. I know sometimes I don't get notifications in a timely manner.

Heather noticed the time between Adam's two texts and shook her head. Fifteen minutes. She typed out a reply and bit her bottom lip when she tapped the send button.

Heather: Adam, we need to talk.

He replied within seconds.

Adam: k

Adam: I'll come a little early for Jake tomorrow.

Heather: OK

In the sunroom, Heather shook her head when she sat on the couch. Marin's slight smile told Heather she knew who'd texted.

"I'm going to talk to him tomorrow. Pray for me."

"You know I will. Pray for me too. I don't know why I can't send Gage a picture."

"What do you think he'll say?" Heather took a sip of tea.

Marin shrugged.

Heather studied Marin. "Do you know you are pretty?"

Marin glanced at Heather, then stared into her teacup.

"Marin?"

Marin looked at Heather for a moment, then her gaze drifted out the window. Heather imagined it had been hard for Marin. She didn't have a father figure to instill self-worth and self-esteem. Her grandfather passed on by the time her grandmother had gotten custody. And Marin certainly hadn't had a father figure in her own father.

"What about a side profile?" When Marin looked at her, Heather quickly turned to show her profile. Marin giggled. "Or from here, over." Heather covered half her face and raised her brow.

"Maybe."

"Let me ask you this. If Gage said you were the most beautiful woman he'd ever seen, would you believe him?"

Marin's lips parted and she tilted her head. Poor Gage had his work cut out for him if he was determined to win Marin over. But Heather could relate. She was a teenager when her parents divorced. Her dad tried his best, but she saw him once or twice a month and that wasn't enough during a time she'd needed his assurance the most.

"I should get ready for work," Marin said.

"Okay, have a good shift."

Marin smiled, grabbed her laundry basket and teacup, and made her way to the kitchen. Heather heard the back door close and watched Marin walk across the yard to the pool house. Never would she have guessed the quiet girl in black would become a dear friend. Having Marin live in the pool house helped fill a void while Shelly was at school. The five-hour drive to Ole Miss might as well be five days. Less than a week, she'd see her girl for Thanksgiving break. Heather couldn't wait to have all her children under one roof.

Catching up on a word game on her phone, Heather's brows lowered when a text from Adam appeared at the top of the screen.

Adam: Are you awake?

Heather glanced at the clock on her phone. It was not yet seven thirty. Adam's pick-up time was ten unless other arrangements had been made. Last night, he said he'd come early so they could talk. But this early?

Adam: I'm out front. I can go grab a coffee down the street if you need more time.

Heather groaned. She'd been wide awake since five and laid awake most of the night, worrying herself about how Adam would react to her boundaries.

Heather: I'm up. Give me fifteen minutes.

Adam: Ok, want your usual from Starbucks?

She certainly wouldn't turn down Starbucks.

Heather: Yes, thank you.

Adam: You bet. See you in a few.

By the time Heather got ready and went downstairs, Adam sent a text that he'd just pulled into the driveway. She opened the front door and took the caramel macchiato from him when he walked onto the porch.

"Kids up yet?" Adam asked.

"Not a peep from either. I saw a hint of light under Ethan's door at three when I went to get a drink of water. He was probably playing video games with his friends. I'm sure he'll sleep until noon." Heather grinned.

Adam nodded and headed to the sunroom. It seemed to be the preference when things needed to be discussed out of earshot of the kids, since it was in the back of the house. He eased down on one end of the couch and Heather took the glider across from the couch.

"Amber left this morning."

Heather lifted the paper to go cup to her mouth and was waiting for the caramel goodness to touch her lips. She pulled the cup away from her mouth.

"What?"

"She's struggling, Heather. She didn't want the baby, then she did, then... She said she needed some time to think."

In the morning light drifting through the windows, Adam's struggle to maintain control of his emotions was etched on his face. She'd be heartless if she told him he needed to tell this to a counselor, not her. His girlfriend had just left.

"How do you feel about that?"

Adam leaned back and stretched out his legs. "Some things were said last night."

You don't need to hear this. Suggest therapy.

"She mentioned something that's ridiculous."

Therapy, Heather. Say it.

Adam looked at her and held her gaze for a moment. The words were on the end of Heather's tongue. Biting her tongue to keep it from moving, she tucked her hair behind her ears and cleared her throat.

"I think guilt from being partly responsible for the end of our marriage is tied up in her grief."

"What do you mean?"

"Well, she feels that the baby's death is directly related to the affair and, to be frank, it's something I've struggled with."

Blistering heat rose from Heather's stomach to her face. The temperature in the room soared. In her heart, she didn't believe God would take an innocent life for that reason, but she struggled with her own feelings regarding the baby and how Adam had treated her when she found out she was pregnant with Jake.

"Adam?"

"Yeah?"

She hadn't realized she'd said his name until he answered. "My heart goes out to you and to Amber. But—" She had to be honest with Adam. "I can't do this anymore. You need a professional that's trained in grief and loss to help you." A dozen more things to say to him popped into her head, but she let them go.

"What about your therapist?"

"No." The word came out unexpectedly and with a bite to it. "I'm sorry." Heather grimaced. "It's a conflict of interest for us to see the same therapist. I can ask if she knows anyone experienced with infant loss."

Adam rested his elbows on his knees and rubbed his hands over his face. "I'm sorry to have dumped all this on you. It wasn't right. It's just that... You've always been the one I talk to about hard things. Well, before..."

Before you tore my world apart?

"I get it. I care about what happens to you, Adam. You are my children's father."

"I'm sorry I hurt you, Heather. Truly sorry." He swallowed hard.

"I know."

"Mom?"

Heather looked up and saw Ethan step into the doorway of the sunroom. His hair was sticking up in all directions, and he looked exhausted. He noticed his father sitting on the couch and Heather held her breath. Ethan had seen his father once since the baby died and no words had been exchanged. Heather's eyes widened as she watched Ethan walk across the room and sit on the other end of the small couch where Adam sat.

"I'm so sorry about the baby, Dad."

"Thank you, Ethan." Adam glanced at Heather and back at Ethan.

"What are you guys doing in here?" Jake walked into the sunroom, pulling his small rolling suitcase behind him.

"I came a little early so Mommy and I could have coffee."

Ethan looked at Heather and knitted his brows together. He stood and said, "I came downstairs to take some headache medicine. I'm going back to bed for a bit."

"Okay," Heather said.

"Bye, Ethan," Adam said.

Ethan lifted his chin to Adam and walked into the kitchen.

"It's those video games. He stares at a screen all day long," Adam whispered.

Heather shrugged.

"Is it time, Daddy?"

"Close enough," Heather said and smiled when Adam looked her way. Spending the weekend with Jake—just the two of them—would do Adam good.

Heather was still working on forgiving Adam for what he'd put her through. Trying to keep her head above water in the wake of it all exhausted her. She had a little over two years to get her life together before the house went on the market. It was time to focus on her future.

Chapter 35

Frida

Three or four of her tiny houses would fit inside Heather's house, Frida decided when she pulled into Heather's driveway. It was a beautiful home. The porch stretched across the front of the house with four white columns. Frida thought of the swing Heather told them about—the one she wanted on the front porch that ended up in the backyard.

She picked up the dish from the passenger seat and made her way to the door. Heather said to bring a Thanksgiving dish she was famous for. *Capirotada* was what she made every year for her family's Thanksgiving. The bread pudding had been dubbed the "disappearing dish" by her family, as it was gone in less than five minutes once the desserts came out.

Joyce opened the door and smiled when Frida stepped onto the porch. "Dah-ling." She stepped aside as Frida walked inside.

"Playing hostess duties?" Frida smiled at her friend.

"Frida." Heather came into the living room and gave her a hug. "Kids, come in here please." Joyce took the dish from Frida and went to what Frida figured was the kitchen. A beautiful young woman with long, blond hair like her mother walked up next to Heather. "This is Shelly."

"Nice to meet you, Shelly." Frida shook Shelly's outstretched hand. A little guy ran up to where they stood, followed by a teenage boy. Frida noticed the truck on the front of the little one's shirt. "You must be Jake and Ethan."

Jake grinned and nodded.

"Nice to finally meet you, Ms. Frida. Mom talks about you all the time." Ethan shook Frida's hand.

"Good, I hope," Frida smiled.

"Always," Ethan responded.

Jake and Ethan returned to wherever in the house they'd come from, and Frida followed Heather and Shelly to the kitchen. Marin smiled from the other side of the island where she was using a potato masher in a bowl of potatoes. She paused and walked around to hug Frida.

"Happy Thanksgiving," Marin said.

"Happy Thanksgiving, honey."

"Is this what I think it is?" Joyce's eyes lit up as she pulled back the foil on a corner of the pan Frida brought. "Oh my. Yes, it is." Joyce wiggled her brows. "Girls, Frida brought this to a few teacher potlucks. I think she tired of all her hard work disappearing in a minute flat." She laughed.

"What is it?" Shelly asked as she walked up to where Joyce was standing admiring the dish.

"*Capirotada*. It's Mexican bread pudding," Frida answered. "I use Mexican vanilla to give it that authentic taste."

"I can't wait to try it." Shelly's eyes brightened and she smiled. Her mannerisms reminded Frida of Heather.

Half an hour later, everyone was seated around Heather's large dining table. Frida suspected it got little use now that Shelly was off at college, and it was just Heather and the boys at home. They took turns saying what they were thankful for. Frida didn't miss Heather's wince when Shelly gushed over her boyfriend, Travis, who was sitting next to her.

"I'm thankful for every one of you," Frida said when it was her turn. "You were the blessings I didn't know I needed." Frida looked at each person lingering on Heather and Marin.

Marin smiled and angled her head. "I feel the same." She glanced at her lap and softly gasped. Frida realized Marin had her phone in her hand. She'd get with Marin after dinner to make sure she was okay.

Frida, Joyce, and Heather found Marin and Shelly in the sunroom. Shelly looked up when they approached and raised her brows. Marin had her phone in her hand and from what Frida could see, she had some type of messaging app open. Marin looked up. She seemed a little pale. Maybe something from dinner didn't sit right with her.

"Are you okay, honey?" Frida asked.

"Gage wants to video chat with her. He has something important to share." Shelly looked at Marin, then at her mother and Frida.

"Why does the thought of him seeing me freak me out?"

"You didn't send him the photo we talked about?" Heather asked.

Marin looked out the window at the darkening sky and shook her head.

Frida sat next to Marin and patted her knee. "What's the worst thing that can happen?"

Marin pushed out a breath and shook her head.

"Say, for whatever reason, he doesn't like what he sees. Then what?"

Marin shrugged. "I don't hear from him again."

"Well, there ya go," Joyce said. "But if he sees anything besides a beautiful young woman, he's blind." She gave a curt nod.

"Honey, no pressure." Frida smiled. "If you aren't ready, then you aren't ready, but what do you have to lose? I know you're fond of each other, but if he can't see your heart then—"

"You don't need him." Joyce's lips twisted into a scowl, and she crossed her arms.

"I can sit off camera, if it would help you feel better," Shelly said. Heather told Frida that since Marin had rented the pool house, she and Shelly had gotten to know each other and become close. This pleased Frida since Madison moved to Mobile. Frida loved Marin's friendship, but having someone close to her age was good for her.

"I can set up some chairs on the east side of the pool and we can watch you through the blinds. You know, support you from a distance," Heather said.

A small smile found its way to Marin's lips. "Thank you for that, but I need to do this on my own. Maybe I'll send him a photo first. Or maybe I'll rip the Band-Aid off and go for it."

"I say rip the Band-Aid off," Joyce said.

"I can help with your hair and make-up." Shelly brushed her hand down Marin's hair. It had grown considerably over the past year and a half and was holding the deep red tint well.

"No," Marin said and looked at Shelly. "I want to be who I am every day; you know? A little eyeliner and run a brush through my hair and I'm done." Marin laughed.

Shelly reached over and hugged Marin. "You'll be fine. You are beautiful inside and out and if Gage can't see that—." Shelly looked at Joyce and lifted her brows.

"You don't need him." Joyce lifted her chin. "Well, girls, it's been real, but I've got to head home."

"Yeah, I should get ready myself." Frida headed to the kitchen for her empty pan.

"I'll walk you out," Marin said when Frida walked into the living room where Shelly, Heather, and Joyce gathered. Frida said goodbye to the girls, and she and Marin walked out to her car.

"What do you think Gage wants to tell you?" Frida asked when she opened the passenger door of her car and placed the pan on the seat.

"Oh, gosh. My mind is all over the place. Maybe he's leaving sooner than he thought he was? He volunteered to stay because someone needed to go home. He stayed instead of someone having to come early. I don't know how all that works." Marin laughed. "But my fear is that he'll want to come here."

"Why does that scare you?"

"Tootles, girls. Have a good night," Joyce said when she walked outside. Frida and Marin waved and watched Joyce drive away in her yellow Beetle.

"It's silly, right?" Marin sighed.

"You have a right to your feelings, but the likelihood of Gage running the opposite direction is slim to none, honey," Frida said. "You've made such progress. You said your therapist said so as well. But, honestly, honey, if you have decided to focus on yourself and not be in a relationship, what is the harm?"

Marin bit her bottom lip. "I don't know. Maybe him seeing me will…" She groaned.

Frida tilted her head. "Spark something in you?"

"Maybe." Marin laughed. "That seems to be my new favorite word."

"The world is full of maybes."

Marin gazed up at the evening sky, then looked at Frida. "I'm so glad God brought you into my life. What if I hadn't gone to the craft store that day?"

"You did. *We* did." Frida patted Marin's arm. "Think about it. What are the odds that all three of us go to the same store on the same day around the same time? Only God can do that."

"I never said anything, but I remember seeing Heather when I was heading to the register."

"Really?"

"I stepped out of the aisle in front of her cart and said, 'excuse me' and she gave me a nasty look. Maybe it was partly the way I looked, but I think it was mostly because Adam had left."

"You see, this is why we should always give people grace. You never know what they are dealing with."

"So true. Okay, well, keep me in your prayers."

"Always." Frida grinned when Marin looked her way. Marin pulled Frida into a hug and went back to the house. Frida climbed into the car and backed out of the driveway. Before pulling away, she looked at the house and thought about the people inside. She loved them as if they were her blood.

"Thank you, Lord, for bringing those girls into my life."

Chapter 36

Marin

The frigid early December air surrounded Marin as she made her way to the pool house. Inside, she kicked off her shoes and flopped down on the couch. She'd just bombed her college algebra final; she was sure of it. The entire test looked as if it was written in a foreign language. The instructor had told the class on the first day that math was a language. Marin thought it looked like some ancient obscure language from biblical times.

Her phone rang and she dug around in her backpack, trying to find it. Somehow it made it to the bottom. Groaning, she pulled it out and raised her brows at *Unavailable Number* on the screen. If she wanted to catch it before the call went to voicemail, she had about two seconds. Drawing in a deep breath, she held it a moment before answering.

"Hello?" Marin waited for the usual pause.

"Hey," Gage said, a smile evident in his voice.

Relief flooded her veins. She'd written an email trying to explain why she felt the way she did about video chatting, but she finally admitted to herself that she didn't know why and deleted the email. But what Frida said a few evenings ago made sense. Marin was working on herself and there was no reason for her to be so anxious about Gage seeing her.

"Hey, yourself. How are you? I'm, I'm sorry I haven't written more. I was studying for my final that was today."

"Oh, how did you do?"

"I think I bombed it." She laughed.

"Ah, I bet you did better than you think you did. How soon will you know? Graduation is next Saturday, right?"

"Yeah. The instructor said by the end of the week."

"So, my return date was moved up."

The air left Marin's lungs.

"That's what I wanted to tell you. I'm flying out of Iraq on your graduation day—December ninth. It will take about five days to travel."

"What? Really? It takes that long to get home?"

"With the flight times and time changes, it can get drawn out. As soon as I sign in at my unit, I'll start my leave and head to Montana."

Marin softly cleared her throat. "I bet your mom can't wait to see you."

"Yeah, she's glad I'll be home for Christmas."

"I can imagine."

An awkward silence rose between them.

"Marin." Gage exhaled softly. "I understand why you feel the way you do about video chatting."

"You do?" Marin didn't understand it herself. How could Gage?

"I didn't say I like it." He laughed. "I understand it. You've been through so much. So many things in your life were out of your hands. You need something to hold on to and this happens to be it."

In a different way, Barb said the same thing. Marin wanted to show herself to him, to see his facial expressions in real-time. Didn't he deserve the same from her? Barb also suggested Marin take baby steps. Heather said for Marin to send Gage a profile shot or half of her face.

"Well, I should get going." Gage's voice interrupted Marin's thoughts. "I only have a few minutes and wanted to hear your voice."

"Okay." An idea sprang to life before the end of the call, but Marin kept it to herself. "It was nice talking with you."

"You, too, and you passed your algebra final. God told me so."

"Oh, yeah?" Marin laughed.

"Yeah." Gage sighed. "Talk soon?"

"Of course."

"Bye, Marin."

"Bye, Gage."

As soon as they ended the call, Marin ran to the bathroom and brushed out her hair. She took over a dozen selfies with various hairstyles and settled on leaving her hair down. After cropping the image to where only half of her face was visible, she opened the email app on her phone and attached the photo. She thought of a few clever things to say but settled on the image only and hit the send button. Now she waited.

Marin checked her email at least two dozen times between the time she'd sent Gage the photo and the two hours before she had to leave for work. Nothing. He was repulsed by her and didn't know how to tell her. She shook the intrusive thought from her head as she pulled into a parking space at Charley's Steakhouse. For once she was thankful for a full parking lot, as she wouldn't have time to obsess over why Gage ghosted her. Was not hearing from someone for two hours considered ghosting?

Inside, Marin clocked in and slipped her phone in her backpack and shoved the backpack in her locker, closing the door. She opened the locker door but closed it again, stopping herself from checking the phone one last time.

"Lord, why do I have to carry this cross?" she whispered to herself as she headed to the dining room to make her rounds. Marin reminded herself that Jesus had already carried her cross, and she needed to put this burden down she'd heaped onto herself. Easier said than done. Marin sighed.

As she approached the bar, she noticed a customer watching her. The man looked vaguely familiar. Probably a regular. As she passed him, he turned on the bar stool, watching her. The hairs on her arms raised.

"Marin?" he said.

She stopped and turned to face him. "Yes, sir?"

He grinned, raising Marin's pulse. "It's Chris."

Chris?

"Stella's fiancé."

"Oh, my goodness. I'm sorry." She managed a half-smile.

"It's okay. We only met once." He glanced back at the bartender, who walked to the other end of the bar as if he'd read Chris's mind. "Can we talk?"

"Sure." An array of thoughts began assaulting Marin. Stella sent Chris to try to get on her good side. What kind of man would go along with that? The bar wasn't busy yet, so Marin walked with Chris to the opposite end.

"I'm sorry for coming here like this. Stella doesn't know I'm here."

Marin arched her brow. What was Chris up to?

"She told me about the letter she wrote a few weeks ago. And," he looked around, "she's told me some about how she has treated you."

Marin had forgotten about the letter. It was probably crumpled up in the bottom of her backpack. Her pulse quickened when she remembered what Stella asked in the letter.

"We met at a grief support group my church sponsors for people who've lost siblings."

Marin angled her head. Stella grieved the loss of Gemma? Marin found it hard to believe Stella could grieve anyone, much less the person she'd claimed had caused so many problems in her life.

The sting of conviction pricked Marin's heart. Conflicting thoughts assaulted her from every angle. She'd held such contempt for Stella over the years, yet Stella was a child of God like herself.

"Will you go to a therapy appointment with her? I think it would help her heal."

Marin opened her mouth but held her tongue when Chris spoke again.

"I know I don't have the right to ask. Just know that she is trying to work through everything and be a better person. She feels God is leading her to make things right with you."

A gentle urging filled Marin's heart. Maybe this was what they both needed to fully heal. Stella had her own struggles because of Gemma. Stella was five years younger than Gemma and Marin imagined she'd disappeared into the background by no fault of her own. Why hadn't Marin thought of it before? Stella was just eleven years old when Gemma disappeared.

"I'll call her."

Chris smiled. "Thank you."

Marin nodded.

He patted her arm. "I can only imagine how hard this is. With the Lord, you can overcome anything."

"He's the only way." Marin noticed the sous chef flailing his arms in the background, and she grimaced. "I'm sorry. I think I'm being paged." She laughed.

"No problem. See ya around."

Marin smiled and headed to the kitchen. The Lord was the only way she would make it through her shift with thoughts of hashing out past hurt and anger with Stella following her around.

THE KNITTING CLUB

The cool night air was a welcomed change from the oppressive heat of the kitchen of Charley's Steakhouse. Marin slid behind the wheel of her car and said a prayer as she made her way home. It was well past midnight, which was typical for a Friday night, but tonight she was more exhausted than usual. The visit from Chris added to her usual stress. That along with —

Marin gasped. She'd forgotten all about sending Gage the photo. Reaching for her backpack in the passenger seat, the car drifted to the right as she leaned over. The right front tire dropped off the side of the road and Marin jerked the steering wheel to the left, causing the car to fishtail.

"Please, God." The car righted itself and Marin gripped the steering wheel tightly with both hands, causing her knuckles to burn. Her heart beat so hard she thought it was going to tear out of her chest. Her hands stayed on the steering wheel—except for using the turn signal—until she shifted into park at home.

Exercising a bit of control, she waited until she was inside before tearing her backpack open and pulling everything out to get to her phone at the bottom. It had settled on top of the wrinkled letter from Stella. Tapping the screen, she saw an email notification from Gage. She gulped and tapped on the notification, watching the email open on the screen. She took a deep breath and held it as she read.

Wow, what a beautiful sight to wake up to. You said your eyes are green, but I wasn't prepared for just how green. And the color complements your beautiful red hair. I can see a hint of a smile. The little gold hoop completes the picture. Well, almost. Haha.

Marin grinned and ran her finger over the hoop in her nostril. She noticed the timestamp on the email. Gage must have gone to bed as soon as he got back to the barracks. Sometimes she'd forget about the time difference. Soon, they wouldn't have to worry about that.

"Wait, what time zone is Montana?" Marin did a quick search. Gage would be an hour behind once he was back home. She returned to the email.

Thank you for trusting me.

Tears gathered in Marin's eyes and spilled down her cheeks. It was a big step for her, especially since she hadn't met Gage in person. Was she being naïve? Shaking her head, Marin realized she had to step out in faith, eventually. It was what people did. She corrected herself. It was what healthy people did using healthy boundaries. And she was on her way to being healthy.

I care a great deal for you, Marin. If you want to be friends, then we'll be friends. If you're okay with exploring more, I am on your timeline. Whatever we are (friends or more) started with us being in different countries. Long distance relationships are HARD. My cousin met his wife online, and we have talked a lot about long distance relationships with me being in the military.

All I wanted to do was thank the woman who made my scarf. If you were 80, I'd still want to thank you.

Marin smiled. At their last knitting get together, Frida told Marin that God used all kinds of ways to bring people together. Joyce had added that He'd brought them together through knitting, and He'd also brought Marin and Gage together through knitting. Joyce guessed God was a huge fan of knitting. Marin and Heather had laughed, and Frida had narrowed her eyes at Joyce.

God was not new to Marin, but having a personal relationship with Him was. She was still learning about faith. Fear tried its best to steal the faith she'd gained. Why did stepping out in faith sometimes feel like stepping out into rush hour traffic?

Chapter 37

Heather

To someone on the outside looking in, they looked like a normal family. Until bedtime came and Adam would sleep in Shelly's bed. She'd be driving in from school the following day for Christmas break, which left her bed unoccupied for the night. It was better than Adam sleeping on the couch.

Heather put fresh sheets on the bed in Shelly's room and ran a dusting cloth over the surfaces. She turned around to head out of the room and gasped when she saw Ethan standing in the doorway.

"You're really okay with this?" he asked.

"Yes, honey. It's one night."

Ethan rubbed the back of his neck. When Adam picked Jake up earlier, he'd asked Heather if it would be okay for him to spend time with Jake at the house. Amber had been admitted to an inpatient treatment program for depression and complicated grief. There was a situation that'd led to her involuntary committal, and Adam had said he'd rather not be at the apartment. Heather hadn't asked for clarification, and he didn't offer an explanation. She could only guess that it meant the apartment wasn't ready for Jake.

Six months earlier, Heather would have asked Adam if he were crazy, but she'd grown since then. Therapy had been a turning point in her healing process. She still gently urged Ethan to interact with Adam. He'd said half a dozen words since the night he'd offered Adam his condolences. But he no longer disappeared when Adam was due to pick up or drop off Jake. It was progress.

Jake's sweet laugh drifted up the stairs, bringing a smile to Heather's face. Ethan looked as if he would roll his eyes, but he didn't. To Heather's surprise, he took the dusting cloth from her hand and went to his room. What was going on in that child's head?

Adam and Jake were sitting on the couch with a large bowl of popcorn between them. Adam looked up and smiled.

"I've got Shelly's bed made up for you."

"Thank you."

Heather nodded.

Jake gasped and looked at Adam. "You're spending the night?"

"Yeah. I've got some repairs going on at my apartment."

"Where's Amber?" Jake asked.

Adam's lips parted and he looked up at Heather, standing not far away.

"Jake, honey, Amber isn't feeling well and she's at the doctors," Heather said.

"Oh," Jake said. "I'll ask Jesus to help her."

Adam seemed to sink into the couch.

"That's a good idea, Jake," Heather said. "Why don't you take your bath before the movie?"

"Okay, Mommy."

Heather smiled at Adam and headed to the kitchen. A few moments later, she stood at the sink washing the cookware and heard someone come up behind her.

"Thanks," Adam said.

Heather turned around. "Of course. Jake in the tub?"

Adam nodded.

Ethan walked into the kitchen and up to where Adam and Heather were standing. For a moment, it was as if she'd gone back in time to the day when Adam told her he was leaving, and Ethan walked in to witness everything.

"Dad, is Amber okay?"

Heather looked at Adam and angled her head. This was Adam's story to tell. Heather didn't know exactly what happened, anyway.

Adam studied Ethan for a couple of seconds. "You're seventeen now and I'm sure you've heard of things like this." He looked at Heather, then back at Ethan. "Amber has struggled with losing the baby and got really depressed and she started having dark thoughts. She's now getting the help she needs."

Ethan's eyes widened and he looked at Heather. "Dad, I'm so sorry. What is going to happen now? Are you staying with her?"

"Ethan." Heather pressed her lips together.

"No, it's okay, Heather. I'm sure this is very confusing. I love Amber, son. This doesn't change that. I'm standing behind her and encouraging her to get the help she needs. I've started going to therapy myself."

"You have?" Heather rested her hand on her upper chest.

"Yes. I've had two appointments. I think it's going to be good for me. Help me work through a lot of things."

"Like why you cheated on Mom?" Ethan set his jaw.

Heather opened her mouth but closed it when Adam held up his hand.

"Among other things." Adam cleared his throat.

"I-I'm glad to hear that. Mom is doing much better since she started going."

"That's good to hear." Adam lifted his brows at Heather.

"Hi guys!" Jake said when he ran into the kitchen. Heather noticed a few drops of water fall from his wet hair to the floor.

"Let's go dry your hair, buddy," Adam said and directed Jake out of the kitchen.

Ethan leaned against the counter and looked at Heather.

"What?"

"How do you do it? Most women wouldn't let their adulterous ex-husbands sleep under the same roof."

"God." Heather smiled. "He's the only way. We need to keep Amber in our prayers. I didn't know it was this bad. I don't know what it's like to lose a baby, but I know her life will never be the same. And your dad? Unfortunately, men are often in the background with pregnancy loss."

Ethan nodded. "Are you going to watch the movie with them?" Ethan tilted his head towards the living room.

"No, I've got a knitting project to finish before Christmas." Heather smiled. "Good night."

"Good night, Mom."

Heather watched Ethan get a large plastic bowl from the cabinet and head to the living room. "Don't make a big deal out of it, Heather," she whispered.

"Good night, Mommy," Jake said when Heather walked into the living room.

Heather kissed the top of his head and looked at Adam. "Good night."

"Good night," Adam said.

Ethan reached across his father and grabbed a handful of popcorn and dropped it into his bowl. On the way upstairs, Heather prayed watching a movie with Adam and Jake would be the start of something new between Ethan and his father.

The smell of bacon roused Heather. Her gaze fell to the chair in the corner where the dark green sweater she'd finished late the night before was neatly folded on the seat. The color would go fabulous with Marin's hair. A yawn watered her eyes. She needed to get the sweater wrapped and put under the Christmas tree.

Once dressed, she made her way downstairs to the kitchen where Adam was making pancakes and bacon. In their nearly twenty-year marriage, Adam had never cooked—or helped with, for that matter—their traditional Sunday morning brunch. It was odd seeing him flipping pancakes.

"When's Shell due in?"

"Late afternoon." Heather glanced at the stove clock. She had an hour until she needed to leave for church.

"Mommy, is Daddy going to church with us?" Jake asked.

Heather caught herself before she could choke on her coffee. She hadn't thought about Adam going to church with them. The first thought that came to mind should have been the last thing she thought of: she didn't want Adam going to church with them. That was bad, right? She should want to welcome Adam to church. But not to *her* church. There were hundreds of churches in south Mississippi he could attend.

"No, buddy. I've got to get back to the apartment. There's lots to do before work tomorrow."

"Oh." Jake stabbed several pieces of pancake, making a stack, and shoved the stack in his mouth. Heather winced and watched Jake closely until he chewed and swallowed the food.

"One piece at a time, Jacob," she said.

Jake sighed and put the last piece of pancake in his mouth. After chugging the rest of his milk, he scampered off, declaring he was brushing his teeth and getting dressed. She'd need to check on him before she got ready to make sure he was not playing with his Monty the Monster Truck.

"Don't worry. If I go to church, it wouldn't be where you and the kids go," Adam said, as he placed a plate of pancakes and bacon in front of her. "Does this meet with your approval?" He laughed when she looked up at him.

"It'll do." She grinned and picked up the plate, along with a cup of coffee Adam poured for her and walked over to the kitchen table. As she settled on the chair, she thought it was a sort of weird to be waited on by her ex-husband. She grimaced when the next thought came at her. What did the neighbors think about seeing his car in her driveway this morning? She pushed the thought aside. It didn't matter what the neighbors thought.

Adam joined Heather and the two sat eating in comfortable silence for a few minutes. She studied him as he gazed out the kitchen window. She'd fallen head over heels for this man when he walked into the room on the first day of economics class. Never would she have fathomed just shy of their twentieth wedding anniversary, Adam Zimmerman would rip out her heart and stomp on it.

"Do I have something on my face?" Adam asked, bringing Heather out of the past and to her current circumstances. Grabbing a napkin from the holder in the center of the table, he wiped his mouth and raised his brows at Heather.

"What happened to us?" Her question surprised them both. It wasn't the first time she'd asked the question of herself. It had been with her since the day Adam walked out, following her everywhere she went—even into her dreams. Was there something she did or said that caused Adam's feelings for her to change?

Adam's lips parted and he pushed out a breath. Balling up the napkin in his hand, he held on to it as if was a life preserver.

Jake squealed, and Ethan laughed. A moment later, Ethan yelled from the top of the stairs, "Jake's okay. He wanted me to put shaving cream on him."

"It's cold Mommy." Jake giggled.

Heather's heart squeezed tight. "Was it Jake?" she said, barely able to hear her own words.

"No." The answer came quickly. "I..." Adam sighed. "I really don't know what it was."

Adam was in denial. Jake's conception was the turning point, but Heather was beyond exhausted of hashing it out with Adam. No amount of pointing it out would change things. They were divorced, and Adam was in love with another woman.

"As the kids' mother, I care about you."

"Same. If I didn't, you wouldn't be sitting here." She smiled when Adam looked at her. "But, I think it's best that this is a one-time thing. Jake is still young and doesn't fully understand."

"I accept that. Thanks for letting me stay."

"Sure."

Adam reached for Heather's empty plate and stacked it on top of his. She followed him to the sink with the coffee cups and made her way upstairs to tend to Jake while Adam cleaned up the kitchen. It was something she never thought she'd see. Adam wasn't one to help with housework. Too bad it took a divorce for him to change.

Joyce removed her red-framed glasses and perched them on top of her head. Holding out the hot pink scarf, she closed one eye and grimaced.

"What is it?" Heather asked.

"It's wider on one end," Joyce said. She folded the scarf in half and held it up for Heather to see. Joyce was right. The scarf was a good two inches wider at one end. "How did I do that using this thing?" She pointed to the knitting loom on her lap.

"It's asymmetrical," Frida said. "It's in style. I'm more worried about the hot pink for Perry." Frida smiled when Joyce shot her a look.

Joyce dropped the scarf to her lap. "Ah, who am I kidding? Perry didn't inherit his mother's fabulous sense of style." Joyce pointed to her green leggings printed with lighted Christmas trees and a red sweatshirt with a giant snowman on the front.

"Give it to Tiff and make Perry something else," Frida said.

"Frida Gomez. It took me six months to make this silly thing. It's hopeless. I am no knitter. Or loomer. Or knitting loomer. Or loom knitter. Or whatever you want to call me."

"And that's okay," Frida said.

Heather checked the time on her phone. Marin was a half-hour late. She'd been worried about Marin since her Aunt Stella's fiancé visited her at work recently. The poor girl was worrying herself sick about going to counseling with the woman. Heather believed Marin felt she had no choice. Hopefully Marin would get good advice from her counselor on whether she should and when. A soft knock sounded on the door.

"Come in Marin." Joyce shouted.

"How'd you know it's me?" Marin said when she walked in.

"I know your knock," Joyce said. "You look lovely, doll."

"Thanks." A light blush swept over Marin's cheeks.

Heather noticed how the way Marin dressed had changed over the past few weeks. She'd been incorporating more colors and some printed items as well. Gone were the days of black everything. Heather had to keep her mouth from falling open when she noticed the pale green eye shadow. She'd never seen Marin wearing anything besides shades of brown and black eye makeup.

"Do I have something on my face?" Marin asked. It was the second time in a week Heather had been asked the same question when caught staring at someone.

"Your eyes look gorgeous, Marin. That shade of green makes your eyes pop," Heather said.

"Thanks." Another blush swept across her cheeks.

"Does a certain gentleman have anything to do with it?"

Marin rolled her eyes at Joyce.

"You don't need to apply any blush. You've got that natural blush going." Joyce pointed to her own cheeks.

"You look beautiful, Marin."

"Thank you, Frida." Marin settled on the couch next to Heather. "And to answer your question, Joyce, this is for me, not Gage or any man."

"You go, girl," Joyce said and winked. "You truly look lovely."

"Thank you." Marin smiled at Heather when their eyes met. Heather imagined Marin in the sweater she'd knitted for her for Christmas, wearing the same makeup.

"All right. Now that Marin's joined us, we need a status update. Marin, we've got everything planned for your graduation party at Heather's next Saturday." Joyce lifted a brow at Heather and Heather nodded. "Good. Is Madison still coming in?"

"Yes, she's staying the night with me Saturday night and driving back to Mobile on Sunday," Marin said.

"Good," Joyce said. They covered the ceremony and menu.

As Heather tallied the headcount, she added Adam and shook her head.

"No?" Joyce asked.

Heather looked up and realized everyone was looking at her. "What?"

"I asked if you were still making your famous punch and you shook your head."

"Oh, I'm sorry. My mind was somewhere else."

"Care to elaborate?" Joyce asked.

"Oh." Heather shrugged. "Adam stayed at the house last weekend for his time with Jake instead of taking him to his apartment. I didn't ask, but I know it has something to do with Amber being admitted to the hospital. He stayed in Shelly's room. Anyway, I found myself asking where we went wrong."

"*He*, Heather. Where *he* went wrong," Joyce said. "We all know where."

"Sometimes the fault lies solely with one person. However, usually, both are at fault. I'm not saying that's what happened in your case," Frida said.

"I know. I asked if it was Jake and he said he didn't know what happened. But that is the marker for me. He was so angry when I ended up pregnant. And it didn't really get better between us. He loves that little boy, but..." Heather shook her head. "This isn't how it was supposed to be." Tears stung her eyes.

"Oh, honey, I'm sorry," Frida said.

Heather closed her eyes, pushing tears down her cheeks. She felt a hand on her back and opened her eyes to see Frida holding out a box of tissues. "Thanks." Heather wiped her eyes.

"It is unfortunate when life takes a different turn," Frida said as she returned to her chair.

"I just never would have imagined this."

"Did you two ever talk about it?" Joyce asked.

"About Jake?" Heather responded.

"Yeah. How did Adam feel about it? From what you've said, Adam is a type A personality. Maybe he felt all his ducks were in a row and little Jake came and knocked them all out of whack."

"We never really talked about it. Just surface level conversations."

"That's why communication is so important," Frida said.

"It doesn't help when you can't identify your thoughts," Marin said and looked up at Frida.

"That's true," Joyce added.

Was that the case with Adam? He couldn't identify his feelings, thus couldn't communicate how he felt?

"If it's something you feel you have to know, maybe talk to Adam about it. But will knowing the truth change anything?" Frida asked. "That's a rhetorical question."

"Yeah, nothing will change. He's made it clear that he's in love with Amber. And you know what? That's okay, because I no longer love him. I mean, not like a wife loves her husband. I love him as the father of my children and as a friend. Well, acquaintance."

"We know what you mean, love. You care what happens to Adam because it affects your children."

Joyce's words hit a place in Heather's heart. She would always carry some hurt for how their marriage ended, but Heather no longer harbored hatred or ill feelings for Adam for the sake of her children and her own peace.

Chapter 38

Frida

Frida looked around the pool house while Marin was in the kitchenette preparing the tea. Heather and Marin had made the pool house quite homey. If she didn't already know, she'd never guess it was a pool house. It looked like a quaint little studio apartment. The room divider Heather found was the perfect touch.

"Thanks for coming over," Marin said when she handed Frida a cup.

"You're welcome, honey. I'm happy to help switch out the buttons on your graduation dress. And I'm glad to finally see your little place."

"I like it. I love being close to Heather and the kids. And it helps that the rent is reasonable." Marin grinned and sipped her tea.

"Any updates with Gage?"

"Well, he wants to visit after the first of the year."

"And how do you feel about that?"

"Excited and terrified."

"Have you sent any more pictures?"

Marin shook her head.

"That's okay, honey." Frida patted Marin's knee. "As long as he's not pressuring you."

"He's not." Marin tucked her hair behind her ears and leaned back against the couch. "How did you know Max was the one?"

"I felt it here." Frida rested her hand over her heart. "I thought about him all the time when we weren't together. Probably when we were together, too." Frida laughed. "Have you ever liked anyone?"

"Not like this. I had a crush on Madison's high school boyfriend, but obviously he'd never give me the time of day. Don't tell her." Marin laughed.

"Your secret is safe with me." Frida smiled. "Max was the only boy I ever liked."

"Really?"

Frida nodded. "Boys weren't something I lent my time to. I was the oldest of eight children and helped my mother care for the younger ones. I had no time for boys. Until Max Gomez came to church one day." The memories of that day came flooding back, bringing tears to Frida's eyes.

"I'm sorry."

"It's okay, Marin. He was my soulmate and I get sad when I think of what could have been."

"Is that why you never remarried?"

Frida nodded. "Maria and I had this discussion. She struggled a lot with dating after Mateo died. I feel as if he was her soulmate. In her case—as with others—I feel there is more than one, but that wasn't the case for me. I never had the desire to be in another relationship."

"Why is that?"

"It wouldn't be fair. No man could live up to Maximiliano Roberto Gomez." A smile found Frida's lips when Max's face filled her thoughts.

"Why am I so scared?"

"First off, you haven't had many healthy male role models, so you don't know what to expect. You know how a man should behave. But from what I've seen, Gage checks all the boxes."

Pink filled Marin's cheeks.

"That being said, sometimes you have to take a chance. If you live in fear, life will pass you by and before you know it, you will be an old lady like me."

"You aren't that old." Marin winked. "You would have been a wonderful mother. The advice you've given me has been invaluable. So have the times you've sat quietly and let me talk and cry."

Marin's innocent words stung. No one but the doctor and the Lord knew Frida was almost a mother. Maybe it was time for her to share that fact with Marin. No, the time wasn't right. This was about Marin.

"Thank you, honey. I know we aren't blood and I'm old enough to be your grandmother, but I consider you my family." Marin smiled and hugged Frida. "Now, get me that dress."

"Yes, ma'am." Marin went behind the room divider where a wardrobe served as a closet and returned carrying a deep green, A-line dress with short sleeves. Green had become Marin's color of choice since she'd changed her hair and began wearing more colorful clothing. When Marin wore green, her eyes stood out more.

"For the life of me, I don't understand why the designer chose these plain buttons for such a beautiful dress. I think those sparkly green buttons you found on clearance at Cathy's Craft Haven will look gorgeous."

"Me too," Marin said.

Frida showed Marin how to use the seam ripper to remove the old buttons and how to sew on the new ones. She wondered if Marin's Grandma Judith ever sewed on a button or if she'd left it up to the alteration shop. Part of her thought that Marin's grandmother might have tried to teach Marin the basics of clothing maintenance, but Marin hadn't been in the right frame of mind to learn back then. By her own admission, she'd harbored a great deal of anger for her grandmother when she'd first gained custody.

A few minutes later, Marin tried on the dress for Frida. At first glance, Frida saw the timid, withdrawn young woman she'd met over a year and a half earlier. Marin had come such a long way. So had Heather, for that matter. The Lord knew what He was doing when he sent her to Cathy's that day. How different things would have been if one of them had decided not to go.

Heather sat in the seat Frida saved and puffed out her cheeks. She looked at Frida and shook her head. "Her cap kept sliding off her head. Thank goodness another girl had a pack of bobby pins. I don't know why we only had two. But she's good now."

Frida smiled and glanced down the row at those that'd come to show support for Marin. Heather and all three kids, Madison and her parents, and Stephanie and Rebecca from Charley's Steakhouse. Frida wondered if Stella would have come if she'd known.

"It's a full house," Joyce said and fanned herself with the graduation program. "Makes my heart sing."

"Mine too," Frida said. As an educator, it warmed Frida's heart to see all the support for the graduates.

"*Tia.*"

The familiar voice came from behind Frida, and she turned around. Maria, MJ, and Phillip sat two rows behind. Frida smiled and turned back around when she heard a tap on the microphone. The announcer introduced the president of the community college and, after a brief speech, the commencement began.

Three graduates in, Jake began quizzing Heather on when it was Marin's turn. Heather tried her best to get Jake to understand that Martin was in the middle of the alphabet. Finally, it was time for Marin's row to stand and make their way to the stage. Jake squealed and clapped. Heather smiled at Frida when their eyes met. The simple joy of a child.

"Kaylee Elizabeth Martin. Associates of Visual Arts," the speaker said.

Travis let out a shrill whistle, and Shelly and Madison hooted. Frida grinned at Marin when she snuck a peek at the audience as she received her diploma. Frida's heart swelled with pride for Marin's accomplishments. She couldn't wait to see what Marin achieved as she pursued her Bachelor of Arts degree starting next fall.

A hint of sadness came over Frida when she thought of Marin's mother. Without a doubt, Frida knew Gemma would have been proud of her daughter, as would have Marin's Grandma Judith. Frida considered it an honor to witness this event on their behalf.

After the ceremony, the group of family and friends stood around talking and taking pictures before heading to the reception at Heather's house. Frida watched Marin and Heather as they laughed and talked. Life had not turned out the way Frida planned, but Frida was happy with the life God had given her. She recited Jeremiah twenty-nine, verse eleven, in her head, as she'd recited many times over the years.

"'For I know the plans I have for you," declares the Lord, "plans to prosper you and not to harm you, plans to give you hope and a future.'"

He had indeed given her hope and a future. It wasn't in the way she'd imagined, but His ways were perfect, and that was what she was holding onto.

Chapter 39

Marin

Marin angled the graduation cake and smiled her best smile for Ethan as he took pictures. It had been a long time since she'd smiled this much. And it was all genuine. She was a college graduate now and downright proud of herself.

Deciding whether to enroll for her bachelor's degree in January or wait until the fall had been stressful. She'd wait until the fall so she could save money. Once classes started, she planned to cut back on her hours at work.

Gage crossed her mind. He was probably in the air now, traveling home from Iraq. He'd mentioned stopping by on his way home, but the thought terrified her. Why? She wasn't sure. Deep in her heart, she wanted nothing more than to meet him in person. They had become closer in the last week, talking on the phone most days, and several emails and instant messages throughout the day and night. She guessed it was because he was returning to the States.

"Here, doll," Joyce said and handed Marin a slice of cake.

"Thanks."

"You bet, you graduate you." Joyce laughed.

Marin smiled and shook her head. She glanced at the stack of greeting cards that held various gift cards and the new leather backpack from Heather and the kids. Frida knitted Marin the most beautiful cardigan.

It was dark brown, reminding her of chocolate, and thick and warm. She couldn't wait to wear it.

"We're going to head out, honey," Frida said.

"Bye." Marin hugged Frida, then Joyce.

"I'm so proud of you." Frida cupped Marin's cheeks.

"Thank you."

"Me too, doll. You are so bright and beautiful inside and out." Joyce squeezed Marin's arm.

"Thank you, Joyce." Marin followed the women to the front door and showed them out. She headed to the kitchen sink, but Heather cut her off.

"No, ma'am. No dishes for the guest of honor. I think Ethan said there's some mail for you on the table in the foyer."

"Okay." Marin made her way to the foyer, where she found a letter from Grandma Judith's lawyer among a few Christmas sales flyers. On the bottom was a card from Gage. He'd asked for her new address when she moved to the pool house.

She made herself comfortable on the couch in the living room and glanced at the *Monty the Monster Truck* Christmas movie Jake was watching. Pulling back the flap on the card from Gage, a smile spread across Marin's face when she opened the card and read Gage's words.

I'm so proud of you. Congratulations! Love, Gage.

Gage had to have mailed the card before she took her algebra final. Chills ran down her arms. He had full confidence that she would graduate. It was a God thing that the card arrived on her graduation day.

Putting Gage's card aside, Marin opened the envelope from the lawyer. She unfolded the letter and gasped when she saw the number of zeros on the attached check.

"Marin?" Jake asked. "You okay?"

"Um," was all Marin managed to say. She rested a shaky hand on her chest.

"Mommy!" Jake took off to the kitchen.

"What's wrong, buddy?" Heather said as she followed Jake to the living room. He pointed to Marin. "Marin, what's wrong? You look a little pale."

Marin held the letter out to Heather and took slow, deep breaths.

"Wow. Okay, so this is your half of your grandmother's estate. This amount is after expenses like the funeral were deducted and her last income taxes were filed. General upkeep of the trust. And the proceeds of the sale of her house."

Ethan walked in and stood behind Heather. "I've never seen that many zeroes before."

Heather folded the letter and gave it back to Marin. Tears filled Marin's eyes as her heart grieved. "I'd rather have Grandma Judith."

"Oh, honey." Heather sat on the couch next to Marin and slipped her arms around her shoulders. "I know how you feel. My sister and I received money from Dad's estate when he passed, and I felt the same. I'd much rather have him here than all the money in the world."

"That amount is pretty close."

"Ethan Adam Zimmerman." Heather narrowed her eyes at her eldest son.

Ethan lowered his brows and looked at Marin. "I'm sorry, Marin. I didn't mean to be insensitive. It's just... That's a large amount of money."

"It is. What am I supposed to do with it?" Marin wiped her cheeks. Jake jumped up and grabbed the tissue box next to Heather's chair and brought it to Marin. "Thanks, Jake."

Jake nodded and sat on the floor in front of the TV. Heather usually got onto him for sitting close to the TV, but Marin figured her sudden windfall took precedence.

"Stella did what she was supposed to do."

"What do you mean?"

"I figured she spent it all. But she didn't."

"Well, she could have gotten into trouble if she did."

Was that why Stella didn't squander Marin's inheritance? Fear of the law and not because it was the right thing to do. Marin still needed to let Stella know a good time for the joint therapy session. Part of her didn't want to go, but the other part wanted to allow Stella the opportunity to make things right.

"For now, I suggest putting it into the bank. Actually, you'll need to open several accounts. The federal government insures banks up to a certain amount per account and this far exceeds it. We'll go Monday if that works for you."

"Okay. I have to be at work at two."

"Ethan, can you take Jake to school on Monday so we can take care of this?"

"Sure Mom."

"Thanks, Ethan," Marin said.

"You bet, Kaylee." Ethan chuckled.

Marin rolled her eyes but couldn't help but smile at the young man she now considered a little brother.

"Coffee in the sunroom?" Heather asked.

"Yes, please."

In the kitchen, the two fixed their coffee and went to the sunroom. Marin noticed the swing moving in the slight December breeze. It was in the mid-thirties, too cold to swing out her thoughts.

"Less than two years ago, I was homeless sleeping in my car and now I can afford not to work for the next, oh, I don't know how many years that would cover."

"Life is strange sometimes."

"Hmm." Marin sipped her coffee, savoring the hint of peppermint in the creamer. "Death is so much more than dying."

"You've got that right." Heather sighed. "There's the emotional side and the business side. I thought we were going to have to take my dad's widow to court in the beginning."

"Oh, really?"

Heather nodded. "Her kids tried to talk her into contesting the will. Dad had it written up where it was divided three ways: me, Michelle, and my stepmom. Her kids said it should all go to her as his next of kin."

"Oh, wow."

"Yeah. Someone dies and the greedy people come out of the woodwork. But like you said, I would have much rather have had Dad."

"What did you do with it?"

"ESAs for the kids."

Marin raised a brow.

"Educational savings accounts."

Marin nodded.

"Have you talked to Stella?"

"No. I've been putting it off. But now that I got that check, I guess I should. It's just…"

"People change both ways. Adam was the ideal husband until he wasn't. Stella was the horrible aunt. Maybe that's changed."

Heather had a point. Marin pulled her phone from the pocket of her dress and brought up the messaging app. She scrolled until she found the last text message with Stella, which was last year.

Marin: Does next Friday afternoon work for you?

Marin hit send and placed the phone on the side table. Less than thirty seconds later, the text notification sounded. Marin picked up the phone.

Stella: Perfect. My appointment is at 3. I'll text you the address.

Before Marin finished reading, Stella sent another text.

Stella: Thank you, Marin.

"Wow, she referred to me as Marin. She hasn't done that since the funeral, and she was mocking me when she did it."

Heather lifted her brows. "All we can do is pray. It's truly in God's hands. God loves us and wants nothing but the best for us. My favorite verse is Jeremiah twenty-nine, verse eleven."

Both women began reciting the verse at the same time. Heather smiled at Marin when they finished. She reached out and slipped her hand in Marin's. "I love you like a daughter, Marin. I thank God every day for bringing you into my life."

"I love you, too." Marin gave Heather's hand a little squeeze before she released it.

"You know, I think I remember seeing you that day in Cathy's Craft Haven."

"You do? Cause I definitely remember seeing you," Marin said.

"No way." Heather laughed. "I almost plowed you down with my shopping cart, right? I was a woman on a mission. I had to find the yarn to make the other sock. In my twisted thoughts, I believed Adam would come back if I made the other sock."

"Oh, I thought you were one of those who was put off by me."

"What? Girl, no. I don't judge books by their covers. Anyway, I've always thought you were a good person. Just broken like me."

"Ain't that the truth?" Marin shook her head and laughed.

"Look at us now, huh?"

"Yep. We've both come a long way. In our everyday life and our faith."

"They go hand in hand. Can't have one without the other."

Marin drank down the last of her coffee and grimaced at the lukewarm temperature.

"What about Gage?"

Marin laughed. "You and Frida."

"We love you and care about you."

"I know. He's probably somewhere in the air now. He was scheduled to leave Iraq today. He wants to meet after the first of the year. We haven't decided on a date yet. He has leave time with his family, then he has to report back to the base in Texas. Fort Hood."

"He's making it a career?"

"That's what he said."

"Send him another picture?"

"No, maybe I'll send him one Ethan took. They turned out pretty good. I hate feeling this way. I keep asking myself silly questions."

"Like?"

"What if he doesn't like what he sees?"

"What if he falls head over heels in love with what he sees?"

"You're not helping." Marin rolled her eyes.

Heather laughed. "He's already fallen in love with your heart. I don't think he cares what you look like. Although I'm sure he likes what he's seen so far."

"I don't want to get involved until I'm out of school."

"Those two years will fly by. Trust me. What kind of job do you want?"

"I don't know. Maybe teaching art?" Marin fought a yawn. Glancing at her phone, her eyes widened. It was after ten. No wonder she was exhausted. "I think I'm going to turn in for the night."

"Okay. See you for church?"

Marin nodded. She'd gone to church with Heather and the kids for the past three Sundays and enjoyed herself. Shelly encouraged her to join the college Bible study group, but Marin hadn't done so. Maybe she'd talk to someone about it tomorrow. Now she would go home, get ready for bed, and lay awake most of the night, stressing about seeing Stella.

It was thirty-nine degrees according to the weather app on Marin's phone, but her damp shirt clung to her underarms. She blasted the air conditioning for a moment before getting out of her car. Walking through the parking lot, Marin glanced at the cars. She did not know if Stella drove the same car. Maybe she used some of her share of the inheritance to buy a big new SUV. Marin noted the white Cadillac Escalade parked in the front parking spot of the building. It looked as if it'd just been driven off the showroom floor.

Stella stood when Marin walked inside. Her curly black hair bounced with her movements. There was a couple sitting in the corner, but they seemed occupied by something on the man's phone. Stella walked up to Marin and flashed a half-smile.

"Thank you for coming."

"Sure."

Stella's gaze drifted over Marin. "You look—different."

"It was time for a change." Marin forced a smile. Any lingering hatred she had for Stella dissipated. The woman standing before her looked more like a frightened little girl than a grown woman.

A tall black woman dressed in gray slacks and a white button-down shirt walked into the waiting room. "Stella?"

Stella smiled and gestured to Marin. "This is my niece, Kaylee. She goes by Marin."

The woman offered her hand. "Hi Marin. I'm Tonya. It's a pleasure to meet you."

"You, too." Marin followed Tonya and Stella down the hall.

The office was set up similar to Barb's office, with a floral print armchair and a brown leather sofa. Marin assumed the armchair was for Tonya and she and Stella would share the tiny sofa. Basically, sitting on top of each other. It wasn't true. At least one person would fit between them.

One. Two. Three. Four. Five. I can do this. Lord, guide my words.

Tonya got straight to the point. "Stella has been struggling with being able to move forward in her life after her mother's death. And through therapy, we believe it is because of lingering guilt over you and your mother."

Marin glanced at Stella, who was sitting closest to Tonya. Stella was studying her newly manicured nails. Marin realized Stella was doing the finger breathing exercise Marin herself learned in therapy. Slowly trace each finger in a five count move. The goal was for anxiety to subside by the time the last finger was traced. Stella was counting too fast to calm down.

"Okay," Marin said and looked from Stella's hands to Tonya. Marin noticed a tear fall from Stella's cheek.

"I'm sorry," Stella said, glancing in Marin's direction. More tears fell from her cheeks, and she gasped.

An uncomfortable sensation settled in Marin's stomach. Part of her wanted to hug Stella and tell her it was okay and part of her wanted to get up and walk out of the room. Instead, Marin sat quietly, glancing between Stella and Tonya. There had to be more to the apology than a simple 'I'm sorry.'"

"I was eleven when Gemma met Kevin. Even at that young age, I knew he was bad news. Mama and Daddy forbade her from seeing him, but she began sneaking out. Sometimes she'd sneak him in the house in the middle of the night."

Marin knew this much from what her grandmother had told her.

"Daddy caught him in her room one time and called the law. He ran before they got there, but he'd left the drugs behind. They had their suspicions that Gemma was on drugs. She had this look about her. She giggled all the time and looked spaced out."

Marin softly cleared her throat.

"I'm sorry," Stella said and looked directly at Marin. "I know she was your mother. I don't mean to talk ill about it. It's all true, though."

"It's okay. Grandma told me some things. I knew she was on drugs and was obviously sleeping with him. That's how I got here."

"Yeah." Stella looked at Tonya and glanced at Marin. "Mama bringing you home brought up all the memories from the past. After Gemma left, they spent an absurd amount of time and money looking for her. And you, of course. She announced she was pregnant and was gone within two weeks. Two years later, Daddy was gone. Mama said he died of a broken heart. He'd lost his beloved daughter and never got to meet his grandchild." Stella cleared her throat.

"I always felt as if I was invisible," Stella said. Marin looked Stella in the eyes. This time, Stella didn't turn away. "Everything was about Gemma. Did you know Mama missed my high school graduation?"

"No."

"She got a call from her private investigator the day before letting her know that his contact reported seeing Gemma in Salt Lake City. Mama caught the first flight out to Utah to see if she could find Gemma. Aunt Linda, that's Mama's sister. She died before you came home. Anyway, she took Mama's place at my graduation. She was going to come anyway, but..." Fresh tears rolled down Stella's cheeks. "The sad part? It wasn't Gemma."

"Stella—"

Stella lifted her hand. "It's okay, Marin. Now, as a grown woman and with the help of therapy, I know you are innocent in all this. Like me." Stella adjusted in her seat so that she was facing Marin. "Do you remember her? Gemma?"

The memories Marin had were not pretty. Was Stella in the frame of mind to know what kind of person her sister was? What kind of mother?

"What was your childhood like? Mama said little about it. Maybe she didn't know."

Marin's lips parted. Did she want to open this can of worms? Marin turned to face Stella and leaned back against the arm of the couch. "Stella, Gemma and Kevin were hardcore drug addicts. They both died of an overdose in front of me."

"Oh, wow." Stella rested her hand on her chest.

"I thought they were asleep, but neither one would wake up. I found someone in the other room, and they got me out of the crack house and to a nearby homeless camp where we were staying. I never saw Gemma and Kevin again. I don't know what happened to them—their bodies—after that."

"How old were you?" Stella tucked a curl behind her ear.

"Ten."

"You said you went to a homeless camp," Tonya said.

Marin nodded and talked about the woman who'd helped her and ultimately directed her to a police officer. Should she tell Stella about the abusive foster parents? Or how angry she was at Grandma Judith for taking her away from the foster family that was going to adopt her?

"I need to say something, Stella," Marin said.

"Okay." Stella looked at Tonya and back at Marin.

"I understand where your feelings came from when I first came to live with Grandma. What I can't understand is how you kicked me out of Grandma's house when she died. Did you know I had to sleep in my car? Did you even care?" Tears blurred Marin's vision. She swiped angrily at her cheeks as the tears fell. Tonya handed her a box of tissues.

"I'm, I'm so sorry. I have no excuse. I was hurting and lashed out. I hope you can forgive me one day."

"Lashed out? I was almost assaulted because I had nowhere else to stay." Marin shot to her feet.

Stella grabbed Marin's hand and tugged. "Please don't leave. I'm so sorry." She tugged on Marin's hand again. "If I could go back, I wouldn't have sold Mama's house. At least not that soon."

Marin relented and sat down, leaving more space between them. She closed her eyes and silently prayed. "Father, please give me strength. I know I'm here for a reason. Please show me."

"I have something for you," Stella said.

Marin opened her eyes and saw Stella pull something out of her purse. She held her hand over Marin's hand and dropped a key.

"It's a storage unit. All of your things from the house and some of Mama's things. Oh, there's some of Gemma's things in there, too. I thought you'd like to see. Everything in that unit is yours if you want it. Your stuff, of course, but you can take anything else. The rent is paid through the end of next year."

"You didn't throw my things away?"

"No, Marin. I'm not that heartless. I should have told you about the storage unit before now. I didn't know how to find you until I saw you that night at the steakhouse."

Heat filled Marin's stomach and traveled to her chest. Stella had Marin's things all along? Why didn't she try to find Marin? Why did she suddenly care?

"You had my number."

Stella looked at Tonya and down at her hands resting in her lap. She twisted her engagement ring and nodded. "You're right and I'm sorry."

Marin noticed Tonya smile at Stella. She recognized it as an acknowledgement of progress. Barb had given Marin the same look a time or two. She watched Stella's mannerisms for a moment. From her own healing journey, Marin learned how her childhood had impacted her as an adult. It was no different for Stella. Stella, in a sense, seemed stunted. At thirty-two, she acted younger than Marin.

The road to forgiving Stella was quite lengthy, and God was the only way Marin could make the journey.

Chapter 40

Marin

Marin's phone rang as she was unlocking the door. She grabbed the phone from the side pocket of her new backpack and grinned when she saw the number Gage had given her on the screen. It meant one thing. He was now stateside.

"Hi."

"Hello, college graduate," Gage said. He sounded exhausted.

"Where are you?"

"Just flew into Baltimore. I'm getting ready to be bussed to the hotel for the night and will fly out in the morning to sign in to my base. I should be home by the end of the week."

"I bet you can't wait."

"You are correct." He laughed.

"Thank you for the graduation card and e-gift card."

"You are very welcome. I hope you can get some good supplies for the fall term."

"Oh, that's for school?"

"Well, with it being Amazon, you can get whatever your heart desires."

"Art supplies."

"That's my girl." Gage chuckled. "How'd it go with Stella?"

Marin let out a little laugh.

"That bad?"

"It was okay. We talked about some things. She's obviously struggling. She was eleven when Gemma left."

"That's the right age to catch on, but too young to do anything about it."

Gage had a way of putting things into perspective. "Yes, and I'm trying to keep that in mind when dealing with her."

"Are you talking regularly?"

Marin laughed. "She just texted about the storage unit. I don't know when I'll go check it out. If it was just my things, I'd have already been, but with my mother's things."

"I get it. Maybe I can go with you when I come for a visit."

Heat filled Marin's stomach. She wanted to see him in person, but was she ready? Butterflies and bees sprang to life in her stomach, fighting against each other.

"Hello?"

"I'm here," Marin grimaced. "When do you think that would be?"

"Oh, gosh, probably not until the spring."

Marin was met with a mix of relief and disappointment.

"I had to give up my apartment for the deployment and put my stuff into storage. I need to find a new place and get settled." A muffled sound came through the phone and Marin heard voices. "Sorry, we're loading in the shuttle to go to the hotel."

"There are others with you?"

"Yeah, about ten of us. By the way, am I going to see you before I see you?"

Marin knew what Gage was hinting at. For the first time, the thought didn't send her anxiety through the roof. "Maybe."

"I hate to, but I need to let you go. I've got to drag my bags."

"Army talk?"

He laughed. "Yeah. I'll call when I get settled."

"Okay."

"Talk soon. God bless."

"God bless." Marin waited for Gage to hang up first. She missed him already. Checking the time, she had a few minutes to change clothes and meet Heather to ride to Frida's for their last knitting get together before Christmas.

In Heather's Suburban, Marin settled into the seat and thought about Frida. This time last year, Marin was sketching Oscar for a special present. This Christmas, she was working on something more special. She opened the album on her phone and found the picture she'd taken of Frida and Max's wedding photo that was displayed on Frida's mantle. Hopefully, she could do it justice. As a backup, she'd started on a prayer shawl for Frida.

"Gage is on American soil now," Marin said.

"That's awesome. I know you're getting excited. Do you have plans to meet in person?"

"He said in the spring. He has thirty days leave with his family, then he has to go back to Texas and find an apartment."

"Ah, the things us civilians don't think about."

"Yeah." Marin looked out the window as they drove.

"Have you two video chatted yet?"

"No. I'm kind of having a hard time crossing that line. It's a silly line, I know."

"Not to you."

"No, I guess not. I've learned a lot about myself from Barb."

"She's good at what she does. She's helped me out so much."

"Me too. My therapy has helped me understand Stella. I keep telling myself that she was only eleven when all this happened. I was ten when my parents died, and I know how that affected me."

Marin's thoughts went back to the therapy session with Stella. Some might think not having a parent at a high school graduation was trivial because of the circumstances, but to an eighteen-year-old who'd been living in the shadow of her big sister's disappearance, it would have meant the world.

Joyce opened the door as Marin and Heather walked onto the porch. She wore a green sweatshirt with what looked like a homemade snow globe filled with little pom-pom snowmen attached to the front.

"Grandkids?" Heather asked, pointing at Joyce's shirt.

"How'd you guess?" Joyce laughed.

"It's cute," Marin said. "Very creative. And earrings to match." Marin pointed to the pom-pom snowmen dangling from Joyce's ears. Marin hugged Frida and took her usual seat on the couch. Oscar sprang onto the couch and stretched out between Marin and Heather.

"What are you working on, honey?" Frida asked Marin.

Marin snuck a glance at the wedding photo on the mantle and pulled out a cowl she'd been working on. "For Shelly."

"That's lovely."

"Heather picked out the color."

"Are you knitting your young man another scarf for Christmas?" Joyce asked.

"No, I got him a gift certificate from his favorite Christian bookstore."

"Oh, I bet he'll like that. Have you done the video thing yet?"

"No."

"No? Why on earth not?" Joyce angled her head.

"I don't know. It's kind of like yanking off a Band-Aid. You know it's going to be uncomfortable for a second, then everything will be okay."

"Here." Joyce reached out her hand. "Give me your phone. I'll yank the Band-Aid off for you."

Marin's mouth hung open and her heartbeat doubled. She looked at Heather and Frida and was met with smiles and raised brows. Even Oscar smiled at her when she looked at him.

"He's probably sleeping. He had an overnight flight and I'm sure he didn't get much sleep on the plane."

"No more excuses," Joyce said, still holding out her hand.

Marin's breathing slowed, and nausea bubbled in her throat. Should she? As if her hand belonged to someone else, she watched it reach into her knitting bag, pull out her phone and hand it to Joyce. Was this really happening?

Joyce scrolled through Marin's contacts and showed her the screen where Gage's name was displayed. After Marin nodded, Joyce tapped on the FaceTime icon and waited. Marin broke out in a cold sweat and trembled. Oscar raised up and rested a paw on her thigh.

"I can hang up," Joyce said after the second ring.

Marin shook her head. It was now or never. Tugging at the neckline of her sweater, she struggled to catch her breath.

"Hey, you," Gage's voice came through the phone.

"Hello yourself," Joyce responded. "I'm ripping the Band-Aid off for Marin."

Marin let a giggle slip, ridding herself of a trace of anxiety. Her eyes widened when Joyce handed her the phone. Gage was sitting up in bed, leaning against several pillows.

"Hi," Marin said and held her hand over her mouth. She stood and walked into the kitchen. When she turned around to lean against a cabinet, she saw Oscar sitting not far away, swishing his tail behind him. Her little furry protector followed her.

"Are you okay?" Gage sat up straight. "I don't want you to feel pressured."

"No, I'm fine. I'm glad Joyce called you." A swarm of butterflies battered her stomach.

"Was the thought of FaceTiming me that bad?" He tilted his head and grinned.

"No, it was a hurdle that I'm glad I'm finally over." Marin wiped her damp palm on her pants.

"You have a beautiful smile." He held his hand over his mouth as he yawned.

"Thanks." Marin's cheeks warmed. She caught sight of the Bible on the nightstand. Frida would point out the well-worn edges. She'd said a man with a worn Bible was a good sign. "You look exhausted. I'll let you go."

"Any other time, I'd protest, but you're right. I'm exhausted. I'll call when I get in."

"Okay. Good night."

"Good night, Marin."

Marin made her way back to the living room, where the only sound was Oscar's soft purring. The eavesdropping women watched her take her seat on the couch. All three wore wide grins. Marin couldn't blame them.

"How's it feel now that the Band-Aid is gone?" Joyce asked.

"Good," Marin said, heat filling her cheeks. "And a little scary."

"Boundaries are okay," Frida said.

"I'm boundary number one," Joyce said, pointing to herself, "and they are boundary numbers two and three." She laughed. "Kidding aside, he seems like a nice young man. All three of us have been where you are. We know how new love feels."

Marin swallowed hard.

"If that's what it is for you. You may never go beyond friends, and that's okay," Joyce added.

Marin wasn't sure what it was, but she knew her feelings went beyond friendship. She believed Gage felt the same. She was twenty-one, getting ready to get her bachelor's degree. There was no reason to rush into anything. God held them in His hands and would guide their steps.

Christmas had come and gone and now they were less than twenty-four hours from the new year. The pencil drawing of Frida and Max turned out perfectly, which surprised Marin. Artists were notorious for being hypercritical of their work. Frida also enjoyed her new prayer shawl and wore it frequently. Everyone else on her Christmas list was enjoying some sort of knitted item or drawing. Marin made Heather a necklace as she was dipping her toe into the world of jewelry making.

Marin and Gage had been video chatting every day since the last knitting get together. He had a few days until he was due back in Texas. He'd found an apartment and had a walkthrough scheduled. If he liked it, he would sign the lease. His belongings would be delivered two days before he was to be back at work. Marin dreaded it, as she knew their communication would be less.

Joyce walked up to Marin wearing a pair of *2024* glasses. "Hello, dah-ling."

Marin laughed when Joyce propped her hand on her hip. "You look...festive."

"Thank you, love. Too bad your young man isn't here for a midnight kiss."

Heat bloomed through Marin's cheeks. If Gage was there, she doubted he'd kiss her. He'd made it clear that he liked her but was taking things at her speed. Marin had no experience with romance. Shelly and Travis weren't shy with their public display of affection, but even if Gage and Marin were in a committed relationship, she didn't see herself behaving as they did. Not that they were inappropriate or anything. But by Heather's reactions, Marin wondered if Travis and Shelly's relationship was healthy.

"Did you enjoy your Christmas with Heather and the kids?" Frida asked when she walked up to Marin. Her dangling *2024* earrings drew Marin's eyes.

"I did. Did you and your family?"

"Yes, but I admit I missed having you. I enjoyed our little quiet Christmas last year."

"Me, too." Marin hugged Frida. "How's Maria and Phillip?"

"The newlyweds are doing wonderfully. And MJ and Phillip get along so well."

"I'm glad."

The women made their way to the patio, where a table was set up with fruit and vegetable trays, finger sandwiches, and desserts. Another table held chilled drinks. The pool house in the background captured Marin's attention. Heather said Marin could stay until the house sold. With the inheritance, she could buy a townhouse or small starter home, but Marin wasn't sure if she wanted to take that step yet.

Heather helped Marin get set up with an investment firm and she had learned enough about investments that she felt confident she would be financially comfortable for the foreseeable future. She'd still rather have Grandma Judith than the money, but she was thankful she was no longer struggling.

"I have an announcement to make," Heather said, tapping a large plastic serving fork on the side of the soda can in her hand. Marin smiled and shook her head. "I'll be joining Marin at the University of Southern Mississippi. And if all goes well, I'll be a CFP in less than two years."

"A who?" Joyce asked.

"Certified Financial Planner," Marin said.

"Oh, that's right up your alley, Heather. Good for you," Joyce said. "Are you starting in the fall?"

"No, this spring semester," Heather said.

"That's wonderful," Frida said and hugged Heather. "I'm proud of you." She rested her hand on Heather's cheek.

"Let's eat," Ethan said when he placed the tray of hot dogs and hamburger patties on the table with the buns and fixings. Jake hovered around the outdoor heater but ran over for a hamburger.

Marin looked around Heather's backyard at the people who'd become her family. The day she'd found Grandma Judith on the floor, she couldn't have imagined she'd be standing here with these people she loved dearly.

"We should have total darkness in less than thirty minutes," Ethan said.

A whistle and pop sounded from down the street. The partially dark sky lit up with a spray of red and yellow.

"Oh, it's on," Travis said and jogged over to where they'd set up the fireworks. Ethan and Jake followed him, but Heather stopped Jake and raised a brow.

"Sparklers, buddy."

"Aww, okay."

Heather and Marin sat on the chairs on either side of the swing where Frida and Joyce were sitting. All four women watched the various displays of fireworks across the sky. Marin thought about Gage. He'd said his family put on a huge display on their ranch each year. She hadn't talked to him yet today. Yesterday they'd talked about trying to connect at midnight to ring in the new year together.

"Hello?" a male voice called out.

"Who's that?" Ethan said, turning towards the side of the house. Everyone stopped what they were doing and watched the shadowy figure make its way to where they were gathered.

"Mommy?" Jake said, a hint of concern in his voice.

"Is it Dad?" Ethan asked Heather as he passed by, heading toward the person. Heather followed Ethan and grabbed his arm, stopping him. Marin's pulse raced.

"I'm sorry. I rang the doorbell and knocked, but no one answered," the man said. "I heard voices back here and saw that last batch of fireworks go off."

Marin's mouth hung open when she saw who stepped into the light at the edge of the yard.

"Is that...?" Heather said and looked back at Marin.

"Gage?" Marin's heart rose to her throat, cutting off the air to her lungs. She hopped out of the chair and headed to where Heather was.

"Marin." Gage walked up to her like he'd known her his whole life. "Hi."

"Wha-what are you doing here?" Marin asked.

"I thought I'd surprise you."

"Mission accomplished," Heather said and held out her hand. "I'm Heather."

"Nice to meet you."

"You, too. That's Ethan, Shelly, and her boyfriend Travis, and this little guy is Jake."

"Hi," Jake said and gave a little wave.

"On the swing are Joyce and Frida," Heather said. The women smiled at Gage.

"Hello, everyone. I'm Gage Harris."

"The pen pal?" Travis said.

"Trav." Shelly elbowed Travis.

"Something like that." Gage laughed.

"Want a sparkler?" Jake asked.

"That would be awesome."

Jake tore off to where the sparklers were and impatiently waited for Ethan to light one.

"What happened to spring?" Marin asked.

"Mom sent me."

"She did?"

"Yep. She said all I did was mope and talk about you and she said I should see you now. She said it was fine since I was home for Christmas."

Marin realized she'd been looking Gage in the eyes. "We're the same height."

"We sure are." He laughed. "Can I give you a hug?"

Marin nodded. When Gage slipped his arms around Marin, tension left her body. He released her and they locked eyes for a moment. She liked they were the same height. It was easier to carry a conversation standing next to each other. Travis was a good bit taller than Shelly and she was always leaning her head back so she could see him when they talked. Marin noticed what was wrapped around his neck.

"You wore the scarf."

"Of course, I did. There's a chill in the air. It's not a Montana chill, but a chill nonetheless." He angled his head and smiled.

Marin laughed.

"Here," Jake said, handing a sparkler to Gage.

"Thanks, little man." Gage waved the sparkler all around Marin. "I always thought you sparkled."

Marin's cheeks grew warm and was thankful for the cover of darkness. "Would you like some hot cocoa?"

"I'd love some." Gage let the sparkler burn out and walked with Marin inside.

Marin got two mugs from the cabinet and removed the lid from the pot of homemade cocoa on the stove.

"Can I tell you something?"

"Of course." Marin ladled hot cocoa into the mugs.

"I think you're prettier than Madison."

She stopped mid pour and looked at Gage. His expression told her he was serious.

"Thank you." She fought the smile spreading across her face but gave up.

She finished pouring the cocoa and returned the lid to the pot. He took one mug and smiled when their eyes met. The room spun, and Marin used her free hand to brace herself on the counter for a moment. They walked together in silence and joined the others outside. Jake ran up to them with another sparkler.

At midnight, Marin froze as she stood next to Gage. His eyes found her lips, but he leaned over and kissed her cheek.

"Happy New Year, Marin."

"Happy New Year."

"May twenty twenty-four be a year of new beginnings and many blessings from God."

"Amen." Marin smiled. They toasted their mugs and took a sip. "I never asked how you got here."

"Uber. I have a hotel reserved for three days. No pressure, but if you want, I can go with you to the storage unit one day before I leave."

"I'd like that." She'd been putting it off, but curiosity had been getting to her the past few days. "I can drop you off at your hotel if you'd like."

"It's late. I can Uber."

"I don't mind."

"Well, okay."

They said their goodbyes and walked out front. Gage looked around. "Where is it?"

"Over there." Marin pointed to a black GMC Sierra. She bought three things before she invested the inheritance: a new laptop for school, a new phone, and a new truck that she planned to drive until the wheels fell off.

"Wow." Gage walked over and did a quick inspection. "That's sharp."

"I think so, too." She grinned and unlocked the doors.

Marin pulled under the hotel's overhang and shifted into park. Her pulse raced when Gage leaned over and kissed her cheek.

"I am so happy I came."

"Me, too." She smiled. "Is tomorrow okay for the storage unit? I have the code to the facility and the key to the unit."

"Yes, that's fine. Say nine? We can grab breakfast first?"

"Okay. See you at nine."

"Good night, Marin."

"Good night, Gage."

Gage climbed out of the truck and made his way inside. Marin waited until he disappeared from view and headed back home. On the drive, one word kept popping into her head. It was a word that had been foreign to her for a long time.

Hope.

Grandma Judith had helped her feel hopeful for the future. Then she died, and Marin's hope died along with her. Finding faith in God and her friends, along with Gage, had given her new hope. She'd progressed enough in her healing journey that she felt she could hold on to that bit of hope even if faced with a challenge.

What was waiting for her in the storage unit? She would have a long night tossing and turning as her mind raced from one scenario to another.

Regardless of what they found, Marin had a feeling her life would never be the same.

Chapter 41

Marin

Marin removed the padlock, and Gage helped her push up the roll-up door. Along the left side of the unit was a row of cardboard boxes stacked two high. In the back looked like furniture covered in bed sheets. Marin's old ten-speed bike was leaning against the right side of the storage unit.

"This is bigger than I thought it was," Marin said.

"It looks like the end units are the full width of the building."

Marin walked to the back where the furniture was and lifted the corner of a sheet. Underneath was her old bedroom set from Grandma Judith's house. She pulled out a drawer, half expecting to see clothes, but it was empty. She went to the stack of boxes and counted eleven.

"They're labeled," Gage said.

Marin looked closer and saw that Stella had written names and contents. There were three boxes that belonged to Grandma Judith. Stella had written *craft items* on one, and *clothing* on another. The last one had *old photos, etc* written on the side.

"These seven have your name on them and that one has Gemma's name on it." Gage pointed to a larger box on the bottom at the end of the row.

Marin removed the box that was on top of Gemma's box and saw that Stella had written *Kaylee's art supplies* on top. She rolled her eyes. Gage pulled Gemma's box to the middle of the floor. Marin looked towards the furniture and saw the bench that had been at the foot of her bed. Gage followed her gaze and brought it over.

Blowing out her breath, Marin sat on the bench next to Gage and brushed her hands across the top of the box. She began picking at the end of the strip of tape.

"Here," Gage reached in his pocket and pulled out a knife, "let me." He opened it and sliced the tape.

"Of course." Marin laughed.

She pulled out the packing paper at the top and stared at the contents. Some items were wrapped, but most were loose in the box. What Marin noticed first was a stuffed teddy bear. She'd remembered seeing a picture of her mother as a child holding the bear. Tears gathered in her eyes. She grabbed the bear and hugged it, closing her eyes. Gage's soft touch brushed away the tears that'd spilled onto her cheeks.

They spent a few minutes going through the box. There was an array of things in the box, including jewelry, a few clothing items, a hairbrush, and a Nickelback CD. Marin pulled a few strands of hair from the brush and held it out to Gage.

"This is my natural hair color."

"I'm partial to red." Gage winked when Marin looked at him. "Last but not least." He handed her what looked to be a book wrapped in packing paper.

Marin's chest burned when she unwrapped the book and realized it was full of her mother's thoughts.

"A journal?"

"Yeah." Marin thumbed through a few pages. Nearly every page had something doodled in the margins. Grandma Judith told Marin she'd inherited her mother's artistic abilities. She came across a page with frowning and crying faces. The date caused her breath to hitch.

Sept 11, '01

We were attacked by terrorists today. I'm scared. Kevin said he'll protect me.

Marin showed the page to Gage, and he raised his brows. Turning back a few pages, she found the entry she was looking for.

Aug 31, '01

I met a cute guy today. His name is Kevin. He's here at the house doing contract work on the roof. He's twenty. Is that too old?

"Oh wow," Marin said.

"What?"

"My mother met my father at my grandparents' house." She showed the entry to Gage. "I wonder if they knew then? I'm sure my grandmother read this journal after Gemma left." Marin skimmed through a few entries. She shook her head when she read about Gemma's drug use and giving herself to Kevin. She found the last page. The air left her lungs as she read.

Dec 10, '01

I'm having a baby. My parents are going to kill me. Kevin said he's always wanted to be a daddy. I'm done. No more pot or meth or whatever. I can't do that to my baby. I am going to be the best mommy I can be. If I have a boy, his name is going to be Andrew Michael, and if I have a girl, her name is going to be Kaylee Elizabeth.

It felt as if a fist pushed its way into Marin's chest and grabbed a hold of her heart, squeezing the life from her body. Her hair had fallen forward as she read her mother's words again. Through her tresses, she saw Gage turn to her.

"Marin?"

Her mouth fell open and a sob slipped out. Gasping for air, sob after sob shook her shoulders. Gage took the journal from her hands, closed it, and laid it on the bench next to him. He wrapped his arms around Marin and held her, rubbing her back and offering soothing words of comfort.

"Let it out," he whispered against her hair and kissed the side of her head. Exhaustion took over and Marin slumped against Gage. They stayed that way for a while—him holding her as her world was falling apart all over again. Finally, she lifted her head, and he offered her the sleeve of his Army sweatshirt, bringing a faint smile to her lips.

"I'm sorry," she whispered.

"Never apologize for feeling your emotions, okay?"

"Okay."

Gage wiped the hair away from her face and tucked it behind her ear. He smiled, but she didn't have the energy to smile back. Staring into his eyes, Marin caressed the side of his face. The urge to kiss him overwhelmed her, but she stopped herself. Not now, not like this.

"I feel the Lord leading me to tell you something," Gage said.

"Okay." Marin sat up and ran her fingers through her hair.

"I swore I'd never tell you this. At least not for a while."

Marin swallowed hard and braced herself. Gage began talking about the day the Socks for Troops box arrived at the chapel. He was there volunteering and was the one who opened the box. The first thing he saw was a blue and green scarf among black and tan socks.

"I opened the card and saw the names. God told me..." he cleared his throat and stared into the empty box at their feet. "God said, 'Gage you are going to marry the woman who made the scarf.'"

Marin's eyes widened and she swallowed hard. A shiver ran down her spine. God told Gage to marry her?

"I said, 'But Lord, what if she is eighty and a great-grandmother?' and he said, 'Trust me.'"

Marin bit her bottom lip to keep a giggle in when Gage glanced at her.

"It took me over two weeks to write that card. I came up with every excuse in the book. I admit, some were…vanity related. Every time I balked at God's urging, He told me to trust Him."

Marin turned to face Gage.

"I got nervous when you took so long to send a picture. When I saw who I now know was Madison, I was relieved. Until—"

"I admitted I lied."

Gage nodded. "But that forced me to get to know you as a person. And…"

Marin waited for Gage's next words as he struggled. Was he scared or did he not know how to put his feelings into words? She reached out and took a hold of his hand.

"I fell in love with you."

Marin's lips parted, but no words came.

"It's okay if you don't feel the same."

"I don't know what love feels like. Obviously, my parents didn't love me. I didn't like Grandma Judith at first. I ended up loving her, but then she died." She looked into Gage's eyes.

"I think your parents loved you in their own way. Addiction is powerful. Sometimes people don't come back from the grip of addiction. By your mother's words, I think she loved you before she knew you. Unfortunately, the drugs won."

Tears stung Marin's eyes.

"I'm sorry. I didn't mean to make you cry."

Marin slipped her fingers between Gage's and shook her head. "How do you know you love me?"

"You mean besides God commanding me to?" He chuckled.

"Yeah." Marin smiled.

"You're always here and here," Gage said, touching his head and chest.

It was the same thing she'd told Frida when they'd talked about her feelings for Gage.

"I can't stop thinking about you. I'm happy when you are happy, and sad when you are sad. Marin, your beauty takes my breath away. Your eyes are so green. That brief glimpse you gave me with the photo. It made me fall more in love with you. And when your face appeared on my phone when Joyce called me." He raised his brows.

Marin looked at the pieces of her mother's life spread out on the floor in front of her. What did she want out of her own life? She had goals. She wanted an art degree and to teach. Would admitting she loved Gage change that? He had a life in Texas. Was he at a place to commit to her? It would mean she'd have to follow him around. He'd already said he was making a career out of the Army.

"Talk to me," Gage said and brushed his fingers down the side of Marin's face.

"You're in the Army in Texas and I live in south Mississippi."

"One day at a time."

"But you want to retire from the Army."

"Things change, Marin."

"You'd get out of the Army for me?"

"I'd get out of the Army if God told me to. I don't make rash decisions. For now, the Army is job security. I'm a helicopter mechanic. That's not necessarily an in-demand career in the civilian sector. Let's take this one day at a time, okay?" Gage lightly squeezed her hand.

"Okay." Marin rested her head on Gage's shoulder.

They packed up Gemma's box and loaded it in the back of the truck along with the bench and the box of Marin's art supplies. She'd go through the rest of the boxes at a later time. Gage helped her unload at the pool house, and she made them hot apple cider. They talked into the night about their lives, getting to know each other better. As the minutes turned into hours, Marin's feelings for Gage grew deeper.

Over the next few days, Gage and Marin spent time with Heather and the kids and Frida and Joyce. It was important to Marin for Gage to get to know her friends and for them to get to know him. They were her family now and were a part of her everyday life. Maybe one day, she'd introduce him to Stella. Her relationship with Stella had more healing to do before then.

Marin parked in short-term parking. Gage held her hand as they made their way to the ticket counter. She stood by his side as he checked in and received his boarding pass. They walked hand in hand as far as she could go without a boarding pass. Gage turned to face her and took her hands in his.

"I love you, Marin." His eyes glistened.

Tears stung Marin's own eyes. "I love you, too, Gage." And she meant it.

"I can't wait for you to meet my mom and dad. And brothers, of course."

"Me either." They'd planned for Marin to accompany Gage to Montana to meet his family in the spring or early summer.

Gage drew Marin into a tight hug and held her for a while. When he released her, she leaned in and gave him a gentle kiss. She held her breath to keep the tears gathering in her eyes from falling. Gage had become a part of her in the short time they'd been together, and she was going to miss him terribly.

Tears fell down her cheeks as she watched him walk up the ramp to the gates. Marin didn't know what the future held for her and Gage, but she knew Who held their future.

Gage's Scarf

Gage's scarf is Marin's first knitted project and is based on my first knitted scarf.

   Size 8 knitting needles
   1000-1200 yards of medium/worsted weight yarn (size 4)
   Cast on 25.
   Row 1: k5, p5
   Row 2: p5, k5
   Repeat rows 1-2 until 67 inches or desired length.
   Bind off.

Note: You can cast on more than 25 stitches (in multiples of 5) for a wider scarf, if desired.

If you knit Gage's scarf, please consider posting a picture on social media and use the tags below.

   #gagesscarf
   #theknittingclub
   @andieyoungwrites (both Facebook and Instagram)

Acknowledgements

Thank you to my husband for your continued support as I pursue my writing dream. Thanks to my beta readers and my editor for helping me bring this story to life.

About the Author

Andie Young began her writing journey in 2020 after a recurring dream, and hasn't put down her pen or put away her laptop since. That dream grew into her debut novel, *A Heart's Journey*. She is a retired therapist and a veteran and likes to incorporate one or both in her writing. When she's not writing, Andie enjoys spending time with her family and their dog, Lucy. Lucy has a cameo in *A Heart's Journey* and *The Journey Home*. Andie is currently working on several standalone books and hopes to release *Phoebe's Garden* in 2025.

Sign up for her newsletter to keep up to date on upcoming releases: http://eepurl.com/hVEPcH

Reviews are important to the success of a book. An <u>honest</u> review with retailers and social media is appreciated.

If any grammatical or continuity errors are found, please contact Andie at andieyoungwrites@gmail.com.

Thank you for your support!

Also by Andie Young

A Heart's Journey
The Journey Home
*A Bouquet of Sunflowers**

Please visit my website to see descriptions of books and find where to purchase.

https://andieyoungwrites.com/my-books/

*A Bouquet of Sunflowers is available free to newsletter subscribers. Please see "About the Author" page to sign up.

Printed in Great Britain
by Amazon